I0675389

TIME IS
FOR
FOREVER

by

Laszlo Gubanyi

Published by New Generation Publishing in 2012

Copyright © Laszlo Gubanyi 2012

Cover by Chris Bamberry

First Edition

The author asserts the moral right under the Copyright, Designs and Patents Act 1988 to be identified as the author of this work.

All Rights reserved. No part of this publication may be reproduced, stored in a retrieval system or transmitted, in any form or by any means without the prior consent of the author, nor be otherwise circulated in any form of binding or cover other than that which it is published and without a similar condition being imposed on the subsequent purchaser.

www.newgeneration-publishing.com

 New Generation **Publishing**

*I dedicate this book to the angel who loved me,
nourished me and inspired me—my wife*

CHAPTER NUMBER ONE

The shout died in his throat as the steel claws of the dragon man closed around his neck. Red eyes with no pupils burned into his mind. As he fought for breath, the deadly teeth approached. The gaping mouth grew, a steaming depth of indescribable horror - closer, closer......

'Carlos! Wake up!'

'Okay. Okay. What is it?'

'Ambulance control called. They are sending us a group of casualties from the oil-plant. There was some kind of accident. They are on their way.'

'I am going! I am going. Be a good girl and get me some more details - will you?'

With a sigh of resignation, Dr Carlos Allegria threw the blankets to a corner of the bed, and for a second stared at his shoes. Could they be the same shoes with which he had walked into this Casualty only two months ago? They were white and shiny then, not like now. But then, if you want to have nice shoes, you should not sleep in them or use them in places where people wet, vomit and bleed on them.

As he walked out to the Casualty reception area, Sister Angelica was just putting down the phone.

'There was an explosion at the oil refinery - apparently one of the woman technicians is quite badly injured. There are also a few dozen of minor burns and lacerations.'

'That is the ambulance arriving,' she added 'you check the woman in the ambulance while I will line up the rest of them for you.'

'Yes boss!' And he was on his way. Sister Angelica, no matter how deceptively young and fragile she looked, was the indisputable authority in this part of the hospital.

Even the Medical Superintendent - called Ogre by his residents, and not without reason - was all smiles and polite when talking to her.

For a new resident doctor - if he wanted to survive the insanely hectic six months term of Casualty duties - it was indispensable to be in her good book.

'I should not be complaining,' he told himself while manoeuvring through the swinging doors , 'I had nearly one hour of sleep tonight. Damn more than I had last night,' he added while opening the ambulance's back door, which had just arrived as he got out.

'She is pretty bad Doc.' The paramedic was lifting the blanket covering the charred body of the woman. She was right next to the explosion.

'Let me check her before you move her out ......'

As he was opening her clothes, her chances appeared to improve. She wore thick, hard-wearing overalls which should have protected her body, at least partially. Her hair was charred, exposing large areas of blackened scalp, with a deep laceration on the left side which started to pump out blood in spurts at the moment he removed the dressings. She was unconscious - probably due to that blow to the head, but breathing deeply and regularly and she had a good, strong pulse.

Although she must have received the explosion right in her face, this was not burned. The skin was blood stained, but intact.

She probably protected her face with her hands - the very deeply burned, blackened hands witnessed this.

'Take her into the emergency room, quickly.' –

A nod from Sister Angelica confirmed that the other patients could wait.

As he jumped out of the ambulance to head to the emergency room, Carlos heard the approaching sirens.

'Please, no more,' he mumbled to himself.

'It is a police siren.' Sister Angelica seemed to read his mind once again. 'I do not think they are bringing more patients, but probably investigating the explosion. As usual they will get in the way, asking questions from everyone, causing a lot of bother and paperwork.'

The police car with its flashing light - switched off now - screeched to a halt next to the ambulance as the paramedics were removing the burned woman. The doors opened and the first to jump out of the car was a tall, very distinguished looking man, who with a gesture of his hand stopped the paramedics. With two long steps got to the stretcher, had a glance at the woman, then with a deep sigh of relief let them pass.

'Thank God she is alive.' - with this he turned around and went straight to the Casualty reception area, without heeding the protesting of the young nurse that he was not allowed to enter there.

'Carlos, Telephone!' - Sister Angelica's voice insisted at the door.

'Take a message - will you, please. I have to put a clip on this bleeding and do something about this head wound.'

'Carlos - you better come now. Dr Manzino is on the phone, and he wants you. Now!'

There was authority in her voice. Carlos knew that she understood exactly what he was trying to do - and if she judged that phone call more important, then it was.

On entering the office, he noticed the tall man standing next to the window, talking on the phone. He recognized him immediately, although had never met him before. Who could not recognize him? Dr Andronicus's picture appeared very frequently in all the newspapers, television; he was like a living legend - if not for the world - at least for this part of it.

He was the Chairman of the National Institute of

Modern Technology - which was the humble name of the society formed by the best brains of the Continent - all dedicated to research projects related to space travel.

Dr Andronicus's name was outstanding even amongst these people. The media had stopped counting the number of his inventions or major scientific breakthroughs in which he was the key figure.

Anywhere, anything new happened related to space travelling, people expected his name to be mentioned somewhere along the line.

'What the hell is going on here?' Carlos was confused. He would not be coming here if something important were not about to happen.

In answer to his questions, Dr Andronicus without a word presented him with the phone, indicating to take it.

'Hello?'

'Dr Allegria? Dr Manzino speaking - now listen very carefully because it is very important that you understand this …'

It was undoubtedly Dr Manzino's voice but it sounded strange. Usually he called him Carlos, had a bit of a small talk before starting to talk business. The tone of his voice denoted that he wanted to use all his authority and that it was very important that he, Carlos, would accept this authority without questioning.

'The burnt woman you just received is Dr Andronicus's wife. He requested from me, and I agreed, that he takes over her care immediately. He wants to take her away. Please - no questions asked now, just stand aside and let him proceed. I'll talk to you tomorrow - is that clear?'

'Clear - but the woman is ……….'.

'No buts. Dr Andronicus assumed full responsibility for her. He brought with him his own personnel to look after her. Our nursing staff has the same orders that you have - stay clear, do not interfere, whatever they do. Is it clear?'

'Sure. But I hope you will tell me more tomorrow.'

'I will. See you tomorrow.'

More confused than ever, Carlos put the phone down.

That woman was dying - needing immediate emergency care to give her at least a chance for survival. This was the only reasonably equipped hospital for a long distance around - and he wanted to take her away. It would kill her - and the man had to know it.

'Dr Allegria,' Dr Andronicus's voice brought him back to the office. He noticed all the nurses standing around and the door to the emergency room closed.

'Who is looking after the....?'

His exclamation was cut short by Sister Angelica's angry, impotent shrug. He did not remember ever seeing her angry - but definitely he would have never imagined her to be giving in to anything.

'Dr Allegria - I am Dr Andronicus - I am sorry to interrupt your routine like this, but I am sure your Superintendent explained to you what is happening. Am I right?'

'He told me that he agreed that you could take her away. But he was not aware of her condition. I assure you that if you move her, she will die. Not very sure about her surviving her injuries even if she stays. So please - let's not waste time ....'

'Dr Allegria - I assure you that we are not wasting time. My personnel are looking after her and I can also assure you that, now that we are here - she will be Ok. Now do not get offended, nobody is questioning you or your hospital staff 's capacity for dealing with the usual type of injuries, but my wife is not the usual type of patient. You see - she had a very major accident years back and in order to preserve her life she has several mechanical devices implanted into her body. To save her now, a medical doctor - no matter how able - simply is not enough. She also needs highly trained microelectronic and computer technicians - and the persons with her at the moment are the same ones who looked after her before. I assure you again - that this - me taking over, is in no way a lack of faith in your abilities. I hope you understand me.'

'I am not sure I do, but my boss says that you are the boss, so you boss.'

Carlos was trying to appear cheerful - whilst trying to work out how to behave in this unexpected situation. ' Do you mind if I have a look at what they are doing to her?'

'I do, I am afraid. My wife's life is far too precious to allow any sort of interruption - even I wouldn't go into that room. But looks like they have finished, as here they come.'

Six men, entirely dressed in white were wheeling out the stretcher.

It was a simple ambulance stretcher. No oxygen, no drips, not any apparatus visible around. The woman's head was completely covered with bandages, the head, neck, shoulders and arms - all bandaged, and the rest was covered with a blanket. Only her face was visible, clear, untouched by the fire.

'You cannot take her like this - I don't care how skilled your men are - look, she is not breathing!' exclaimed Carlos, trying to push one of the men aside to get to the woman, but it was like trying to push a ton of bricks away. He couldn't even move the man.

'Dr Allegria,' The soft voice of the woman stopped him frozen, looking at her with such an expression on his face that at any other time would have been ridiculous. No one laughed now. Everyone was staring at the woman.

Her large eyes were open, with a faint smile around her lips.

'Dr Allegria,' she whispered, 'thank you for your concern, but I am well looked after. Trust them please.'

No one moved or made a sound while she was taken out. Only the sirens of the departing ambulance made them return to reality and to look at each other questioningly, utterly confused.

'Dr Allegria,' Dr Andronicus's voice sounded much friendlier now, 'I very much appreciate your understanding and you're not interfering with my wife's departure. Speed was essential and someone else, with less understanding - could have caused delays. Allow me to express my appreciation by helping you and your staff. Allow my personnel to look after the patients in your waiting room while you rest. This is not a request - this is only an expression of my gratitude - please accept it.'

With a gesture, Carlos indicated that as far as he was concerned, he could take over the whole place. He was still shocked about the woman's miraculous recovery. Too many things happened too fast for him to assimilate all of them.

'Sister - I assure you that you will find this place completely ordered and clean after our departure. I know the workload of a Casualty nursing staff. Please let my men help you by cleaning up after themselves.'

'Thank you,' was Sister Angelica's cold answer. She was at least as confused as Carlos, but the idea that someone else was ordering around in her Casualty infuriated her.

However, there was nothing she could do about it, just stand aside, fuming and watch all those men in white moving around. One thing she had to admit, they were good at what they were doing.

The patients were treated and sent home, the place cleaned, ordered until it shone as new. And everything was done in a very quick, efficient manner. Not a wasted action, not a useless movement. The efficiency of these highly trained people was just amazing. But what really confused Sister Angelica was that all the men were dressed exactly the same - all in white - and all of them seemed to be doing everything. They were treating patients, writing prescriptions, collecting rubbish and cleaning floors - but there seemed to be no distinction between doctors and cleaners - everybody seemed to be doing everything.

'It cannot be,' decided Sister Angelica, 'it must be that I find it hard to distinguish them , dressed all-alike'.

Then it was all over. Dr Andronicus and his crew filed out - the last persons carrying out bags of rubbish.

Then suddenly and as unexpectedly as they arrived - they disappeared with the same quickness.

The noises of their departing cars had faded in the distance a long time ago before anyone understood what was exactly happening.

'Phew! Now what the heck was all that about?'

They were all still sitting in the office, staring at each other and the now empty Casualty. Everything had happened so fast that it still did not sink in what was going on. It was like watching a movie, aware of the action but not part of it.

'I do not believe all this really happened!' The little red headed nurse looked around dreamily, 'in any minute my mother will walk in to wake me up.'

'OK, girls - get moving.' Sister Angelica was the first one regaining a kind of normality, 'we are not getting paid for dreaming. We still have a few hours left of our shift and if I know the Ambulance Control - they will make sure we are not sleeping. So get ready for the next round.'

But there was nothing to do. The place was absolutely clean; everything was exactly where it was supposed to be. It was uncanny how those people knew where everything belonged.

'Carlos - I would like a word with you.'

'Yes Sister,' it was only the two of them in the office now.

'I would like to hear your opinion.'

'About what?'

'About what? For Christ's sake - what do you think I am talking about? About what happened here tonight.

'Oh that. Well, I do not know. A lot of different things happened here tonight and most of it does not make any sense to me. I mean, if you take them one by one, they appear logical and all right - but put the lot together…'

'What do you think? I think that something very, very weird happened here tonight.'

'Not necessarily. I mean lets analyse things one by one. The explosion- it was quite natural. We see here people from worse accidents every day. The burnt woman - she appeared like anyone would appear after being that close to an explosion. That she happened to be the wife of Dr Andronicus, well, it is possible. There is a lot of high-powered, secret government-research going on in the laboratory of that oil plant. That our Medical Super agreed to discharge a critically ill patient to a private person's care - well, unusual, unethical, probably against the law - but Dr Andronicus must have the power to force his way. By the way, I am really looking forward to our superintendent's explanation tomorrow.'

'But let's keep going on. Dr Andronicus's explanation about his wife - I find it a bit hard to

14

swallow but I got no reason to disbelieve him. After all, the man is known as a kind of miracle maker with his inventions.'

'The miraculous recovery of his wife - now there is something I do not understand. Had anyone else told me the same, I would not have believed it. But I have seen it with my own eyes. I have to accept it as a fact, because it did happen. Which by the way, proves the point that he was right.'

'Yes. That was a beauty. You should have seen your face - I deeply regret I did not have my camera with me.'

'Well what do you expect? In one minute that woman was deeply unconscious, in shock, just about dead, and the next one, with a smile on her face she tells me not to worry about her, she is fine.'

'What do you think about his crew?'

'Now that is another thing. Those men. They were fantastic. I have been watching their treatment and I tell you - they knew what they were doing.'

'What about the rest?'

'What rest?'

'The others who made the cleaning and packing?'

'I don't know, I did not watch them. There were too many of them. Too many things going on at the same time to be watching it all. One thing which did surprise me was their being so clean. I mean, doing all the potentially dirtying work, dressed all in white. I could not see a stain, a mark anywhere on those white shoes or clothing. I do not know how they do it. Like look at my shoes. I spent less than five minutes with that woman - and she managed to bleed all over my shoes. Not that it is the first time it's happened, but how do they stay so clean?'

'I would suggest keeping those blood stained shoes as a museum piece.'

'How come?'

'Because they are the only evidence in the whole hospital that anything happened here tonight.'

'I still don't understand you.'

'Well you told me your checklist about tonight's events - let me add to it mine, OK?'

'Go ahead.'

'They cleaned the whole place, and I mean they cleaned it. They washed the floors and the walls in the emergency room, cleaned all instruments used. Collected every little bit of rubbish, used dressings, soiled linen and took it all out. It was like that cleaning whirlpool in the TV commercials. Two blinks and the place was clean.'

'So they are well trained, efficient. So what?'

'Let me finish. I said they took all the rubbish and dirty linen out and ....'

'So what? They wanted to be helpful ....'

'Will you let me finish? Thank you. As I said - they took out all the rubbish and dirty linen. But that is not all. I checked the bins outside - they are all empty. The laundry room, where we collect the dirty linen - empty.'

'What do you mean empty?'

'Empty! There is nothing there.'

'So where is the rubbish?'

'That is a good point.' Sister Angelica sat down with a mocking grin on her face, 'and that is exactly the point I came here to talk to you about. How do you explain it?'

Carlos looked at her with suspicion in his eyes. This whole thing started to look more and more like a joke. Like the silly pranks they used to do to residents to make them appear stupid in public. But not Sister Angelica. She would not tolerate a joke in her domain, much less participate in it.

'Now hold it for a minute, let's see if I got it right.

This Casualty produced tonight, as every night, a large pile of rubbish. Papers, used syringes, soiled dressings, blood stained bandages and so on. It is incredible the amount of rubbish I see the cleaners take out every morning. So you mean to say that all tonight's rubbish disappeared or that tonight there was no rubbish produced?'

Sister Angelica stamped her foot in anger. 'You know that there was plenty of rubbish. Just remember, for example, that pile of gauze you used to clean the blood from that woman's face. Dressings, towels, sheets - all full of blood. Where are they?'

'Well? Where are they?' Carlos was still missing the point she was trying to make. She just did not make any sense.

'I don't know. But the only explanation I can give is that they took it all away with them.'

'Now that is silly. Why would they do that?'

'I don't know! I don't know! She exploded. I do not understand the whole thing that happened here tonight - but it disturbs me. I feel it in my guts that something is not right, that there is something more here and we cannot see it. I had this feeling all night and put it down to resentment for invading my territory, for taking over, pushing me away and that there was nothing I could do about it. But when I noticed that they took all the rubbish and the dirty linen away with them - then I thought ....'

The emergency buzzer interrupted. The Control notified them that an ambulance was on the way with a cardiac arrest.

The ambulance came to a screeching halt outside the main door in less than four minutes after - by that time the emergency room was ready, all staff present, waiting with the resuscitation trolley next to the only bed in the room - with all instruments, drugs displayed, connected, ready to use.

As the ambulance's back door opened, Carlos jumped up into the car and with one glance took in the situation. A middle aged fat man lying on the stretcher, lips and ears deeply blue, face covered by the oxygen mask and the hand of the paramedic holding it, pumping vigorously with the other hand. The other one was kneeling on the stretcher with the palm of both hands rhythmically pressing on the chest, trying at the same time pressing and co-ordinating with the pumping of oxygen of the other one, watching the man's face and keeping his precarious balance on his knees.

A quick check. No heartbeat. No spontaneous breathing. Pupils small. Colour not too bad.

'Let's move him!' He took over the pressing over the lower chest while the stretcher was rushing along the corridor and the man was placed on the hard board on the bed in the emergency room.

The team was good. They went through together the same procedure many times before, and everything went smoothly. Everyone knew exactly what to do and when to do it, everything was previously prepared, ready for use.

Carlos always wondered what a cardiac resuscitation would look like to an observer. It must appear to be a turmoil of hands and feet and equipment. But to him everything went as clockwork.

By the time he inserted the tube into the trachea to maintain an open airway and started the bicarbonate drip running, the nurses had connected the patient to the cardiac monitor. The small screen lit up with the lines representing the irregular functioning of the failing heart.

'Look at that!' Murmured one of the nurses.

How come I did not notice that flaming red head

before - said Carlos to himself - *better check her out after we finish with this mess.*

'Sister! Charge the defibrillator ....'

Sister Angelica was already holding out for him the charged plates of the defibrillator.

Everybody stepped away from the bed - Carlos placed the electrodes on the chest and pressed the red button. The strong electric current went through the man, throwing his arms and legs into the air.

'Beautiful! Sinus rhythm! ....'

-'Naturally, he is in good hands,' Carlos commented, 'mine.'.

This type of remark usually provoked a lot of responses from the nurses - but not this late in their shift. They were all tired and ready to go home. They also knew that this resuscitation was unusually easy. He was left to finish the paperwork, do the formal admission, and write out the orders for the next few hours and to notify the specialist of the admission.

By the time he finished, there were all new faces around him, the nurses of the new shift, all fresh and sparkling and giggling. He still had an hour or so until his replacement arrived, and so much energy at this time of the morning felt like an insult to his numbed brain.

It happened like this every time. He could go on without rest until work was to be done, without feeling tired. The moment he finished and sat down, the lack of sleep hit him like a blow to the head.

A glance towards the waiting room confirmed his fears – people had started to arrive for the routine morning treatments - dressings, plaster checks and so on.

There is nothing urgent, they can wait - he decided. *If I don't lie down for half an hour I might kill someone.*

**

'Carlos - wakey wakey – it's nearly eight o'clock.'

'So what? If it is nearly eight o'clock Dr Rodriguez should be around. Wakey - wakey him.

'That is just it. He is not coming.'

'What do you mean he is not coming?'

'Just what I said. He is not coming. He is sick or something. Just rang. Which means - my dear boy - that you are IT again.'

'Thank you. Just what I needed. Give me a few moments to have a shower and to make myself look more human. And while we are on the subject of shower - what about coming and washing my back.'

'To wash your back and what else?'

'That's it. I don't think I could manage anything else the way I feel just now.'

'Just what I thought. I do not accept backwashing invitations from unfit gentlemen.'

'And if I repeat the invitation tomorrow - after I have slept?'

'Then I will say no, naturally. Now get lost and be back in a flash.'

**

'Hi! I thought you said you would fix yourself up to look human.'

'Sister - I will answer that remark after I am fully awake - in the meantime what about a cup of coffee?' Carlos resented Sister Wilson's bouncing vitality. A tall, very pretty brunette, whose torrid love affairs were in every conversation, especially when she was not around - but about whose private life no one really knew anything.

'No one has the right to have so much energy at this

20

time in the morning,' he mumbled to himself.

'Where do we start?' he asked out loud. 'I just passed by the waiting room and it is full of people. Don't they have anything better to do than to come to see me? I mean, it is good to be popular, but not today, please.'

'Correction - they are here to see a doctor - they do not know they will get you.'

'Then tell them they will get me, and let them go.'

'OK Carlos, let's start in the holding area. Bed number one - nine-year-old girl. Dr Salim sent her in with appendicitis.'

'I bet she has a temperature and a sore throat.'

'How did you guess?'

'Well, it was a guess, but it was easy. Did you ever see Salim come up with the right diagnosis? I mean - that man is dangerous.'

'What about seeing her before you send her home?'

She had tonsillitis, and she was sent home with a prescription.

On the next bed there was an asthmatic woman. The next one was a screaming, vomiting child. On the next bed there was a drunk, swearing that there was nothing wrong with him, he just slipped and fell over - and now he wanted to go home. His right leg lay in an odd position - he had broken his hip.

Prescriptions, drugs, X-rays.

Beds emptied and filled up again in a non-stop, continuous process.

Carlos was in his element now. He was floating like in a dream, very alert and aware of what he was doing, noticing and recognizing everything, but completely unaware of anything beside the patients he was treating. Unaware of the passing of time, unaware of the world outside. Somebody put a plate of sandwiches in front of him while he was writing the admission papers for a young woman who was about to lose her baby, so he ate.

Somebody put a cup of coffee in his hand while he was looking at the X-rays of the little boy with the broken arms, so he drank.

The feeling was very familiar by now and he allowed it to take over and carry him through the day. He knew by experience that the moment he stopped working this feeling of unreal energy would disappear and the tiredness and the lack of sleep would take over.

So he did not stop. Kept on and on suturing wounds, putting dressings on, taking off plasters of Paris, admitting and discharging patients. He did not see faces - only wounds, illnesses.

He was not aware that now, again, he was working with a different group of nurses, as there was a new shift on late in the afternoon, and the constant stream of patients from the waiting room towards the beds made sure that he was occupied.

And then suddenly, he had little to do. The Casualty was still full with patients, but things seemed to be done before he got there.

The woman in the diabetic coma had all her drips going, catheterized and ready to be admitted before he got to her bed.

That screaming child in the corner already had her finger sutured when he asked the mother what the problem was.

Only then he realized that there were two other interns moving in between the beds. He resented their smooth, rested faces. He resented their interruption, their intrusion into his domains, taking over his patients. But most of all he resented them making him slow down because he disliked the feeling which came with slowing down.

Carlos sat down wearily in the nurse's room. Away

from the people, with his feet on the other chair, he was sipping his coffee, trying to focus his clouding mind on his sneakers. (Why am I wearing sneakers at work?) Then he remembered his bloodstained shoes, which he kicked under his bed this morning, which reminded him of his bed. (What the hell am I doing in here?)

It was a physical effort to get up; his legs and his whole body were heavy and aching. Felt better once he started to walk. He felt lucky that there was no one around to talk to - so he could go straight to the quarters to sleep.

He just made it to his bed.

**

The next day he received an outside phone call in Casualty.

'Hello. Carlos? Hi. Sister Angelica speaking.'

'Hello Sis, it's been years since I talked to you on the phone.'

'Cut the clowning and tell me - did you watch the news this morning?'

'Of course! I was passing the time in Casualty watching TV. Now there was this little red headed nurse next to me who...' ....

'Okay. Okay. Do me a favour, it's important.'

'You sound serious. What is happening?'

'Look. I do not want to talk about it now - but it is very serious. Please, watch the news - then I would like to talk with you. Contact me at the hospital - I will be on duty by that time.'

'And I will be off - so I can watch TV. Okay - I will do it - but I would prefer to know more about why. What particular segment of the news do you want me to see?'

'There is a short clip about the opening of the new

23

Science and Technology Exposition at the University. Please watch it. If you have a video - tape It. I missed to tape it this morning.'

'And that's all?'

'Yes. You will understand when you see it.'

'Okay Sister. I will call you tonight.'

'Goodbye Carlos.'

**

By eight o'clock Carlos was at home. Although he had dinner at the hospital, on his way home he went through the usual debate - should he stop to eat something or trust himself to his very limited culinary performance. Normally it was an easy decision - and he bought something to take home.

But today he was desperate to get home. That phone call in the morning, he could not get it out of his mind. It was a strange call for sure. Not only the unexplained part that she wanted him to watch the news, but the mere fact that she called him. That was unusual.

Sister Angelica was a very unusual person. On one side, she was the undisputed boss in the Casualty Department and everyone knew what she was thinking, what she liked and what she wanted because she always told that to everyone. And everyone jumped to obey what Sister Angelica wanted him or her to do. On the other hand - no one knew the real her. No one knew why everyone called her Sister Angelica - and most of the people did not even know her surname. Very few people knew about her private life - and they did not talk. In spite of her good looks - she had no known friends at the hospital - and the few doctors who were trying to get friendly with her learned to get out of her way.

For her to call an intern on a private matter was

unheard off. Which, together with the seriousness of her voice made that phone call something very important for Carlos.

One look at his fridge confirmed his fears - it was practically empty - except for some leftovers here and there. He was lucky that he organized a daily delivery of eggs and bread – many times this saved him from a hungry night.

Carlos put milk and a large piece of cheese in the pan. When it melted, he added six eggs, stirring the mixture till it was firm. With the pan in one hand and the packet of bread in the other, he sat down in front of the TV.

He had to get up again as he forgot to get a fork - and at the same time he got the carton of milk. Why bother to make coffee?

He was set to watch the news.

**

Sister Angelica looked up from the records she was writing – 'Can I help you?'

She was alone in the nurse's room. The Casualty was fairly quiet now and she wanted to be alone. She had a lot of paperwork to catch up on.

The tall man standing in front of her desk looked confusingly huge, towering above her. He looked massive in his brown suit, with his very short black hair, square face and large, dark-framed glasses.

'Sorry to bother you Sister. Dr Andronicus sent me. He was afraid that he left you with some bad impressions of the other night and sent me to answer your questions - if you have any. Do you?'

'The man has nerve - I have to admit that.' She stood up and started to walk around the small room - to try to hide her surprise and her nervousness. 'Yes I do

25

have some questions. For example - where is his wife now, like I was watching the news this morning and…'

'I was afraid you would ask that question' - the man interrupted - taking off his glasses. The light in his eyes startled her.

'Your eyes. Your eyes are…' Then she just stood motionless - looking into those unusual eyes.

The lines on her face smoothed out, her body relaxed visibly.

'I understand,' she murmured at last, and with a marked slowness in her movement she went back to her work at the desk.

The tall man did not move. Kept watching her working on the records with renewed energy, then he slowly turned, left the room, closing the door behind him.

Sister Angelica wasn't even aware of his departure.

**

Carlos missed the ten o'clock news. The clatter of the pan falling to the floor woke him up, sweating, flushed, his heart racing, with the receding fright still in his eyes as he looked around.

The dream was back again. The same dream, again and again with its message of utmost fear. He did not remember the origin of the dream - but it went back a long way. But recently it was appearing more and more frequently until he was practically reluctant to close his eyes and sleep - so deep and powerful was his fear.

And it wasn't only the fear. That was bad enough. But after awakening, it left behind a feeling of invasion. An invasion of the deepest levels of his privacy and the feeling of impotence - the inability to defend himself was expressed in anger. An anger blind and violent which was building inside, and which had no target to lash out to.

The fact that it always attacked him in his sleep - when he was defenceless. When he was trying to bring it on remembering the dream, daydreaming - it did not come. When he could have defended himself - when he could lash out against the very fabric of the dream - it did not come. But he felt its presence all the time - lurking somewhere in the borders of his subconscious - to jump on him when he was defenceless.

The anger born in the shame of the fright was burning on Carlos's face. Sister Angelica will be furious with him. For some reason it seemed very important that he would watch the news and it pained him that he had failed her. Perhaps he should ring...

She wasn't even upset. Her voice was calm, and cold and officious - as always.

'Don't worry Carlos ...... it is okay. Forget it.'

'But what was it all about? It did seem very important when you called me.'

'It seemed to be important at the time - but I was wrong. It was all a mistake - so forget it - I have to go now. Sorry to cause you any problems - but really it was a mistake and I'd rather not talk about it. Please forget it. Okay?'

'Okay Sis. Anything you say.'

'Good-bye Carlos.'

'Good-bye Sis.'

Carlos kept looking at the receiver in his hand as if there would be a clue to the conversation.

This did not sound like her at all. The living example of a perfectly organized and functioning machine, Sister Angelica just did not make this kind of mistake. To ring him up urgently - breaking all previously-established behaviour, asking him to do something with that unmistakably tense, urgent tone in her voice, then come to tell him to forget it, it was not important...

Something was not right. He had the impulse to call her again and demand some kind of explanation. But what would he say? She just would repeat what she already said.

He needed an argument. A reason to justify calling her again. Something to prove to her that this denying of importance cannot be true. Like if he had made a recording of her morning's phone call...

Recording...

He had set his video to record the news, as she suggested. It should be all there. All the answers should be there.

Carlos relaxed on the sofa while he switched on the TV with his remote control.

Now we will see what all this is about.

**

And he nearly missed it again.

Amongst the usual, mainly boring news items - the clip about the opening of the exposition was very short. Just a few words from the commentator - then a short pictorial sequence of the guests arriving in long black limousines. Carlos was not surprised at all when Dr Andronicus was the first one getting out of the car. He was always present on affairs related to the scientific world and he had the looks and the presentation for the media to use any opportunity to get him on film.

When he turned back to the car to help the next person out - Carlos went suddenly cold, rigid with tension. He suddenly knew what would happen. He anticipated the apparition of the slender, white-gloved hand from the darkness of the depth of the car, followed by the graceful figure in the long, white dress.

And for a few seconds the screen was filled by her

smile, by her astonishingly blue eyes - looking directly into the camera.

Then everything was gone - and the commentator started to talk about some problems in Afghanistan.

Carlos played the tape again and again, until every little detail was in his mind. Then he froze the picture - showing her face, occupying the whole screen.

It was her. There was no mistake about it.

That smile. The blue of those eyes.

It was "his" burned patient in Casualty from the other night. This woman was dying in his Casualty from very serious injuries a few hours ago.

How long was it now?

This film must have been taken a little over twenty-four hours after she was taken away from Casualty, in a stretcher, all bandaged up. And talking to you - when you expected her to be practically dead – he reminded himself, throwing a bit of doubt over the accuracy of his assessment of her. But whatever her physical state was - her injuries were unmistakable. That deep, bleeding laceration on her forehead...

He studied the screen. There was no mark - no blemish on that face. The golden hair went towards the back and to the side in a wide, soft wave, exposing her very high forehead.

It could be covered with makeup, Carlos told himself. He did not really believe it - but it was more acceptable to think that the wound was still there. He studied the hand in slow motion as it appeared from the car.

Those fingers were working!

Fully covered by her long gloves, the right hand rested on her husband's arm - the left clutching the small, silvery purse.

Carlos remembered the burned hands. The claw-like, black, charred hands - the muscles, the tendons burned beyond recognition. He shuddered.

Those hands were not repairable. Those hands were beyond repair. They could not function ever again - there was nothing left of them to function.

And in twenty four hours...

This woman cannot be the same. No way!

And then again - his eyes told him that she was the same woman. His gut feeling told him that she was the same woman.

At the hospital, Dr Andronicus called that woman his wife. The commentator called this woman Dr Andronicus's wife...

Still - it could not be.

And still again - there is no way to mistake her for anyone else. Her face was known to everyone. One time or another - that face was on the front page of every larger magazine of the country - and also overseas.

The blonde beauty had her own name well recognized in the scientific world, in the field of biochemistry, and when she married Dr Andronicus - the media called it a union of minds. That they were very right was proven by the results of their working together. The main attraction for the present exposition was one of their combined successes - a new system of rocket propulsion.

So the lady was too well known, by everyone, to be able to be mistaken for any other.

But those hands... it could not be.

The white gloves could not be covering the burned hands he remembered.

Suddenly Carlos remembered Sister Angelica's telephone call. Remembered the tension, the feeling of importance he noticed in her voice. He could well understand her now. This was something...

Carlos was going to call her, but his hand stopped

halfway to the phone.

Their last conversation. She appeared relieved when he said he missed the news. Her insistence that it was not important - that it was all a mistake...

That it was not important! - Carlos felt anger - an impotent anger building up inside him. Too many things out of place. Like in a jigsaw puzzle - the important pieces did not fit. Nothing seemed to fit.

The dying woman perfectly fit in twenty-four hours.

Sister Angelica arguing with him to see something important - then telling him it was not important - then he finding out it was very important.

His head started to throb, the tension building inside.

He had to see those hands again.

**

'Do you have an appointment?'

The porter behind the long desk eyed him suspiciously while the empty hall of the huge department building echoed hollow his voice.

Should have known there would be a tight security system around here, thought Carlos - they are too important to allow any nut to approach them- including me, he added as an afterthought.

'Look! I do not have an appointment. I am not expected. I am a doctor who treated Mrs Andronicus recently and I can assure you if you do not let me up it will mean trouble for you. So why don't you just ring up the lady and see what she says. Okay?'

'I guess I can do that. But if she says no - out you go. Is that clear?'

'Crystal clear. Now go and call her.'

'What was your name again?'

'Carlos Allegria. Dr Carlos Allegria - tell her I am

the doctor who was treating her at Central Hospital last week.'

'Hello? Perez speaking - your porter at the main desk. Sorry to disturb you Mrs Andronicus - but there is a gentleman here really insisting to see you. Yes. His name is Carlos Allegria - he is a doctor and he says that he met you at Central Hospital last week. I do not know. Yes. I checked his credentials and he seems to be who he says he is. Yes. Yes. I understand. Thank you.'

'Well. What did she say?'

'She says you can go up in twenty minutes. Take the elevator on the left. Top floor.'

'Which apartment?'

'Top floor. They have the whole top floor.'

'Poor people. They must be starving. But what seems to be the problem with you?'

'What do you mean?'

'You have the face of somebody who just stepped on something soft and suspicious.'

'There is nothing wrong. She just surprised me. I am turning away dozens of people every day who are insisting to see her for one or other reason - but between the two of us - you are the first one for a long time I am told to allow to go up.'

**

'Dr Allegria? Come in please.' Mrs Andronicus looked just like her picture, as Carlos knew she would. Elegantly dressed in white and silver - appeared to be just getting ready to go out. She was wearing long, white gloves, which reached nearly up to her elbows.

'Can I offer you something to drink?'

'No thank you'. Carlos had difficulty of keeping his eyes off her hands.

'My husband is not at home at the moment - but I

expect him shortly. You see, he is coming to pick me up, as we are due at a reception in less than an hour. I do not intend to rush you, but we did not expect your visit and...'

'I'll try to be short Mrs Andronicus. It is hard to explain the reason for my visit - because it is not entirely clear to myself.'

'Perhaps you could start by explaining your comment to the porter about seeing me at Central Hospital.'

'Yes. Well it is a good place to start - I guess. I was on duty at Casualty last Wednesday night - when that accident happened at the oil refinery - and you were brought in by Ambulance. You probably do not remember much as you were unconscious at the time.'

'Was I...? Sorry - I do not want to interrupt you. Please continue.'

'Well, to cut things short, you had shocking injuries - which by itself would not call my attention in any special way - as I see them practically every day. But what did call my attention was that a little over twenty-four hours later you appeared on television, fit as a fiddle. From what I know about medicine, this is impossible - however - I am sitting here - looking at you - and do not know what else to say. I guess I came to see you to find some sort of explanation.'

'Dr Allegria - I do not know how to tell you this, but...oh - hi darling - Dr Allegria - this is my husband, Dr Andronicus.'

The man thus introduced was unmistakably the same man he saw at Casualty the other night.

'Hello dear. Glad to meet you doctor - his handshake was firm and friendly - Perez, down at the desk told me we had a visitor - but I did not really understand the rest of what he said.'

'You better sit down, because he has a strange story

to tell. This gentleman is Dr Carlos Allegria - who is working at the Casualty at Central Hospital - Perez checked him out - so we can take him seriously. Dr Allegria was just telling me when you walked in, that he treated me in Casualty for some very serious injuries a few nights ago. He also expressed his surprise about how well I look now.'

'And what did you say?'

'I did not have time to answer anything - as you walked in just when I was going to...' ....

'I beg your pardon,' Carlos interrupted. 'Do not mean to be rude - but could somebody fill me in. I have this distinct feeling of being the centre of a joke, which I do not understand.'

'I am sorry to give you that impression - but you see - it is you who owe us an explanation. I can assure you, that my wife has never been near the hospital you mentioned.'

Perhaps for the first time in his life - Carlos found himself short of words. Suddenly there was nothing for him to say.

He planned this visit - this interview with the Andronicus's very carefully. He prepared himself for every possible outcome. He knew how to behave if they would not talk to him, or if they would react with anger, violence, if they told him off or if they would try to trick him with some scientific explanation. But that they would simply deny that the whole thing happened - he was not prepared for that.

Because it did happen. He did see them. He did talk to them, and now they are sitting here, all nice and smiling, expressing concern and friendship - and lying to his face.

Or are they?

His confusion was deepening as the Andronicus's concern was increasing. He accepted a drink with a nod of his head, and slowly, haltingly, looking for the words, was answering their questions.

He slowly related the whole happening - the accident at the oil refinery - his sleepless night at the Casualty - her arrival and departure with her husband shortly after - and the confusion which stayed behind.

During the conversation Dr Andronicus left the room, and by the time he returned Carlos was at the end of his third cup of coffee and also seemed to have some of his wits with him.

'I don't believe you! I cannot believe you!' he blurted out at last.

'Dr Allegria - please change places with me - and look at what is happening tonight from my point of view.' Dr Andronicus's voice was soft, friendly and very persuasive. 'A young man I have never seen before arrives at my home - stating that my wife had a very serious accident a week ago - while she is standing next to me appearing perfectly healthy. He also states that he saw me at a hospital where I know I have never been before. He states that I arrived there with a group of doctors and orderlies - a group of people I wouldn't know how to contact now.'

My first thought was that he's confused me with someone else. Then I contacted Medical Records from his hospital - to find that there is no record of anything as described happening there. Then I contacted Ambulance Control - and there is no record of any burnt patient taken there from the oil refinery. Then I contacted the oil refinery and they denied any explosion or accident happening there for the last eight months. Now - looking at it from my point of view - what do you expect me to think about all this?'

'There was no accident?'

'None whatsoever!'

The figures seemed to change - the proportions of

the room switch - the colour - the sounds had an unreal quality, dreamlike...

Dreamlike - Carlos grabbed the first seemingly logical thought in his mind. It must be a dream. The whole Casualty affair must have been a dream...

He remembered his experience with the Karate school - during the first years of his medical training. He was passing by Columbia Park - noticing for the first time the large black and white sign of the Karate club. For a long time he was looking for a place to learn Karate, but could not find a class which fitted to his timetable or his valet.

He decided to check out this club. He walked up the long flight of stairs, which finished directly into the Gym. The class was in progress - so he stayed to watch.

He liked the training, just the right amount of roughness with a lot of sweating. At the end, he talked with the teacher, finding out that he could train after the university classes. The price was not cheap - but reasonable - and they agreed that he would start next Monday...this was Friday afternoon.

On his way out, Carlos called in the sports goods store just next to the Gym's entrance, enquiring about the price of Karate suits. He talked to the owner, who said that he was supplying this and many other clubs with equipment. As a new member of the club he could get a discount...

The next Monday Carlos arrived early to Columbia Park - as he wanted to have plenty of time to choose the right Karate suit. He got off the bus - and the shop was not there.

The entrance to the Gym was not there. The Karate club, the whole building was not there...

Over the years he learned to accept the possibility that he probably dreamed the whole thing. But still, when he passes by Columbia Park, he automatically searches for the sign which should be there...

'Are you feeling Okay?'

Carlos slowly returned to reality. It must have been a dream. Things like this do not happen in reality.

'Dr Andronicus - I am sorry to disturb you tonight - and I also want to apologize to take up so much of your time. You must think I am mad - and quite honestly - you might be right. I do not understand what really has happened. Everything I told you was the truth - at least the way it appeared to me. Now it seems I've got a lot of figuring out to do.

'Mrs Andronicus - I would like to ask you one more favour before I go. Something, which is very important for me. The woman in my memory had both of her hands burned very badly. The kind of injuries she had are not repairable. If you could show me your hands, if I can see your hands with my own eyes, I would have some proof - some kind of reality around which I could collect my memory and build some sort of sanity into my life. Could you do this for me?'

There were no words needed. The blonde figure pulled off her gloves with a fluid motion - and extended both her hands to him to be inspected.

Her fingers were soft and delicate and pink. The skin was perfect – without a blemish.

Perhaps too perfect...

Carlos had sufficient surgical training to recognize things, which were staring right at him. The pink softness of that perfect skin... it was recently grown, new skin. Although perfect in appearance, his trained eyes recognized the recently regenerated tissues.

Those hands were extensively damaged not long ago.

**

37

The roughness of the bark of the large tree felt soothing to his back. Pressing his head against the tree, Carlos searched the top of the building for the windows which should belong to the Andronicus's. With a conscious effort he was trying to slow down his heart, which appeared to be pumping in his throat.

While slowly achieving some resemblance of calmness, Carlos was trying to put together the pieces of tonight's happening. He was remembering the appearance of friendly concern of the Andronicus's. How convincingly friendly they were. How honest, how open they were. They nearly convinced him that he was dreaming the whole thing.

They nearly convinced him!

The sight of those hands!

What did she think of him? That he was entirely stupid? That he would not recognize the obvious signs of a recent injury?

Or did she not care? Why should she?

The expression on his face should have been obvious to her. His faltering words of apologies and his precipitous retiring.

He just did not know what to say. The only thing he could think was to get out of that place, to get away and to order his thoughts.

He could not remember clearly how he got to this park - and for how long was he standing there looking up at the building.

**

High up - in one of the top floor's windows there was a flicker of movement behind the thick curtains. In the thickening shadows there, a very tall, heavyset man in a brown suit was looking down directly at Carlos. With intense concentration on his square face, he slowly took off his large, dark-framed glasses...

**

Down in the park, Carlos was still trying to sort out his ideas, getting more and more upset by the minute.

The face of them! With that friendly concern for his well-being - they were - they were lying to his face. How they must have been laughing inside at the sight of his confusion.

He was ready to doubt his own mental sanity!

They were toying with him, leading him by the nose! A thick anger was rising inside Carlos. Anger towards the Andronicus for lying to him. Anger towards himself for not realizing that they were lying - they looked so honest and friendly.

The growing feeling of anger was choking him. The pressure was building inside. A pressure, which felt more and more overpowering. More and more threatening.

Suddenly it started to feel like it was not his own anger any more. It felt more and more like a pressure from the outside, invading, pressing in, threatening.

And this feeling of pressure in his mind brought fear.

FEAR!

THE DREAM!

The burning pressure of those red eyes, the fear...

But he was not sleeping now. He was not unaware now. He was not defenceless now.

Carlos lashed out, sending a wave of hatred towards those eyes. And in that wave of hatred was all the anger, all the frustration he was building up this afternoon.

All his anger and resentment towards the Andronicus, all the feelings of frustration, shame and confusion which were building up inside, all the feelings of hurt, pride, impotence in expressing his anger - all that was sent as a scorching blow towards those eyes...

**

On the top floor the man in the brown suit faltered, and with his hands pressed against his eyes slowly sunk to the floor.

He was unconscious before he reached the carpet.

**

'Ted - how could this have happened? He nearly killed Raulfe.'

Edward Andronicus appeared calmer to his wife than she knew he was.

'Raulfe said that he - Allegria - is a latent Psi - locked in a defence module.'

'How can he be a latent and at the same time locked in a defence module?'

'I do not know. It does seem to be contradictory. But also remember that Raulfe is a trained mentor. I tend to believe what he says.'

'How does he explain what happened?'

'He could not. Partly probably because he was not in the condition for a prolonged conversation. We will have to wait until he recovers to find out more details.'

'Okay. That leaves to my next question. Why did you send Raulfe after Carlos?'

'He is Carlos now - eh! Do I detect a trace of emotion behind those composed features?'

'Yes. You do. I was feeling sorry for him until I thought him an innocent victim of our mistake. Now I do not know. It seems to me that it is he who is dealing the cards.'

'Not quite. Raulfe said something about how Allegria might not have been aware of what he was doing.'

'How could that... Okay, okay. We'll wait until Raulfe recovers. You still did not tell me your reason for sending him after Carlos.'

'I had to. Remember what happened when you showed him your hands.'

'I had to show him - the way he was putting it I had no alternative.'

'I know, I probably would have done the same myself - hoping that he will not recognize the regenerated tissues as such. But he did recognize it. It was clear on his face.'

'But he said nothing. He even denied it. He even said something about me not being the burned woman.'

'Lor dear - you are missing the point. It is exactly that. That he did not say anything is the problem. Why didn't he say it? Why did he not call us liars? Can't you see? He must have had a reason to make us believe that he does not know the truth. He must know or perceive something about us, which makes him careful. I must know what that something is.'

'And this nearly cost Raulfe his life? We are starting to make too many mistakes.'

'How could I know that he would be able to do this? He gave no indication of any Psi capability. You yourself know how low is the incidence of Psi awareness amongst these people. To find a latent one, and with this power - it was unexpected. And this makes him even more important. We cannot just let him go without fully investigating him.'

'And whom do you intend to send to contact him. After what he did to...'

'My secret weapon. You.'

41

'You must be joking, Raulfe was the most qualified amongst all of us for this kind of job - and he failed. I could not get close to Carlos without being burned out.'

'Yes, you could and you will. First of all, Raulfe did not fail - he was taken by surprise. And second, for this job you are much better qualified than him.

'You are a woman.'

**

'First tell me more about this patient of yours.'

'So, you did find something!' Carlos had difficulty refraining from grabbing his friend and shaking him until he said everything he knew. 'I told you everything I know. A young woman with no known past history - severely burned in an accident - removed from Casualty before receiving therapy - showing an incredible amount of healing one week later. That is all. Now - your turn.'

'Okay. Yes, I did find something. I am not sure what it is - but I bet my bottom dollar it is more than what you bargained for.'

'Go on.'

'Let's take it step by step. When you appeared in my laboratory with your bloodstained shoes, asking me to analyse it, I thought you were joking. Matter of fact I was so sure it was a hoax - that the only reason I accepted to do it was to teach you a lesson.'

'Come on, I would not joke about anything like this.'

'Carlos - I am your friend, but I am not stupid. I know your reputation.'

'I am not that bad.'

'You are worse. I remember that poor surgical registrar who passed a night trying to remove a tattoo from a cadaver because you convinced him that the

Rabbi would not allow him to be buried in the Jewish cemetery.'

'I did not lie to him. The Rabbi would not let him be buried in the Jewish cemetery.'

'Of course not. He was an Arab - his brothers are still fighting the Jews in Palestine.'

'You see - I was not lying. I just forgot to tell him a small detail.'

'Sure. And I also remember when you quarantined forty medical students - just because one of them was trying to take your girlfriend to the Xmas party.'

'How did you know about that one? That was not in this...'

'Rumours - especially rumours about you - have a way of getting around. I also know about...'

'Okay, okay - you made your point. So when did you change your mind about me?'

'I did not change my mind about you. I changed my mind about your blood sample. Look at that slide. No. The one under the microscope.'

Carlos was looking at the blood sample with disappointment.

'I cannot find anything wrong with the blood.'

'I hope not. That is my blood, put there only to illustrate my point more dramatically. Change slides - look at this one.'

'This is a pile of nucleated cells. This is not blood. Hold on - I mean - this is not adult blood. You are trying to pull another one - or is it just another illustration? This is foetal blood.'

'Nope. This is it. Tell me what you see.'

'This cannot be that woman's blood.'

'I do not know whose blood it is. I only know that it is the blood which was on your shoes. Now tell me what you see.'

'Nothing special, except that they are nucleated cells

- just like a normal, early foetal blood. Perhaps a bit paler - but that could be your staining. The nucleus looks awfully large in relation to the size of the cell.'

'Now look at this slide. What do you see?'

'They are suspended, unstained cells. They are...hey, this is far enough - Carlos kicked the chair out from under himself - I am supposed to be the joker in this outfit, right? So what the hell are you trying to prove?'

'What do you mean?'

'Those cells are alive. The blood sample I gave you was dry for nearly two weeks.'

'Yes. And this is why I started to believe you. The sample you gave me was obviously old - however when I suspended the cells in normal saline before staining - I noted they were too well preserved. They were alive.'

'They could not be.'

'They are.'

'Do you swear that these cells, frolicking under the microscope are the same ones I gave you on my shoes?'

'Yes, I do. So help me God.'

'Cut it out. Then - how do you explain it?'

'I cannot. I am just a dumb pathologist, doing a dumb job, giving you a dumb fact. I am not asking dumb questions.'

'Do you have any more dumb facts?'

'Yes I do. Look at the slide again. Can you see anything else?'

'No, just what I told you. Nothing else, except...'

'Except what?'

'Something sparkling.'

'Good boy. Now increase the light intensity.'

Carlos increased the illumination to the slide. 'The sparks are stronger. They are all over.'

'Correct. Now if you could increase the light even further - there would be so many sparks, as you call them - that the whole fluid would look luminous.'

'What is it?'

'Hold your horses. Cover half of the light - like this. So you can see half of the visual field clear, with your cells well visible - and the other half is dark, black. What do you see?'

'Both fields, the light and the dark are equally full of sparks. It looks like the reaction caused by the light spreads to the part where there is no light.'

'Hey - you are cheating. It took me two days to figure that out. In lay terms, what you are seeing there my boy - is the conduction of light energy from one point to the other.'

'Then this is not blood?'

'Why not? Our blood has a special pigment, which has the capacity to tie down and transport oxygen. Our body gets all of its energy from chemical reactions for which we need the oxygen. This blood - although it has the same capacity for the transportation of oxygen - it appears also to have the capacity to transport raw energy.'

'Luminous energy.'

'Nope. I tried sounds, heat, and electricity, even a small dose of radiation. All energy sources appear to produce these same sparks.'

'It sounds like we both read the same science fiction books.'

'Yep. In a minute there will be a knock on the door - and the little green men will walk in, demanding that you take them to your leader.'

'Now seriously. What do you make out of all this?'

'That you accidentally stumbled onto something I do not know anything about - and I am not sure I want to know.'

'What kind of woman would have blood like this?'

'Well, you can call her a woman because you did

see her - I did not. The being to which this blood belongs retained the regenerative capacity of very primitive organisms - and this regenerative capacity seems to be boosted by an unlimited supply of energy. Does this answer your question?'

**

The next few weeks were a blur of activity for Carlos. He accepted extra night duties. He stayed in for the weekends. The time he had off he spent sleeping - exhausted. He put all his attention, all his energy to his work, talked only when he had to. He did not want to think. His mind closed to the outside world - nothing existed outside the hospital.

The nursing staff recognized the signs of mental stress, and left him alone, respecting his privacy.

Every now and then a nurse or a sister tried to get close - to make him feel better - but he refused any social contact. This was so out of character that they all accepted it as the result of an inside conflict and no insult was taken.

His mind refused to accept a situation he could not handle, and he did not know how to handle this one.

Carlos had a fairly clear idea what those blood test results meant - or he thought he had, but it was something too big, too strange, he was too unprepared to handle it. Deep inside, he was afraid of what he would find if he kept on looking - so he stopped looking.

He closed his mind - and decided to wait only for further developments - expecting things to mature, to organize inside him.

And they did. After a few weeks, he started to feel better, his feelings were clearer, his ideas started to organize, like a jigsaw puzzle - the pieces started to fit together. He found himself more and more able to carry the responsibilities for his finding.

He was just starting again to ask questions to himself - when she made the next move.

**

Carlos was coming out from Casualty - with a group of nurses, their shift just finished. They were tired, but as usual, a very boisterous group. No one noticed the bright red sports car on the other side of the road until it honked, and the blonde driver waved to them.

'Now you really upset me,' complained Sister Wilson. 'Am I not good enough for you? Do you have to look for girls outside?'

Carlos put his arms around her, looking deeply into her eyes. 'My darling Sister, you are just the woman I need to curl up with in front of the fire on a rainy day.

'But... it is not raining tonight – he finished quickly - so I'll see you tomorrow. Bye!'

Across the street he bent down to the driver of the red car.

'Hello Mrs Andronicus. I was just looking for someone to give me a lift.'

'Hi. I could say you are a liar - as I have seen your car in the parking lot, but I won't. Get in if you are going my way.'

By the time she finished, Carlos was buckling up his seat belt next to her.

'That didn't take you long. I also noticed you did not ask which way is my way.'

'Dear Lady, anywhere you are going now is on my way.'

She was a good driver, but there was a lot of traffic on the road, even at this time of the night, so except for a few furtive glances towards her passenger Lorraine

Andronicus kept her eyes on the road.

Carlos looked very comfortable, relaxed - with his eyes half closed - enjoying the ride.

'You are not very talkative tonight.'

'You see - I was just telling myself, Carlos my boy - you do not need small talk with this lady. When she is ready, she will talk to you.'

'You didn't even ask me where we are going,' she accused.

'I did not need to. We just passed for the second time in front of the Central Library. Obviously we are not going anywhere. You came here to talk to me. So I will just sit - and wait - until you are ready. And I am not in a hurry, this chair is very comfortable.'

'You don't miss much, do you?' She gave him a half-hearted smile.

'Okay, let's talk,' she said while parking the car on the grassy part on the side of the road.

'This is good for my reputation - but I am not sure about yours.'

'What do you mean?'

'You parked in the most popular lover's lane of the area.'

'I am sorry. I do not know this area too well. It seemed a good place to stop. Do you want to change?'

'No. It is fine for me.'

'Okay. Now.' She took a deep breath like someone plunging into deep waters. 'The reason I wanted to talk to you was that I feel I owe you an apology. It took so long because I was trying to meet you casually, like by accident. However - we appear to move around in different worlds - so I decided to see you tonight.'

'Apology accepted - with the condition that you tell me what you are apologizing for.'

'For not telling you the truth.'

'What is the truth?'

'That it was me in the Casualty the other night.'

Carlos was almost sorry that it came out so easily. He expected a long discussion, lies, promises, but now that the cards were on the table he realized this is not what he wanted.

Because now he had to face the truth, take responsibilities and also accept the consequences of his actions.

Whatever is the truth, which will come out of this present conversation - will have a very profound influence on his future. He was just not sure he was ready to face it.

He had no choice.

'You do not seem to be surprised.'

'I am not. But I am surprised that you told me. And now that you told me - where does that leave us?'

'What do you mean?'

'Well, do you really feel, that with this, you telling me that it was you - the whole thing finishes? Don't you think that once you started, there is a lot more to say?'

'Like what?'

'Well, besides the obvious, like how the hell did you heal so fast, I can think about two other questions right now. The first being - why did you deny that it was you?'

'And the second?'

'Why did you decide now to tell the truth?'

'Well, the second question is easier to answer. I felt guilty. Guilty about involving you, although accidentally, in something that can only cause you harm. On noticing the mental turmoil or confusion that our denial caused you - I felt that I owe you and although I cannot answer all your questions - at least I can give you peace of mind by accepting that what you remember is the truth.

'As far as the other questions - I am afraid I cannot give you the information you want. All I can tell you is that you accidentally stumbled onto something you are not supposed to know about, and that this is important enough to upset a lot of people. So I ask you to stay clear. Please, do not ask questions, do not make waves. There is nothing you can achieve, except to bring danger to yourself.'

'Warning was a better word. What you just said has a definite taste of a threat.'

'If there is a threat, it is not coming from me.'

'Then where is it coming from?'

'Nowhere. Your accidentally acquired knowledge was a threat for some people, but not anymore. It is all arranged - it does not matter what you say, or to whom you say it -you do not have any shred of evidence to support it. If you insist on your statements - you just make yourself look ridiculous.'

'You forgot that dozens of other people witnessed the same things that I did.'

'Dr Allegria, believe me - you are the only one who remembers anything about that night.'

'And how do you explain your healing?'

'I do not have to. I simply deny I have ever been hurt - don't you think they will rather believe me?'

'At this rate of healing - in a few days time I would believe you myself.'

'Exactly.'

'But how do you explain it to me?'

'I cannot. I would love to, but cannot. Believe me just to be here with you now - could cause big problems for me.'

'Doesn't your husband know you are here?'

'Of course not. As far as he is concerned you ceased to be a problem when he made the supporting evidence disappear, rendering the situation non-existent.

'And where does that leave me?'

'Nowhere. I mean - your position in life does not change. You remain the same Dr Carlos Allegria you were before, and in the inside, richer with this unusual experience.'

'About which I cannot talk.'

'No, unless you want to be laughed at.'

'And what about what I know?'

'What you know! Tell me, what is it what you know?'

'That somewhere, someone has a method for accelerated healing that he wants to keep secret?'

'The world is full of this kind of secrets. Every research institution has its own secrets, which disappear after they finish their investigations. This healing method will be published in a few years time when we feel it is safe to be released.'

'Who is "we"?'

'Do not push your luck. There are things it is better for you not to know.'

'But I do know.'

In the ensuing silence, Carlos nearly felt sorry for her. She looked so fragile, so beautiful...those incredibly blue eyes looked into his, pleading.

'You cannot,' she whispered.

'I do.'

'How?'

'I analysed your blood.'

She appeared to shrink, became smaller - even more fragile. The pallor spreading across her face made a contrast with the smooth gold around it.

'Carlos,' she said slowly, completely facing him on the seat, with her hands softly touching his face.

The touch of those hands sent shivers of pleasure along his spine.

'Carlos - please remember this. Whatever happens, I am your friend. Remember this. I am your friend.'

From her wristwatch, next to his ear, came a piercing, high-pitched sound.

In less than two heartbeats, Carlos was unconscious.

**

'I had to bring him in.'

'I know Lor, you have done the right thing. The question is, what are we going to do with him now?'

'You cannot erase. He is a barrier.'

'Did you try?'

'I couldn't even try. I tried to probe him. All I could get was a few loose surface thoughts. When I tried to go deeper he attacked me. What a power! I was lucky I could break contact before he burned me out. I can understand now what happened to Raulfe. And he is a mentor.'

'He seems to be a very unusual specimen.'

'Unusual is not the word. I am a fully qualified empath - and have never even heard about anything like this.'

'He couldn't be that bad.'

'He is worse. He is like two different persons at the same time. At the conscious level he is completely non-psi. He doesn't even believe in mental capacities. And at the sub- conscious level - wow - what a power!'

'Isn't that what a latent psi is supposed to be?'

'But he is not latent. At the deeper levels he is very much active. He is locked in a permanent defence - attack module. And the defence part at least seems to be very deeply established in the time pattern. It gives the impression that he has to be on a constant guard against a continuous psychic attack. But where is the attack coming from?'

'Did you get a danger reading?'

'I could not. And the other thing I do not understand is how all this high-geared psychic activity can go on without him being consciously aware of it?'

'It is possible, if the psychic attack is directed to the subconscious - without having any relevance to the conscious part of the person.'

'How can that happen?'

'Like in a dream.'

'Yes. Providing the subject is aware that it is a dream.'

'Correct. And it has to be a dream which keeps constantly coming back causing a deep level fear - awareness.'

'Is that possible?'

'It is possible, I guess. Highly unlikely - but possible... he is waking up. You must have given him a very small dose.'

'I gave him a full decibel range.'

'He must be as strong as a horse.'

'A horse would be dead.'

**

'Good morning Dr Allegria. Welcome to my house. How do you feel?'

'Like someone chewed on and spat out. What am I doing here?'

'Congratulations. I had hopes that you would not come out with the classic "where am I?" of the comic books.'

'It is fairly obvious where I am. Come to think of it - it is also fairly obvious why I am here.'

'We will come back to that point shortly, but first I would like you to rest for a while to clear your head completely. Please drink this - it will refresh you.'

Carlos looked suspiciously at the tall, yellowish drink in Andronicus's hand.

'If I cannot trust an innocent looking wrist watch any more why should I trust the drink in your hand? That watch trick really gave me a surprise.'

'That watch trick, as you call it, is the result of a very highly-developed technology. It was specially designed to render people unconscious - without causing them any harm. The same use of that "watch trick" should prove to you that you could take this drink, as there is no harm intended to you.'

'Then why was I brought here in this way,' Carlos took the drink and examined it closely, 'I mean, if it is for my good I would have come willingly. Hey - this really tastes good!' After a small taste he half emptied the tall glass. The drink was cold, but Carlos could feel it warming up in his stomach, sending an invigorating, soothing feeling along his body. Suddenly he felt much more alert - much stronger physically and mentally.

'This is a great drink, whatever it is. It's a pity it is not available in the shops.'

'You forgot to ask if it was drugged - and it was. It has a light stimulant added to help you feeling better. We need to put a few things clear and I want you with a clear and alert head. How do you feel?'

'Fine. Let's clear things up.'

'At this stage, I only want to clarify your present position in here.

As you know - you happened to acquire certain knowledge - which is kept from the public.

The things you know could be used to prove the existence of people who do not want to be known. You present a certain amount of danger to them.'

'Why don't you shoot me? Sorry - I did not mean to give you ideas.'

'The idea did cross my mind, and believe me it

would be the simplest thing to do. However, our people do not enjoy violence. Which doesn't mean we are not able to use violence when there is no other way.'

'Who is "our people"?'

'That is a point we may touch on later.'

'Why not now?'

'Dr Allegria - remember your situation. You are in this position for knowing too much. Do not make things harder by trying to know more.'

'Sorry. I am listening.'

'I do recognize the fact that you acquired this knowledge by accident - and probably due to my mistake - but we cannot allow you just to walk around, calling attention to us.'

'And if I promise not to talk?'

'I am afraid that would not be sufficient. I do not doubt your word, but there is too much at stake to take just that.'

'What else do you want?'

I am not sure yet. We have to work out something. Something which will convince us that our secrets are safe. Sooner or later we will find it.'

'And until then I am your prisoner.'

'Yes. Although I have never liked that word, it does explain the situation. I feel like I owe you an apology, but there is no other way.'

'I fail to see how I could be dangerous to you. Who would believe me anyway if I would want to talk?'

'I think you are missing the point. You are not staying here because you are dangerous to us. You stopped being dangerous to us when you were brought here. You are our guest for your own sake - to make time while we work out a way we can let you go.'

'Because you cannot erase me...'

In the sudden silence there was an intense feeling of tension building up in the room. The Andronicus's exchanged a quick glance .

'Why did you say that?'

'I - I do not know - I am not sure. It just came out of my mouth - I am not even sure what it means. I think it was something you said while I was waking up.'

(How can that be? That was said in.....)

(Shush. He might be aware of mind speech...)

'Yes. I probably did. It is a technique by which parts of a man's memory can be removed permanently from the mind. The problem is that it causes a certain amount of brain damage. That is why I said we cannot use it on you.'

'Thank you for the consideration.'

'You are welcome. As I said - we do not want to cause you any harm. Okay - now one more thing. Before I show you to your room, I would like you to meet another member of our group. Raulfe would you come in please?'

(Ted - you are pushing him too hard.)

(I have to see his reaction.)

Carlos tensed up on hearing the heavy footsteps, and by the time the large body of the man filled the door-frame, he could hardly hide his shaking hands.

The tension mounted - until the fear filled him. A fear which paralysed the mind, a fear of those burning red eyes...

Carlos stood up, shaking his head to clear it, to face the man.

(Did you feel it? How can he have such a powerful control-response - and not be aware of it?)

(He was aware of it all right. Although he did not know what it was, he was able to displace it from main focus and function, pretending to ignore it.)

'Dr Allegria,' Mrs Andronicus was doing the introduction, 'this is Raulfe - Raulfe - this is Dr Allegria, who will be our guest for a while.'

'Hi!' Carlos said it with a secure voice he knew he did not have. The man was too big - too powerful. He reminded him of...

'Little man, we have unfinished business between us! We will meet again!'

'Raulfe's rumbling voice was still echoing in the room as he turned around and walked out. His movements were surprisingly fast and fluid for a man of his size.

'What did he mean by that? That we have unfinished business?'

'Raulfe is full of surprises - you will get used to his manner soon enough.'

'Oh - there is one more thing I want to call to your attention. This room - like all the others - are fully equipped with alarms and observation devices. Everything that is happening in any of these rooms is constantly being monitored.

'The reason I'm telling you this is that your room will not be locked. You can use the toilet facilities at the end of the corridor - but please - do not get any ideas. I would prefer not to make your stay here any more unpleasant than it has to be. I hope we can find a comfortable solution to our problem, so you do not have to stay long.'

'What do you mean by a comfortable solution?'

'That we keep our secrets and you keep your life.'

**

The bright moonlight from outside filtered through the curtains and made weird patterns on the wall. The figures seemed to come alive when the curtain moved in the breeze. The freshness of the air came through the half opened window, without the street noise. The window was too high for that.

Carlos was observing the moving, changing patterns on the wall. He could not sleep, which was a rather unusual experience for him. He expected this to happen the night before - after his unexplained arrival to the Andronicus's place, but much to his surprise he had a very good night's sleep.

Tonight was different. He felt it the moment he went to bed. There was a tension building up inside - a kind of expectation for something to happen. Something bad.

The day was uneventful. The Andronicus's were very polite, very apologetic - but had little time to spend with him. The food was excellent, in the form of cold meats and salads prepared the day before and kept in the fridge for him. There was a great variety of drinks to choose from, but he preferred to keep his head clear.

He spent the day roaming through the empty rooms, looking at the paintings, objects of art, watching TV or reading books. There was a large room in which three of the walls were covered with bookshelves from ceiling to floor stocked with a great variety of books. In another situation he could have spent weeks or months going through these books.

There was no telephone. The apparatus itself was there, but all the calls went through the switchboard downstairs - and he was not given an outside line. When he mentioned to Dr Andronicus that he was expected at work and that he should call in – he was told that he already had. At least someone did in his name. As far as his job was concerned - he was at home sick.

The shadow patterns moved again as a current of air moved the curtain. The tension was mounting. Something was about to happen. Something dreadful. The air was thick and hot and Carlos had difficulty breathing. He got up and opened the window fully to let some more air in. There was something wrong. There was something definitely wrong. This feeling of tension, mounting fear - he had never experienced it before. Except in his dream. That's it, the Dream. But he was not asleep now...

At the end of the corridor there was the sound of a door opening and closing. The heavy footsteps. Not furtive ones. Confident, heavy footsteps. They stopped at his door.

Carlos knew it was Raulfe long before the door opened and the huge body stepped in.

'Little man - as I said before - we have unfinished business to attend to...'

As the panic struck him Carlos was trying desperately to concentrate, holding himself erect by grabbing the window frame behind him with both hands. He was acutely aware of the sharp edges of the aluminium window as they pressed against his whitening fingers, the cold air, which was blowing the curtains now that the door was open and the faint street noises from far below.

(Why do I fear him so much? - He is just a man) - But deep inside, he knew this was not so. There was more - much more in the waves of hatred he was able to perceive quite clearly.

'Yes little man. I know about your dream. Your dragon man has come to finish you off, once and for all.'

He appeared to be changing. He seemed to be growing larger, wider; his open mouth was getting bigger, and bigger, and bigger - the luminous eyes turning into a burning red...

Carlos closed his eyes.

The anger welled up inside him. Anger feeding upon many years of frustration, of being a helpless victim.

Anger for being attacked always when he was defenceless in his dream.

But not now.

He was fully awake now.

He could defend himself now. He tensed his body, hands in fists by his side ready to leap, to crush against his enemy. From deep inside his mind a searing bolt of anger, blinding hatred struck the dragon man.

The image of the dragon faltered for a split second and he perceived Raulfe's mocking voice in his mind.

'You are strong, but I was prepared this time. I will show you now what real power is.'

Carlos' body suddenly went limp. He lost control of his muscles, his knees buckled under him and slowly sunk to the floor, as if a terrible weight had fallen onto his shoulders. He could not focus his eyes. He could only hear his own gasping breathing.

And those red eyes were pressing, burning fiercely into his mind. The pressure was still mounting.

The Dream never got this far.

He always woke up in terror, much before this.

Carlos wished feverishly to finish the dream, to wake up. He could not take this for much longer.

But this was not a dream. This was a screamingly painful reality.

Those red eyes burning deeper and deeper into his mind. His brain was expanding, swelling, hurting, paining.

Carlos, through the deep clouds in his mind, was aware that he was screaming. He heard the scream as from a great distance, this high-pitched scream of someone in extreme agony.

Then something burst.

A blinding flash of light, a piercing scream, a tearing bolt of pain.

Then everything froze.

Time stopped.

Carlos looked around in the room. Raulfe was still standing, facing him, near the open door, with an expression of deep concentration on his face. He was not moving. He was not breathing.

A bead of perspiration that was running down the side of his face stopped in midway.

There was no movement in the room. The curtains were still, so still that he could distinguish every thread, one by one, forming the intricate designs of the shadows on the wall.

He noticed that the plush carpet was more worn on the right side and that small dirt particles clouded the edges of the window panes.

He saw the street, down there, far below - so clearly as if he were standing on the curb.

He could read the number plates on the cars, the title of the main article on the newspaper lying next to the driver.

And nothing moved. Everything froze. Time itself stopped.

The man at the corner - with one foot lifted in the air as if stopped in the middle of stepping up onto the curb.

The driver with one immobile hand out of the window - like trying to shake the ash of his cigarette which was glowing but did not seem to burn.

The droplets of water had frozen in the air after the taxi had just passed at high speed through a puddle, only to be stopped about a meter away.

He saw his own body lying on the floor, hands covering his eyes, head tilted back, mouth open, frozen in a long scream.

Then everything clicked into place, and he understood what was happening.

He understood the Dream. He understood what Raulfe was doing. Poor old Raulfe, so intent in doing him harm, so deeply into the mental module of his puny attack that he left his physical self-unattended. His physical body undefended, vulnerable.

He knew exactly what to do.

As he got up from the floor time started to flow again. The man at the corner put his foot down. The water splashed on the wall while the taxi sped away.

Carlos kicked Raulfe in the lower part of his stomach, putting all his weight in it, and as the body came falling forward like a toppled tree, he lifted his knee, hitting him in the face.

As Raulfe was desperately trying to get back into the physical module, he had no defence against the searing bolt of pure mental energy.

**

'I don't understand this. How could he do this to Raulfe?'

'Lor dear, remember that we are all mortals. Even a mentor can die.'

'But not like this. This is not supposed to happen.'

'You are right. I know that you are. I didn't mean to sound the way I did, but I do not have an explanation of what happened in here. I know as well as you do that as far as mental capacities are concerned a mentor is the strongest thing our civilization can produce.

'That a mentor cannot be subject to a complete mental burnout - causing physical death.

'It just cannot happen. There is no power able to do this.'

'But it did happen.'

'Yes, it did happen. There is no doubt about that. Which means only that we are dealing with a power beyond anything we know. And this is where your friend comes in...'

'Carlos...'

'Yes, Carlos Allegria.'

'Aren't you pushing it a little, Ted? I mean - I learned to accept that a latent psi resisted a mental attack. I learned to accept the idea that the same latent psi nearly killed Raulfe through a surprise rebound defence module. I have also observed that this same person was subconsciously aware of our mind speech. But that he is able to burn out a mentor - well, sorry. It is just too much.'

'Did I say anything about a latent psi?'

'You said Carlos.'

'Yes. I said Carlos. But not Carlos the latent. Carlos the fully operative psi, with a capacity...'

'You better explain this.'

'Okay. Let's reconstruct what has happened in there. Let's start with Raulfe. Remember how he reacted when you brought Carlos with you? I should have recognized the depth of his resentment for being beaten by a latent. I should have realized how deeply he was hurt emotionally. But I did not. I thought it was safe to leave them together. And he came for revenge. I do not think he planned to kill Carlos, not at first. But he needed revenge and he could not fight a latent psi.'

'You mean...'

'Yes. He woke him up to operational potential. You remember the techniques - quite simple really. For a mentor I mean. We have not been using it for centuries because it is a barbaric method causing a lot of unnecessary suffering. However, this did not particularly bother Raulfe.'

'But why was it so important for Raulfe to fight Carlos? Okay - he was upset about what happened, but this seems to be too much.'

'What do you mean too much? Do you know what would have happened to Raulfe when we got home? He would have been the laughing stock of his Guild. A mentor beaten by a latent psi. You have to accept that it does sound like a bad joke. He had to do something about it, and the only thing left for him was to fight Carlos again. He had to "wake" Carlos - and he got more than he bargained for.'

'But how could Carlos do this to Raulfe? He was completely unprepared, untrained.'

'I do not have the answer to that. He obviously found a way to beat a mentor.'

'So, in summary what we have here is a fully operational psi, with the capacity of burning out a mentor. Completely untrained without any idea of what he has - roaming free in a planet where there is minimal psi activity.'

'Exactly. Meaning that we have to find him quickly, before he causes problems, for himself and us.'

'He does not seem to need our protection.'

'You are missing the point again Lor. Let me put it to you with this example. Let's take you. You have been trained in psi activities since before you were able to walk. You know how to control yourself. You know how to control your environment. And with all this training, would you like to go out and mix with people without the filtering protection of your medallion?'

Lorraine shivered at the thought... in spite of the stifling heat in the room.

'No I would not like that at all.'

'Now think about Carlos. Suddenly open psi - brain, with practically unlimited capacity to receive, being unable to control this capacity - receiving simultaneously the emotions of thousands and thousands of people. To feel at the same time the fears, the hatreds, the loves, the pains of all the people around him.'

'I did not think about this,' she whispered to herself.

'We better find him before it is too late.'

**

The first thing Carlos was aware of was that there was someone in his room. There were several people in his room. He sat up, clutching the blankets with stiff fingers, the heavy, cloudy feeling of the restless night still on his mind.

The room was empty.

But the feeling persisted. People all around crowded in. The feeling of pressure increased in his head. People all around. People from far. People from the same building - they all seemed to be right next to him.

The pressure was mounting and with it came fear. (It is not the dream. It cannot be. The dragon-man is dead.)

He opened his eyes again.

The people stayed - although the room appeared to be empty. Then he remembered Raulfe and the people went away, not fully - but further away.

Poor old Raulfe. So pitiful in his resentment, and at the same time, so confident. The way he took upon himself the dragon-man's role. That was a mistake. He could perceive the intense fear in Carlos but could not have guessed that this particular fear would wake up a violent outburst based on old resentments.

I should be grateful to him, murmured Carlos to himself - he opened pathways in my mind I never thought existed. (The people in the room retreated further.) It is a pity he had to die... and it was not my fault. I just fed back to him what he was giving me. A little stronger perhaps. Repeated the pattern of his own energy flow. I wasn't even sure what I was doing. How the hell would I know that the bastard wanted to kill me?

The people around started to approach again.

'Go away,' he shouted to them. 'I know you are not here! I have to concentrate to keep them away. It looks like, after all, Raulfe did not do me any big favours by breaking my walls down. True it imprisoned me, but it also protected me. These people are probably not even aware of the fact that they are invading my mind.

'I have to concentrate to keep them away...'

He ran his fingers along his body. His skin was hot and wet. His stomach was smooth to touch. The hips and his waist, his breasts were firm, smooth, as his hands went around them, the feeling was...

BREASTS!

Startled, he opened his eyes, and for an instant he could see the reflection in the partly fogged mirror, as she stepped out of the shower. Long hair wet and her skin steaming from the hot water...

'Hey - this was not too bad - maybe I was too hasty in judging...'

The pain was intense - still, what made Carlos cry out was more the surprise that the pain.

'What the hell...'

He was rubbing his leg vigorously - although he knew deep inside that it was stupid to do so.

'Next time I fall I'll break my neck...'

Now that was a stupid thing to say. How can I fall? I am sitting in bed. And talking of beds - what about getting ready for work...

The pain again. It was even stronger as he hit the same part of his skin in the second fall (I cannot stop. Must hurry. I am late for school.)

That stupid kid - Carlos fumed - at least fall on the other leg the next time.

He got out of bed, the floor feeling unusual under his feet. The carpet had a feeling of grass, sand, a hard cement feeling to it and as he lifted his head, he felt a few raindrops on his face.

'I wish I had a drink at home.'

Carlos remembered the drink that his Pollack patient brought him. He said he distilled it himself out of prunes. It was very useful in the past, quite a few times. Not for drinking of course, as it would have burned the skin off his tongue, but it was excellent to remove stains from metal surfaces.

'What I need is a shot of Valium to calm down this brain receptor going berserk, but alcohol should do the same.'

The bottle was still under the sink.

Carlos put about a finger high in a glass - the rest filled with water. Not anticipating its flavour, he drank down the whole glass in one mighty gulp...

It was fire which exploded in his stomach. Fire, which started to burn from the tongue and like a volcanic eruption burnt its way down to the stomach.

'Hell's fire,' he gasped, trying to catch his breath. 'How can anyone drink this stuff straight?'

As his stomach was empty, in a very few minutes he started to feel its numbing effect on his brain.

The people retreated a bit further.

'Ah, I got your number now. One more drink and you are out of my life...'

With the brakes screeching the high bus was rushing towards him. There was no time to move.

Carlos heard himself screaming with fright, in a weak, childish voice. He was frozen. He could not move. The fright froze him...then the impact, the pain. Then the black...

Carlos got up from the floor, shaking, rubbing his back. The pain and the starting bruise was quite real. He hurt himself falling over the chair...

His head hurt. A heavy, throbbing pain. Every sound in the room was like a knife to his brain. It was difficult to open his eyes - the light was intense - it hurt. 'I cannot keep this up for much longer. This is no life...'

The pieces of broken glass looked inviting on the table. She took one of the sharp pieces and pressed against her wrist. It didn't really hurt. The blood felt warm as it ran along her fingers, dripping down to the floor...

Carlos opened his eyes with fear. No. He had no blood on his hands. There was no broken glass on the table.

'I am going nuts. Raulfe my boy - you did not kill me last night, but you are still trying.

'I need another drink. I have to numb the brain receptors - doesn't matter if I get drunk in the process.

'And I will have to stay drunk until I learn to control it.

'The pain...

'I have to drink...

'Get them out of my mind...'

**

The light was hurting his eyes - but it was a subdued light.

The soft light coming through the white curtain from the outside.

There was a faint antiseptic smell in the room.

Carlos felt unusually heavy and tired - but very nicely warm and comfortable at the same time. He felt that he should do something. That there was something he should find out - he should investigate.

He tried to get up.

He was so tired, so nicely warm and comfortable.......

He went back to sleep.

**

The next time Carlos opened his eyes the light was not hurting him. There was no tiredness in his body.

Matter of fact, what woke him up was that he was terribly hungry.

He sat up in his bed, feeling good, mentally getting ready to face the day. In his euphoric state of wellbeing, everything appeared to be fine. The sunshine filtering through the long white curtains, the creamy colour of the clean walls, the crisp gray-blue of the nurses' uniforms...

NURSES!

Carlos suddenly finished waking up.

The young woman sitting at the desk near the window had to be a nurse. The cut of her uniform was unfamiliar to him - but it was unmistakably a nurse's uniform.

And he was definitely not in his room. The place had a warm familiarity to it but Carlos was sure he had never seen it before. The predominantly clear pastel colours gave the room an unreal, hospital-like appearance.

The nurse lifted her head. 'Good morning sleeping beauty! About time you decided to wake up and join the living. How do you feel?'

'I don't know. Let me work out first who I am, then where I am - and then I might tell you how I am.'

'You are a little green man from Mars who just landed in his flying saucer.'

'In that case - take me to your leader.'

'Nothing doing. You just stay in bed. My leader will come to see you shortly. I buzzed him as I saw you waking up.'

As if confirming her words, there were footsteps outside the door and after a short knock a tall man walked in wearing a long white coat.

'Good morning Dr Allegria.'

'Dr Andronicus! I should have known. So, I am your guest again.'

'It appears to be the case. Although the circumstances happen to be quite different.'

'I fail to see the difference. Unless, of course, you have found the solution to our problem.'

'Our problem?'

'Yes. Now let me see. Your words were "to find a way by which you can keep your secret and I can keep my life."'

'Oh - that problem. Well, I can assure you that my secrets, and also your life, are both quite safe. Take my word for it.'

'I take your word for it. Now, can I go home?'

'Dr Allegria - in that closet there is a change of clothing - not your own of course as yours were beyond salvage when we found you - and any time you wish, you can leave. There is no lock on your door.'

'What about right now?'

'No one will try to stop you. However - I would strongly advise you against it.'

'Could you tell me why?'

'Of course. First of all - you have probably realized that you are in a hospital. No one keeps people in a hospital unless they have a health problem. So - what about if we talk about your health before you leave?'

'A good point. What is my health problem?'

'We can come back to that later if you wish. Let me point out to you the other reasons why I think you should stay at least for a while longer. Ok?'

'Go ahead please.'

'You are being given drugs which speed up the self-repair of your body - but at the same time cause a euphoric detachment from reality. We should stop them at least two days before if you want to leave on your own. These are the two simple reasons. The others are a bit harder to explain.'

'If you care to explain, I am not really in any hurry. And by the way, I do believe that euphoric bit. I feel fantastic.'

'I am glad to hear it. But let's bring more facts into the discussion. Please look at yourself in the mirror.'

Carlos accepted with insecure hands the small mirror offered to him by Dr Andronicus.

'His mind took a lot of time to register the face he was looking at. It was a very thin face, with deep, dark rings under the eyes, the cheekbones straining high against the dry skin covering them, the lips thin, dry, crossed with numerous deep wounds and scabs.

'What did you do to me?' Carlos' voice was a hoarse whisper while he kept his eyes on that face.

'I was trying to save your life. What you see is the look after nearly a week of intensive recuperative nutrition. You should have seen yourself before.'

'One week...how long...?'

'Which is the last day you remember?'

'When I left your house that night. It was the twenty seventh of February.'

'Klarin, please bring me the newspaper from the desk in my office. I am in doctor Allegria's room.'

(The room must be bugged thought Carlos - he's talking straight into the air. If someone brings the paper in now - it means that we are being monitored).

The door opened and a young nurse handed in the paper.

'Thank you dear. Now - Dr Allegria - would you care to look at this paper? It is three days old - but it will serve our purpose. Please look at the date.'

'Second of April - it cannot be.'

'It is. And three days more. We found you nine days

ago in a ditch drunk to your eyeballs. You were not a pretty sight. Three weeks of solid booze and barbiturates will not improve your health.'

'I am not a heavy drinker and I do not touch drugs.'

'You did this time, and I tell you one thing - it probably saved your life. Or at least your sanity. Knocking out the brain stem receptors, you very effectively blocked the intrusions into your mind.'

Carlos shuddered at the memory of his room full of people.

'At least that part is over,' he exclaimed in a weak voice.

'It is not. Not quite.'

'What do you mean? I feel just fine.'

'Fact number two - that chain with the medallion you are wearing around your neck.'

'I was wondering about that. What does it mean? You are all wearing something similar - even the nurse who just walked in with the paper.'

'Good clinical eye doctor. Yes - we are all wearing one. Our medallions are identical but for their colour. You will learn later the meaning of them. In the meanwhile, I suggest to you an experiment. Take off your medallion - but have it ready to put it back around your neck.'

Carlos wasn't sure what to do. Without understanding why, the idea of taking off the medallion suddenly appeared very distasteful to him. Like hundreds of alarms going off in his head, warning him not to do it. He lifted his hands towards his neck, but they stopped half way there undecided.

'It is alright.' The assurance came as from far away. 'It is safe to take it off for a short time.'

With the chain in his hands, medallion off, Carlos faced Dr Andronicus defiantly. However, before he could have said anything, the expression on his face

72

changed to that of surprise, and then to fear.

There was sheer terror in the jerkiness of his movements on putting the collar back on. He lay back on the bed exhausted and it took quite a while for the deep lines on his face to smooth out.

'What happened?'

'A necessary cruelty. There was no way you would have accepted this if I just tell you about. The receptor pathways opened in your mind by Raulfe are still open and you are still unable to protect yourself from the involuntary intrusion of neighbouring minds. The medallion protects you with an electromagnetic wave barrier which is tuned into your own emission/receptor wavelength. But it can only protect you while you are wearing it around your neck. This is the main reason why you should stay here with us.'

'If this is all true - why could I not go home wearing the medallion? Why couldn't I go home?'

'The reason is simple. The medallion is not the instrument which protects you. It is only a computer terminal, which connects you to our central computer, which in turn provides you with the barrier impulses adjusted second by second to your present receptor state requirements. I am afraid the functionally-effective distance in between your medallion and the computer is limited.'

'You mean I have to stay tied to your computer for the rest of my life?'

'Yes and no. I mean - yes- you have to remain within effective working distance - although this being several thousands of kilometres – it is hardly restrictive.

'And no - by this I mean you will be going through, if you are willing, an intensive training on mental controllability, and eventually will not need the computer's protection.'

Carlos closed his eyes. It was hard to concentrate.

His mind felt clouded, jumping from one statement to the other, failing to make connections many times.

(There is something wrong here, he fumed inside. I cannot grasp it but I feel it in my bones. I feel a hidden truth behind all this logic.)

'I am sorry, but I must be more tired than I thought I was. If you do not mind, I will need a bit of time to digest all the facts you just dumped in my lap. But suppose I will be able to accept them as fact, it is still not clear to me why you would do all this for me? Why would you bother helping me?'

'The answer to your question is quite simple. We feel responsible - although unintentionally - of being the causing force behind your present problems. We feel we contracted a debt with you and we are paying for it by trying to get you out of your present mess.'

**

Carlos had very little recollection of the next few days. Everything around him appeared to be quiet and calm. He spent the days sitting in his bed, looking out the window with unseeing eyes.

The hospital staff left him alone - respecting his manifested desire for solitude, respecting his need of understanding the recent changes in his life. They only entered his room when they had to, they did not talk to him, and they did not expect anything from him.

With his mind's eyes turned to the inside, Carlos did not often show awareness of his surroundings. He did not seem to notice the food which was placed in front of him - but he ate when he was told to do so, moved when he was told to move and passively allowed them to wash him and clean him when they wanted to do it.

His days and his nights were spent in silence.

But inside, it was different.

Time passed with a turbulent roar.

Though Carlos was aware of the changes in himself, he felt detached from them.

In his mind he re-enacted again and again the events of Dr Andronicus's last visit. Again and again analysing it word by word, checking for hidden meanings in every gesture. Trying to grasp the full implication of the conversation.

Although he felt fully alert and rational he had the conviction that there was something escaping him.

He felt it in his bones that something had happened - something very important - and that he should know about it - and that although the clues present should make it obvious to him, it was also eluding him.

He also replayed in his mind his own participation in the scene, having the conviction that there was something wrong with his own behaviour too.

That he did not talk and behave as he probably should have. That, in some way he could not understand, his emotional response was not the correct one.

That's it! - Exclaimed Carlos's mind - the emotional response... - or rather the lack of one.

His head was clear; his logic appeared to be sharp. He understood the implications of Andronicus's statements but it did not touch him personally.

As if all this was happening to someone else.

While Dr Andronicus stated that he will not be able to leave this place for a very long time, Carlos remembered that he was wishing they would serve the same soup tonight as he had last night.

He felt that this probably was not the correct emotional response from him, but at the time it seemed appropriate.

His logical mind fully understood that the computer technology required to validate Andronicus' statements, was highly advanced. He should have heard of it, but it seemed unimportant. Like if it was a useless news item from the other side of the world.

It must be the drugs they are feeding me - the idea sped through his mind, only to drop out of sight again amongst the heaps of unimportant, unrelated thoughts one dreams of and tries unsuccessfully to grasp.

**

Then one day Carlos woke up - and he knew he was awake.

The colours, the shapes in the room, the sounds that filled the air - suddenly had meaning for him. His senses absorbed the surroundings. The touch of the sheets, the warmth in the air, the pastel colours of the walls, the words which were slowly drifting towards him...

'...back with us?'

'Pardon?'

'I said I am glad you are back with us.' The bright red hair of the nurse made a startling contrast to her blue-gray uniform.

I must be getting better, Carlos thought to himself, she looks quite delicious. Loudly he said 'thank you, I am glad to be back, wherever this back is.'

'How do you feel?'

'Fantastic. If I knew I would wake up like this every time, I would sleep more often. But talking about coming back, I am not aware of having gone anywhere.'

'Don't be smart. You know exactly what I mean. You were not drugged that much.'

'Drugged?'

'Yes. Your doses were doubled to accelerate your healing which of course knocked you out of reality completely. You can talk to me now because it was stopped forty eight hours ago. Your blood stream is almost completely clear now.'

'I remember feeling happy about most things.'

'Happy? You would have been cracking jokes in front of a firing squad.'

'So that is where I am destined to go. To the firing squad.'

'Highly unlikely. Unless of course you are not getting out of bed so I can make it.'

'Why don't you make the bed with me in it? I even could...'

'You are not listening. I said I want to make the bed, not you.'

'Splitting hairs. If I were you I...'

'Get out of bed!'

'Yes sir, straight away sir. And while I am doing it permit me to present to the administration my complaint. The way you are treating a poor convalescent patient. Threatening him with a firing squad and all that jazz. It could have permanently damaged my delicate emotional stability and... and talking about convalescence, am I?'

'Are you what...?'

'Am I cured, saved, repaired to my original perfect self?'

'I thought you were - until you started to talk.'

'When you told me the drug that was supposed to heal me was withdrawn, I just assumed that I was well. And, while on the subject, what was really wrong with me?'

'I think you should ask those questions to Dr. Andronicus - he asked me to tell you that he is coming to see you tomorrow.'

'Why not today?'

'He said that he wants to talk to you when your head

is clear, not like last time. He said that there are a lot of decisions to make.'

The mention of Dr Andronicus's name had a very sobering effect on Carlos.

He suddenly made contact with the real reality. The pretty face of the nurse disappeared in tomorrow's shadow.

Decisions to be made!

He did not feel fit to make any decisions.

He was confused, disorientated, felt himself drifting helplessly without a foothold in reality.

He did not even know where he was!

He was plucked out of his safe environment and after a series of events which by themselves were enough to make anyone doubt his own sanity, he found himself in a room, helplessly undressed, without knowing where he was, why he was there, and who the people he was dealing with were.

'This is hardly a situation in which you can make decisions,' Carlos exploded in anger. 'I need time. I need to organize my thoughts. I need time to think, to understand the situation.'

I need to get out of here!

Now!

The clothes in the closet fitted him. They were not new but they were clean. There was money in the pockets, a small roll of paper money and a few coins - and Carlos was sure he had never seen the kind before. However, they felt familiar. He knew their values and he could read the writing, in spite of the very unusual letters.

There was also a map in the pants pocket. A street map - with a cross marking probably his present location.

'So he was not lying,' he murmured to himself. 'At least not in this. Let's see if the rest of what he said is true also.'

The door was unlocked and there was no one in the long corridor. Most of the large number of doors were locked, and the sounds were unmistakably night sounds.

Snores, whisperings, and soft footsteps were all around him.

He did not stop to ponder about the sounds. On turning around a corner he suddenly found himself in a large hall. Opposite him were the half open main doors, going directly to a dark street.

It was night time - Carlos was quite taken back by this discovery, and this upset him even more.

'Damn that windowless room. It was stupid to assume that it was a morning just because I happened to wake up. But it will not make any difference.'

To his surprise, Carlos gained the street without any problems. The night was fresh, but he was not unduly cold. It was a busy street; there were a lot of people walking about.

It was one of these streets where there is no traffic and all the width of the street is for walking people.

The large shop windows were all lit up, but most of the shops were closed. The open shops were selling different foodstuff - in some of them he could see people sitting at tables and eating. There was one very close to him, just across the road, and through its open door Carlos could smell barbecued meat.

'Just like home,' he murmured. 'Except it is not home.'

Suddenly he lost his hurry. He had - really - nowhere to go. Deep inside he had hoped, until this very minute, that when he gets out of the building he would be just a few blocks away from his home. That all what Dr Andronicus said would prove to be a lie and everything would go back to normal once he got home.

This did not happen. Step by step everything turned out to be as he was told. Even the part about being at a different place.

A place where he was no longer a threat to Dr Andronicus and his people.

And that is why he was able to get away so easily.

He was not guarded. There was no need to do it.

He was in a foreign country. There was no mistake about that. The very sight in front of his eyes now was proof of that. The way people dressed, the signs above the shops - in the windows, the names of the streets, all written in characters he had never seen before. The money in his pocket was more proof.

But what country? How can he find it out?

How can he approach someone on the street and ask "Excuse me, but could you tell me what country this is?"

The food smell from the shop across the road made him remember that he'd had nothing to eat since he woke up. The protesting of his hungry stomach started to make him irritable.

'There is no reason why I should not eat there. I have money; I am not in a hurry. Besides, I might learn something by talking to the people.'

When he got to the shop's entrance, the attendant was just wrapping up a very big hamburger-looking thing for a customer. The aroma on a hungry stomach was irresistible.

'I would like to have the same, with a glass of that drink please.' Carlos pointed to the yellowish fluid in a large container above the counter.

'You name it, and I'll make it for you. Just give me a couple of minutes to prepare it.'

The attendant seemed to be in a good mood, like he enjoyed his job. There was something strange on his face when he talked, but Carlos forgot about it when he looked at the man's chest.

He was wearing a medallion . Blue in colour, but otherwise exactly like his.

He looked around. Everyone was wearing the medallion. There were several colours, blue the most common - but everyone had one.

People out on the street - they all had medallions. And not just that, they were all wearing them outside their clothes, - they were all displaying them like an identification disc.

Carlos also noted that he was the only one with a black one around his neck.

'Here we are Sir.' The attendant's happy voice brought him back to his food. 'That will be two and a half Zerints, Sir.'

Carlos paid automatically - with his eyes fixed on the man's face. The attendant noted the perplexed expression on his face.

'Everything OK Sir?'

'Just fine. Just fine.' He nearly stuttered. He picked up his food and drink and left the shop in a hurry.

'I am going mad!' he nearly shouted as he stormed along the street, ignoring the strange glances from other people.

'This is too much. I am going mad, and all this is just a hallucination - or I am asleep and dreaming all this. This or that. There is no other alternative. I cannot live in films - this is no movie. He was not speaking English although I heard him speaking in English.'

After a few moments of rushing along the street, his body, not used to physical effort for a long time, was sweaty and exhausted. Carlos felt relief when he found a bench in a small square opposite a tall building.

The first strange thing he noticed about the attendant's face was the way he talked. Carlos never made a special study about lip reading but he was sure that those cheerful words did not come out of the man's mouth. The expression on his face, the eyes, the gestures of his hands and body all went along well with the voice he heard. But the mouth moved differently - it was saying something different. Like the thing that used to happen in foreign movies when they changed the voices to English. Everything was OK, providing you did not try to lip-read.

The hot packet in his hand and its aroma reminded him of his hunger. It tasted good, perhaps because of his hunger, but he could not make up his mind about what it was made of. He put all his attention on eating, trying to anchor his raging mind into some kind of reality. There was a limit to everyone's coping capacity...

After a short while his heart beat slowed down and he seemed to think clearly again.

I am not getting anywhere fast. Let's go through this scientifically - step by step. Let's see what I know about this place.

Fact one - it belongs to Andronicus's people. In here lies the fact of his wife's burned hands and the technology required to produce the miraculous cure.

Fact two is Raulfe, the things he did to me and the changes that happened in me. In here belongs also the fact of the medallion. I can accept its activity on mental functions as true. I have tested it several times by trying to take it off and putting it back on again fast.

Dr. Andronicus said that the medallion is only a means to be connected to a central computer. I think I can accept that too as a fact. The size of the medallion seems to be prohibitive to the complex function of what it does to me. To perceive, to analyse, then to react and cause a change in my mental function - you would need a sizeable machine - no matter what the technology. So I am connected to a computer via the medallion.

Then so would every other person who wears a medallion! His mind was racing feverishly now. Some of the pieces started to fit together - every person is connected to a computer through the medallion - probably the same one Andronicus spoke about. A large central computer. I could talk to a Chinaman in English - he could talk to me in Chinese - and we both would understand each other perfectly. The computer could pick up the Chinese sounds in my ear and feed me back the translated version. All I would hear is him talking English. And if the computer is a really good one, the voice and the vocal expressions would come back unaltered. The visual parts do not need to be altered, unless I am deaf and rely on lip reading to understand him. - I am sure I would not understand a word of what he is saying if I take my medallion off. Maybe I should try it to prove the point.

Fact three is... hold on! I have not finished with the medallion yet. If every person is connected to the same computer, then everyone is connected to each other through the machine. That is how Andronicus asked for the newspaper in my room, talking to thin air. His medallion related his message to the computer; the computer sent it to the nurse via her medallion. Who needs a telephone?

His mind was racing again, the tension building. Pressure mounting. Tension.

Fact three is...fact three is...Carlos closed his eyes. Tight.

With cramped fingers, white with tension, he squeezed the edge of the seat by his sides.

The pain was not enough to distract his mind from the flashing pictures of...he bit his lip.

The sudden pain seemed to take his mind away from...he bit his lip again.

The saltiness in his mouth was a welcome

distraction.

Slowly - very slowly he felt some sort of calmness returning. With a strength he did not know he possessed, he forced down the tension to a sane level.

Thanks Raulfe - he sighed - at least I got something good out of our meeting. I don't think I could have taken this much before.

With his eyes closed he allowed the memory of what he saw to drift slowly back to his mind.

The tall building, right in front of him - across the plaza.

The large, full moon above and beyond it, bathing everything in moonlight, leaving the side of the building facing him in darkness.

And the reflection of the moon in one of the windows facing him...

He stood up with uncertain movements - with stiff and aching muscles all over his body. And, holding his breath, he very slowly turned around.

He opened his eyes, forcing himself to look with deep apprehension, because his mind already knew what his eyes would tell him.

There...there was another moon in the sky. A second one.

CHAPTER NUMBER TWO

The central cargo terminal corridor of the warp ship was always the children's favourite place to play. Not just because they were not allowed to be there - although this was probably part of its attractiveness – but because of its huge proportions, impressive even to minds used to interstellar travel.

The other, main reason, was that, due to its central position, the gravity in this corridor was less than a quarter planetary standard - allowing the children to produce "feats of strength". Where else could you jump four to five times your height or lift twenty times your own body weight? This area was the busiest place on the whole ship when arriving to or leaving a destination orbit, swarming with all sorts of heavy machinery, moving, rearranging the cargo in the holds; but during the warp-transfers this was an empty place.

Officially the corridor was off limits for all but the personnel on duty, but unofficially the children were encouraged to go there. As far as the personnel were concerned, this was about the only place on the ship where they could not possibly do any harm - and the mere vastness of the place ensured its soundproofing. The times when the children were meeting in this corridor were the only times the security personnel could relax a bit. In all the other times those small hands were always breaking or taking apart something, which caused quite a lot of problems in planetary etiquette. They had to be controlled, but this was quite a task - as every one of them was the son or daughter of someone important. What could you say to the Narssean Ambassador's small daughter after she clogged up the waste disposal chute with a very expensive tablecloth?

Or what do you say to the son of the Chairman of

the Kingloican Banking Corporation when he sneaks into the switch panel room and neutralizes the gravity control in the swimming pool? Did you ever try to swim in large chunks of water floating in the air?

However, the group was unusually quiet today.

About eighteen of them - aged between six and fifteen - were standing around a small girl sitting on the floor. The girl, about eight standard turns old - with long, golden tresses forming rings over her head - had wide hips and very wide shoulders, which denounced clearly her Lanornian origin.

Contrary to her exuberant temper and to her always being the leader of the pack in the "feats of strength", she was sitting on the floor with her face hidden in her hands and her wide shoulders shaking as she cried.

'It is not my fault! How could I know that no one had told her?' the tall Kandonian boy - with his characteristically wide set eyes - explained to the others. His eyes were sparkling with anger but he kept a respectful distance from the sobbing girl. Lanore was a planet rich in heavy metals - its gravity four and a half times the planetary standard, and one does not pick a fight with someone who had the muscles to live under such gravitational pull.

'There was no need to talk to her like that.' The tall, very thin girl from Tarnandolin took her friend's side.

'I was only…'

'Yes, precisely. You were only telling her that her little sister is an old woman by now.'

'It is true!'

'I know it is true, but is that a reason to unload it on her so suddenly?'

'She was with us during the orientation lecture. I have seen her. She heard the captain mention that by now the back planet, from where we all come from is more than eighty full turns older than since we left it.'

'It is not true!' the sobbing girl was screaming now. 'My little sister is not an old woman!'

'It is true!' the boy persisted, stepping prudently further back.

'Don't cry Sonori.' The long arms appeared even thinner on the broad shoulders. 'I am sure your father can explain all this better to you.'

The mention of her father worked like magic. They were all children of planetary dignitaries, well-versed in the protocol. The reminder of her father brought with it the immediate need for self-control.

'I am OK now.' Sonori stood up wiping her face with the back of her hands. 'But tell Tullin - is it true what he said?' Her eyes were asking for a denial, but the impotent gesture the tall girl made was affirmative.

'I do not understand. We are on this ship for such a short time. My sister is two full turns younger than I am. How could she be so old now?'

'Hey S'lak - get your computer brain here and explain it to her. And on the way - I wouldn't mind to understand it myself.'

'I do not think she is old enough for the mathematics of it yet.' S'lak - the small boy from L'Stvan - was obviously proud of the fact that he was the "brain" in the group. 'Matter of fact I don't think you would understand it either.'

'I don't want the mathematics of it.' Sonori stamped her foot in anger. 'I just want a plausible relate/explanation so I can understand the thing.'

'I can do that if you want it. How much do you know about time vectors?'

'Nothing. We have not finished the normal space vectors.'

'Well let's make it simple then. Just imagine that we are all standing at the edge of a large river - looking at the water. You might be looking constantly at the same spot - but the river you see there is not the river it was a short time ago. Do you understand this?'

'Look, I might be eight but that doesn't mean I am stupid. Everybody knows that, as the water flows away and new water comes in from upstream, you are constantly looking at a different river.'

'Correct - now imagine that half of us get into a boat and start drifting, allowing the water to carry us down stream. For the people on the shore - the water is constantly changing - however - the group in the boat does not matter how far they go - is floating always in the same river - surrounded by the same water. They are flowing with the river. Is that clear so far?'

'It is - so what?'

'So the warp ship is our boat - able to go with the flow of the river - which is the time. People in the ship are always in the same time/span. People who were left behind are out of the way of the time current. For them the time flow passes by - meaning that they are getting older.

'Is it clear now? You are practically in the same time frame all the time while you are on this ship, but for the people you left behind, the time is flowing past.'

'Then how do you explain the fact that I overheard my father talking to the Hhruahran's planet just before we left the back planet? He said that we would be with them in a few short spins.'

'It is simple, Hhruahran's is ahead of us and the back planet is behind us. The time flow affects them differently.'

'How differently?'

'I do not know.' S'Lak blushed. 'We have not gotten to those equations yet. It has something to do with the directional time warps. On selecting the time warp, which kind of short circuits us to our destination, we compromise ourselves to the time flow of the planet in front of us - our time becoming identical to its. The planet behind us is not affected.'

'I still don't like it,' pouted Sonori. 'Why should this happen to us?'

'Use your head. It had to be you.'

'What do you mean it had to be me? Why should I have to lose my sister?'

'I didn't mean it that way,' S'Lak corrected himself quickly.

'I did not mean you as a person, but you - people from Lanore. Remember Hhruahran has a six standard gravity. Only a lenovan has a chance to survive on that planet. Even you will find it hard for the first few turns.'

'So just because we learned to adapt to a higher gravity we also have to learn to live with the monsters?'

'What monsters?'

'The Hhruahrans...'

'Why do you call them monsters?'

'Well, I don't really know them, but Karlon said...'

'I should have known,' Tulling burst out, facing the Kendonain boy. 'Why, you low born bug-eyed toothpick - your race is further away from the human standard than any of ours. How do you dare call anyone a monster?'

'Just look in the mirror before calling on human standards,' Karlon retorted. 'Besides the Hhruahrans are not even of human stock.'

'So what. That does not make them monsters.'

'What about their colour?' Sonori came unexpectedly to the boy's help.

'What colour?'

'I have seen it on the orientation tape. They are of all different colours. Brown, red, even blue.'

'Sonori dear. Did you have the audio on or did you

just look at the pictures?'

'What difference does that make, Tullin? Some of the colours are quite nasty.'

'Did you or did you not listen to the tape?'

'I did not. I only saw the visual. So what? I did not like the look of them and I do not think I will like the sound of them.'

'What I meant was that if you had listened to the tape, it would have explained to you that all those pictures you have seen were taken from the same person.'

'Do you mean they change colour when they want?'

'They do. I mean they don't. I mean - you are confusing me Sonori - I mean they do not do it on purpose, it happens to them.'

'You mean the different colours are signs of different stages of development.'

'No. It is not like that. It is the way they show their feelings - S'Lak, help me out, will you?'

'You should have listened to the tape Sonori.' S'Lak was again using his professorial voice. 'It is all there. The Hhruahrans have a very hard, rigid skin. No one knows for sure if it is a natural adaptation to the high radiation levels on their planet or if it is an artificially-engineered genetic adaptation to their violent life style.'

'What do you mean? Who would want to have thick skin?'

'Well - if sticking a knife in between your ribs is an everyday happening in your neighbourhood - then you would be happy to have thick, metal-hard skin too. Anyway - as they do have a very rigid skin cover, even on their faces, naturally they cannot have changing facial expressions.'

'What a boring race.'

'Not quite. Their skin has very high pigment content, different pigments located in different cellular units. These units are able to expand or contract, with the result that when the cells containing the red pigments are expanding and the rest contracting they will look red. When the red cells contract to a very small size and the browns expand they will look brown.'

'How reptilian.'

'Not quite - the difference is that of the reptiles of Argin the colour change is due to the direct influence of the environment. In the Hhruahran's case the colour shift is emotionally correlated. Once you get used to the meaning of each colour, you can read their emotional state better than on our facial expressions.'

'You seem to know a lot about them.' Sonori was trying to look impressed.

'I know a lot about many things.' S'Lak was not trying to boast. The others knew that for his race, knowledge was the main reason to live.

'I still don't think you know everything. That remark about the knife in between your ribs - I do not think that is right.'

'It is right. They are a nasty and violent race. They are born out of violence - they live fighting and the only normal death for a Hhruahran is a violent one.'

'You are wrong there. We had a Hhruahran living in my father's house for a short time. She was a nice person. On the rough side I admit - but nice. She was very strong, but never hurt anyone.'

'A Hhruahran who never hurt anyone! You must be joking. Or we are talking about two different races. She could have been a Tikri from...'

'No. She was a Hhruahran. She was sent to my father when our medics failed to help him with his eyesight.'

'Now hold on. We are talking about different people. Your father's Hhruahran must have been a healer - a very special Hhruahran. There are very few of them and they are specially trained to develop hereditary healing talents. They are trained to help people, which is quite different from the ordinary Hhruahran who are trained to kill. Do you know that murder is quite a socially acceptable thing, providing you have a good reason for it?'

'What a barbaric planet!'

'Not really - if you consider that...'

The shrill note of the shift change warning interrupted him. Soon the place would be full of heavy-duty machinery getting ready for the orbit transfer. It was time to get away.

It was one thing to be known that they were here, but a very different thing to be caught.

**

'You cannot see beyond your nose plate,' Kiara exploded. 'Our race is finished. Lost its right for existence. We are turning into a race of soft-skinned degenerates.'

'I think you are exaggerating there.' Her friend's voice was blue-soothing - but it did not sound very convincing.

'Am I? Well. I will tell you the facts of life. Let's analyse our people. The Hhruahran have the strongest built body in the known universe. The muscles powerful, the reflexes built with the predator instinct. The skin in-laid with ultra hard protective plaques. You could not design a machine more suitable for the fight than our bodies.'

'Tell me something new.'

'Look at our society - everything is designed to praise the strong, the powerful... our songs and our stories are about wars and heroic deeds. Our children play with war toys - worship war heroes. Our adolescents compete in games of physical violence. During our adult life we strive for power - success is measured by our influence on society. We eat to strengthen muscles, we sleep to restore body energy, and we copulate to create a warrior. Every aspect of our life is dominated by physical violence.'

'I do not understand you. This is the way it is supposed to be. We are descendants of a warrior race and we are proud of the fact that our people dominate all the races we got in contact with. As you said, the Hhruahran's body is the most perfect fighting machine in the known universe. We are physically and emotionally built for battle - and this naturally reflects on our society. So I cannot see what you are getting purple about.'

'Because the whole thing is phony. It might have been true in the past, but not anymore.'

The Council Assistant paled to a brown. She was used to Kiara's outbursts, but she was starting to touch subjects of greying content.

Kiara D'Charkoon disregarded the early distress coloration of her friend.

'This whole warrior race myth is phony. The last war we had was over a hundred full circles ago. We have had no revolutions for thirty. Our government is structured on military power - however, we had no military coups, not even intended ones, for twenty full circles. I have not seen a good street fight in months.'

'This will show you that we have an efficient Government, that the councils controls...'

'Efficient, my antlers. How could you control a strong warrior race with laws in which capital punishment is only something from the past?'

'Just what do you mean?'

'That we are turning weak. Physically weak.'

'You must be joking. I agree that we have not been involved in any major wars lately, but that one I put down as a success of the Council. The powerful do not have to fight. The powerful do not have to prove herself and in the intergalactic scene we achieved a lot in the recent turns, without wasting our resources on war. And if you look around, just as you said it before, our whole society is based on physical power. Anyone who wants to be someone strives to achieve status in the War Games of body entertainment. You can't say that is a sign of physical weakness.'

'You are helping me to make my point. You see, a few turns ago I went to the Archives to get some notes on the original design of the healer pods. By mere accident I happened to stumble upon the yearly War Games statistics. Do you know that for thirty-seven full circles there was no official record of new achievements? Do you know what this means? It means that for thirty-seven full circles we were not able to produce an athlete on this planet who could improve on any of the old records.'

'I was not aware of this…'

'Next I checked the official records of last year's War Games. The achievement looked impressive on paper - until I compared them to the records fifty full circles ago. And guess what? They are so inferior that they nearly belonged in the children's section.'

'Come on! That is a bit too hard to believe.'

'Check the figures yourself. They are available in any branch of the Archives.'

'Okay. Let's suppose your data is correct. It is easy enough to check it. What does that mean to you?'

'That our race is developing new trends. That our science and technology is full of new achievements, making our life more comfortable. That there is a new tendency to develop the mental aspect of our life, weakening the physical. I guess you could call it progress, as the same thing is happening to all the other races at different speeds. But ours is the only civilization based entirely on physical violence and a civilization as such cannot survive these changes.'

'You exaggerate again. Our scientists and technicians were always the leaders of the universe. And as far as the mental part of life goes, you should know better. You are coming from a healer family going back countless generations. You could not be more mental than that.'

'Yes. Our technology was always very advanced. I accept that, there is nothing new about that. But what kind of technology are we talking about? We used to talk about the technology of weapons, travel, communication systems and so on. What are we talking about now? The technology of producing food, clothing, heating systems for winter, cooling systems for summer. Why, my grandfather would have died first than accept the idea that he needed a warm place for the winter. Just look at the heroes of today.'

'I do not agree with you...'

'Of course you don't. No one does. No one seems to see the signs. Just look at yourself sitting there, comfortable, dressed more ornamental than functional, sipping your drink. Why - the same drink of old was designed to nourish travellers on long distance space flights. Your great-grandfather would have died of shame if someone would dare to suggest that one of his descendants would take nourishment for pleasure alone.'

'Kiara D'Charkoon.' The council faced her with her imposing frame fully erect, a deep grey on the angular face. 'I am your friend, and because of that I will not take this as I should. People do not like to be reminded of grey/shame facts. Because the facts you state are true. But the meaning behind it - you got it all wrong. As a healer, you can see things only on a small scale, on an individual basis. On that level you are right. All those things are happening to us. But you have to be an organizer to see the whole picture on a galactic scale. We are not fighting any more with our neighbours on the other side of the hills, armed with sticks and stones. Our enemies are on the other end of the Galaxy - armed with weapons, charged with strange energies. You cannot fight technology with muscle. Look at our neighbouring planets. All the physically-oriented races are dominated by the ones with high technology - and these are bested by the ones using mental energies. Our civilization, based on tradition, cannot cope with them. Muscle is no match for machine - as the machine is no match against someone who is able to control its driver's mind. We have to evolve to keep on top and that means we change our ways. We did not stray from the warrior's way.

'We are going through a transitory period, gathering new energies, new powers and when we are ready, the galaxies beware.'

Kiara D'Charkoon closed the healing pod's lid with disgust. She was tired and irritable.

Her rest period was long overdue and her body resented the lack of adequate nourishment. The use of the pods always left her system very low in energy and she needed large amounts of high energy concentrates to recover its optimal function.

Thank the Star that she was finished for the day.

This is not really what she had in mind when she accepted the post.

To be the First Person's private healer means

position and influence in the sector. When she was first offered this post it seemed like all her dreams came true. It was a prestigious position. A position through which she could do anything she wanted, she would be free to study, to experience.

The reality came to her very quickly.

When she met the First Person, she realized that the illustrious person behind the scenes is just another, bad-tempered old woman.

That she was expected to attend her, calm her and heal her, or if nothing else, just to make her feel good, irrespective of working or resting periods.

And if there was nothing else to do, the First Person's house was always full of visitors, business acquaintances who would benefit from her services. Matter of fact - Kiara started to suspect that her services were part of the price in their negotiations and that the old woman was using her talents to obtain favours or obligation/bonds from her business partners.

There weren't many fully trained pod operators around. Kiara straightened her body with pride while she was walking home. The House of D'Charkoon was the best known healing house of the Sector - and she, Kiara, was the first born of her mother...

She still remembered her mother's voice, cradling her in her arms next to the fire. That she was to grow up to be a big girl, bigger and stronger than all the other ones, because she was a D'Charkoon.

Kiara D'Charkoon...

She smiled at the memory. It was a long, long time ago. A lot of work, a lot of suffering behind her.

Was it worth it?

(Look at me now, mother - the First Person's private healer. Did I do well, as you expected me to?)

Her feet felt heavy - but the pride in the thought gave them wings. Her steps sounded strong and confident along the empty corridors.

She did not have far to go. Her retiring place was very close to the one the First Person occupied. This filled her with a feeling of importance at the beginning - but very soon she realized that this proximity was not a tribute to her person.

She had to be close - so that she could call her at any time, irrespective of the time of the day or what she was doing.

But still, she was the First Person's healer. It was her, Kiara D'Charkoon, chosen from amongst thousands of other aspirants.

(Mother, are you proud of me now?)

The House of D'Charkoon was always one of the leading houses amongst the crystal healers - but she was the first D'Charkoon who was offered this position.

Her hand automatically closed around her pendant - absorbing the heat, the green energy into her blood.

Green for the House of D'Charkoon - the memories of those first years of her life always caused a cold shiver along her spine.

She remembered clearly when her mother was talking about her to her older brother (her mother said this was a false memory, as she was too young to remember, but she did), saying that she, Kiara, will be impressed with the black crystal of the House on her first birthday.

That the House of D'Charkoon was the only House whose members were able to tune into the perfect pitch of the carbon based crystal. Only a very powerful mind was able to control the high quality output of the black energy.

The other Houses had to be content with crystals of a lesser crystalline purity - and as such they had a lower level healing capacity.

Her first birthday was approaching amongst great expectations. The excitement was infectious, and she, who was supposed to be too young to do so, was part of the Big Hope. And then - it happened.

She failed to impress.

They were unable to tune the black crystal to her brain waves. She was not receptive.

The first born daughter of the House of D'Charkoon failed to impress!

Their enemies had a field day with their shame. Because the shame was great. It shook the very foundations of the House.

This failure meant that there was an impurity in the D'Charkoon's bloodline.

Many Houses were broken for much less than this.

Kiara remembered how inexplicable it was for her, that sudden change from a happy, expectant atmosphere to that shameful sadness which followed. She was calling her mother for strength, to be able to cope with this influx of inexplicable feelings...

And her mother was woken up in the middle of the night by the powerful crystal to crystal call...

The rest was on everyone's lips for years to come.

That Kiara D'Charkoon's apparent failure to Impress, was due to the fact that she was already tuned into the green magnetic vibro/crystal from Shainain's outer moon, which was accidentally an inside component of one of her toys.

And the fact that the D'Charkoon's tradition would carry on through a stone of lesser energy was eclipsed by the knowledge of the fantastic mental potentials of the girl who was able to do it.

Because no one, no one ever, was able to tune herself into the wave lengths of the crystal energy...

Kiara's voice-print opened the door to her cubicle. She called her retiring place her cubicle - although it wasn't anything similar to the place she occupied during her training period.

It had three very spacious rooms, all furnished with too much luxury, with excessive thought for body comfort, Kiara thought.

Except the one next to her bedroom. In this room, she insisted to have her own way.

This was her work room. In this room she spent all her spare waking time.

As always, Kiara went straight to this room.

The lights came on at the sound of her footsteps and from their hidden place from behind the panels near the ceiling they illuminated the whole room with their bright, blue white light.

The long shelves along the walls, loaded with books, contrasted sharply with the undecorated cleanliness of the white-painted walls.

The only other furniture in the room was the long, solid work table in the middle, bearing on its top, like on an altar, the large slabs of green stone.

Kiara touched the stones with affection, as if they were alive.

For her, they were.

These slabs were the results of nearly two full turns of hard work. Stones of this size were very expensive. Besides, they had to be cut to her specifications. Every piece had to fit with the other perfectly, so when they were together the flow of green energy…

She saved every credit she earned to buy the stones, and every moment of her spare time to find them, to polish them, to fit them together.

Very soon she will have a full set, and then…then she will know.

Kiara did not notice the lighting up of the communicators screen until the First Person's hoarse voice shook her out of her thoughts.

'There you are dear - I am glad I did not have to wake you.'

Looking at the old woman's' face on the screen, Kiara made a conscious mental effort to keep the purple/red off her face. (I have to remember to turn off the incoming visuals. Anyone could watch me without me even noticing it).

'Yes Great Lady - how can I serve you?' (She must have noticed my red/anger, but she probably knows that it was not directed towards her. It startled me, having my privacy interrupted.)

'I do not want to impose upon you Kiara, but I have this terrible warp in my head-plates and it is imperative that I sleep tonight. Tomorrow I preside the Leader's Council and I have to have my full potential, you know what they are like.'

Yes, Kiara knew. She accompanied the First Person a few times to these meetings, and each time she was surprised by the amount of aggressiveness and violence expressed there. Excessive even by her standards.

(Yes, to survive a meeting like that, one needs to have her full potential).

'I am on my way - My Lady.'

The old face disappeared from the darkening screen while Kiara was leaving the room.

I will not see much sleep this night were her parting thoughts.

**

And the green energy fought the pain. A searing white in the green, a burning, twisting warping of the plates. (She must be very strong to take all this without a visible colour shift).

Kiara needed all her power to control the pain and to not to break the contacts, but then, slowly, the green

101

was winning and she flowed with the green along the new pathways, soothing and calming until there was no more white.

By the time she withdrew from her mind, the First Person was in a deep sleep - a peaceful blue-pale on her face.

**

'Mother! What are you doing here?'

'If that exclamation means that you are glad to see me then I think you should let me in.'

'I am sorry. Please come in.' Kiara stepped aside to let her mother in. 'I really did not expect to see you here.'

'Thank you. Apologies accepted. Did I interrupt anything important?'

'Not really. I just got home and had no specific plans for the evening. I hope you can stay for a while.'

'That is up to you. Make me feel comfortable, offer me something to eat and I might consider it.'

'Please sit down while I prepare something. I do not have many reserves, as I am not eating at home, but I won't let you starve.'

'What do you mean you are not eating here? Where do you eat?'

'I usually eat at the First Person's place. And before you make a remark about it, there is nothing personal in it. Her place is like a big Hotel. I have never seen less than twenty people in her dining room. Besides, the First Person herself eats alone in her chambers.'

She does not like company, but always has people around so they are available when she wants them.'

'It sounds practical - if you can afford it.'

'She can. Believe me - she can.' Kiara put in front of her mother a tray with a tall green glass and sandwiches.

'A moncato! Every time I drink it, it reminds me of you. Remember how you used to bring it to me every morning when you were little?'

Kiara had to use her control to prevent a visible colour shift.

Daira D'Charkoon was not one for idle chatter. She was making time to bring up a subject and found it difficult to do so.

'Mother - why don't you tell me what you are doing here?'

'The green is very perceptive.'

'The black should talk.'

'Where do you keep your crystals?'

(So that is it. I should have known. She heard about me buying the stones, and her conclusion, even if wrong, is a natural one).

It was one of the dangers of being a crystal healer. The communion with the crystal energy was able to offer such a feeling of ecstasy that the healer sometimes succumbed to the pleasures of the union flow. Kiara heard of several cases like this mentioned during her training. Such a person, a prisoner in the web of pleasure energy, required the proximity of larger and larger crystal masses to satisfy her needs. The end result was always a mind burn out.

(She thinks that I…)

'I will show you mother. They are in the next room.'

Daira approached the green stones in silence. She touched the large slabs with her hand, as if to make sure they were real.

'So it is true,' she whispered.

'What is true, Mother?' (I will not make it easy for her. She has to accuse me straight to my face).

'There are rumours about you.'

'What rumours?'

103

'Don't be coy with me,' Daira exploded. 'You know very well what I am talking about. Those,' she pointed to the crystals, 'and I want a quick explanation.'

'That depends on who I am talking to. My mother or the head of the House of D'Charkoon.'

'What is the difference?'

'To the head of the house I owe an explanation with due respect. From my mother I demand an explanation for what she is thinking of me.'

'And what do you expect? Everyone knows you are buying large quantities of your Crystal of Impression. Everyone comments on your solitary lifestyle, so unnatural for your social position. You live alone; your social life is non-existent. The way you dress is a disgrace, and although I perceive health around you, you have lost a lot of weight. So, as your mother and as your superior, I want an explanation. And you know this is not just interfering with your life. You are the heir of the D'Charkoon tradition and too much depends on you to ignore your actions.'

'I am sorry. You are right mother, as usual. But the explanation you seek is not a simple one. The only thing that I can assure you right now is that I am not caught in the pleasure web and that I do not intend to be.'

'Thank the stars for that.' Daira's colour shift was obvious. Kiara recognized that it was an expression of trust that her mother permitted her to see her emotions.

'Then tell me what are you doing with such a vast amount of crystal? You know the dangers of having it so close to you.'

'Mother, this does not apply to me. A long time ago I already found the balanced flow of the crystal energy. It is an instrument for me - nothing else. A powerful one, but unable to touch my emotion/core.'

'How did you do it? I do not think that I could be

able to live so close to so much black without being affected.'

'You don't have to worry about that. No one is able to afford so much black under one roof. Your crystal is too expensive.'

'Maybe so - but how can you be sure that it does not affect you?'

'About a full term ago I went to the Karandza mine to select my slabs. I went down the shaft, cut into the middle of the green mountain. I could draw on the energy of the crystal around me but it did not affect my judgement. If that amount of green did not affect me, those few slabs will not either.'

'Daughter - you are full of surprises. But tell me about your crystals.'

'Well - I have spent many full terms making plans, polishing my theory and thinking and re-thinking about it many times - but now that I want to tell you about it, it seems too flimsy.

'Like, what I do is what I feel I have to do, not what I know I have to do. And what I hope to get - well - I have no way of knowing what I will get.'

'Meaning that you are acting like a crystal healer is supposed to act, following emotions.'

'Thank you mother. I needed a morale boost. Anyway, what I intend to do is an expansion of the use of the crystal energy. You know that in a healing session - the healer connects with the crystal, focuses wave lengths and directs the energy channels into the subject's body. This energy flow is twofold, a doing/feeling flow, and while the healer flows with the energy in - at the same time they receive an emotional output from the body.

'The healer perceives the functioning of the body in shades of emotional static flow.'

'Kiara - remember whom you are telling all this to.'

'I am sorry mother - I know that you were using crystal energy before I was born - but I have to present my point in a way that it makes a bit of sense. Bear with me a little longer. Okay?'

'Fine. Keep going.'

'Now - the quality of the structural/functional picture obtained through the emotional pathways, the depth reached, the capacity of producing the changes requested through the active channel mode - these all depend on the innate impact energy of the crystal - and the synchronizing capacity of the healer. And I have always wondered that the traditional ways of establishing the healer contact would be the right one.'

'Do you have a better one?'

'I do not know it yet. I watched you heal many times. I have talked to other healers a lot lately, and it seems to me that I am not using the crystal the way you and the others are doing. Not by choice, mind you. Without realizing, I learned to apply a different contact system.'

'Explain.'

'The way you are using the crystal, and correct me if I am wrong, is to use the crystal resonance to focus the wave length of your mind; and while your energy does not mix with the crystal's energy, the crystal pattern is the mould only, it is your energy pattern alone which does the probing and correcting. Am I describing it correctly?'

'Yes. You are.'

'Good. This means that, working this way, the energy pattern of your crystal is all-important, but its size is not. A small piece of crystal can be as good a mould as a larger one. Correct?'

'Correct. But you must have known this for many full turns.'

'I had an idea, but not a very clear one, as I do not

work this way.'

'How do you do it?'

'When I flow in and mix with the green energy I am not looking for a pattern to follow. Perhaps partly due to the electromagnetic properties of my crystal, the energy feels to be alive for me. I feel - I perceive a pulsating, live energy, which I instinctively accept as my equal. I mix with it - I flow with it. There is no role differentiation. I absorb the green into me. I gain its energy and flow along with it into the subject to search and to correct. But at that stage there is no me or the green anymore. There is a definite feeling of a powerful "we" which is much stronger than the "I" or the "Green".'

'This is certainly an unusual use of crystals. However, it does not explain your collection.'

'I am getting to that. Now - as soon as I realized that, for better or worse, my crystal ways were different, the first thing that jumped to my mind was that the rules which regulate your ways might not be true for mine. And very soon I was able to prove it to myself. That I was right.'

'Just slow down there. You were right in what?'

'That in my way of doing crystal contact, the size of the crystal is important. That within certain limits, I can absorb much more energy from a larger stone and my capacity of penetration and manipulation are sharpened the more energy I carry into the subject.'

'Sounds fascinating. You should inform the Council about this.'

'I am not ready for that yet. I need more proof before I can do that.'

'Is this what you are doing now?'

'No. I have gone a step further. I feel that to obtain maximum contact energy it is not enough to increase the crystals' size. But if I could place the subject bodily into the crystal - the dimensional flow pattern would be perfect for a deep energy contact.'

' You cannot put a person into the crystal.'

'No. But I can do the next best thing. I can build a healing pod using only crystal material. In this way - the person will be literally inside the crystal.'

**

Although her mother left quite late, Kiara could not sleep. She was lying in her bed with her eyes shining with excitement in the darkness. Sleeping was the last thing on her mind, she felt like jumping, like shouting, and it was hard to keep all this excitement inside.

Her mother approved! Her project was found valid by the Head of the House!

Kiara was making plans for her crystal pod for more full turns than she cared to remember. For her it was a real, well-worked-out plan. Worked out in every detail in every possible emotional pathway, but she kept it for herself.

No one ever knew about her plans. There was no one to whom she could mention her problems, her sleepless nights spent in doubt. No one knew about the frustrations of the dead ends or of the elation she felt when she found the way.

Her way! But it lacked reality for the same reason that made it safe.

There was no possibility for open failure - as no one would know if it failed, because no one knew about it. There was also no confirmation of the trueness of her feeling.

But for the first time, she could explain it to someone. To her mother - who listened, who understood.

And who approved!

The real elation came from the knowledge, that it was not her mother who listened. Kiara knew that the person listening to her explanations was the Head of her House - who was listening - and judging - in her official status.

And she approved!

With this, many turns of planning and wishing suddenly turned into reality. Her crystal pod was not only part of her dream anymore. It was a fact. An officially-presented and officially-approved plan. Approved to be built. It became a reality!

Her mother liked her idea. Even went so far as saying she wanted to make it an official research project of the House of D'Charkoon.

With the connections and with the financial backup of the House!

Kiara could have all the crystals she needed straight away, professional help to build her pod and research facilities to establish the psycho-functions.

It was like a dream. Her mother even looked hurt when her helping offer was refused.

Kiara buried her head in her pillow with a sigh. It could have been so easy. So perfect. Everything she was dreaming about for so long was offered to her on a plate. And she refused! It seems insane! The offer was a genuine one with the intention only to help.

But as she was staring at the dark with a kind of sadness in her heart, Kiara knew she was doing the right thing.

The pod had to be hers - and hers alone. The whole functioning of the idea was based on the assumption that she would be able to identify herself with her Impression crystals, to fuse her mind to the crystal flow and with its symbiotic energy expansion to be able to enter beyond the physical limits of her subjects' body and psyche. To go so deep into the causative vectors of the psyche that not even a healer resonating with the energy of the black crystal would dare or would be able to go.

But for now - she has to be one with the green crystal flow and the crystal has to be a part of her. She cannot lose out in this psychic oneness due to the knowledge that part of the crystals were purchased/belonged to someone else. She could not give herself completely to the green flow knowing that what she was doing was not hers alone.

No. It could not be done!

She has to do it by herself, the hard way!

She has to work, sweat for every bit of crystal, and build her pod when she could afford it.

She has to have the feeling that she has full command of the emotional time flows, that the battle is only her own.

Her mother understood this. Her black crystal was glowing on her chest in sympathy - crystal resonance.

The green and the black blended so nicely together.

**

'It... nearly...got me...this time.' The words came out rasping while she was fighting to regain control of her breathing. The famous Hhruahran fighting machine, like any other, had its weak points. One of them was that, while it consumed very large amounts of oxygen, its supply was limited to the capacity of the chest plates. When the physical activity passed a certain level, there was a shortage of oxygen, and the machine's function decreased in performance.

'No one said it would be easy,' she murmured to herself, while dodging a spiked tentacle, trying to approach the beast from behind. 'But this is ridiculous. You cannot kill this thing.'

As if answering her thoughts, there was the deafening high-pitched scream of the Doanx, and the sickening, crunching sound of D'Kian being crushed under the tremendous weight of its forelegs.

'That leaves only two of us, it won't last much more now. If I could only get behind those shoulder plates...'

The Doanx had a weak spot, just behind his thick neck - where the neck and shoulder plates fused, and formed a raised rim across the back. A kind of blind spot, which the animal could not see clearly, and could not reach with tentacles or claws. But to get there, you had to gnaw yourself through a forest of teeth and claws.

The Doanx they confronted today was fully alert and hungry - well prepared for the fight, which was made clear by the fact that there were only two Hhruahrans left out of the ten that started the challenge.

D'Ktuan's far senses were very aware of the masses of spectators watching the fight and felt a grim satisfaction knowing that they were not cheated in their expectations.

It was a good fight, straight from the beginning. A good alert Doanx and the ten best fighters of the Zone.

She managed to grab one of the spiked tentacles as it whistled by, just missing her head. Immediately it curled around her arms and started pulling her towards the cavernous mouth.

Out of the corners of her eyes, she saw the other tentacles approach. If they grab her too, she would be helpless.

She did not resist the pull, instead ran towards the beast and just before reaching its head, she gave a tremendous jump, using the tentacle itself as a rope, she pulled herself up and in a large arc landed right behind the neck plate. Her talons dug deep into the soft, unprotected flesh, while the sharp, spiked tentacles

111

whistled ineffectively above her head.

The animal could not reach her there.

She wished she had a knife or any other weapon - but that was one of the rules - Hhruahran machine against the beast machine, and the best equipped to win.

This was on the surface in favour of the Hhruahrans - as their natural body armament was formidable to confront any enemy.

But not a Doanx.

You could not kill a Doanx.

Not that a Doanx had any special armament. Quite the opposite. It had the usual set of fangs, claws and a nasty temper - helped by an enormous body weight - but its main defence resided in its decentralization of functions. A Doanx had many weak points, but had practically no vital organs, nothing to be killed by. Its nervous system was spread in several equivalent parts along its spine, it had several independent hearts distributed to supply different parts of the body, even his breathing was distributed amongst several independent systems connected to the outside through deep vents in the skin plates.

Such an animal could bear enormous wounds without really being harmed by it. This is why it was chosen as a valid opponent to the ones who aspired to the higher honours of the War Games. And the real objective of the challenge was not to kill the Doanx. No one ever killed a Doanx.

The winner of the challenge was the last survivor out of the ten.

D'Ktuan was treading in slippery, bare flesh now. Was digging her heals in deeper and deeper behind the neck plate. With her bare hands she was tearing out large chunks of dripping flesh. The beast was screaming in pain, trying to reach her at the plates...

Now was the time for her companion to…

The sickening crunch told her it was too late. There was, of course, no shouting or screaming with the crunching sound.

It was a Hhruahran who died!

The Doanx reared up on his hind legs and shook the body violently. D'Ktuan lost her hold on the slippery flesh and was thrown off in a wide arc, landing in a very undignified posture in the dust far from the animal.

The high trumpets sounded the end of the Game.

D'Ktuan stood up, dusting her body.

This is not the way it was supposed to happen.

She was the last survivor. Technically she won.

But this was an empty victory.

There was no conquered enemy. No kill.

There wasn't even a last victorious act to finish the battle with pride.

The last act of this battle was her biting dust.

Swatted away like a fly.

Her blood started to boil.

She won. She outlasted all the others - but she had no victory.

Her blood was screaming for victory, for a kill.

She faced the beast.

There was a sudden silence in the Arena.

Then a low, approving murmur, growing into a deep roar.

They were all Hhruahrans. They knew the taste of victory.

They wanted a kill.

D'Ktuan was not thinking any more. Her pride, the Warrior Madness was pushing her far beyond her endurance.

With a tremendous jump, she missed the whirling tentacles and struck the wide neck plate. Vaulting over it without breaking the fluidity of her jump, she landed behind the plate - on the same blind spot as before, in the middle of the gaping wound.

She dug her left arm deep into the quivering flesh, looking for a bone to grab, to anchor her body to the bleeding animal.

'And I will stay here until one of us dies!'

With her talons and her right hand she was digging the wound deeper and deeper. Large chunks of flesh were falling to the ground around the screaming, bouncing beast.

But D'Ktuan was glued to the animal. There was no power strong enough to remove her now.

She was digging deeper and deeper into the wound, until she was completely surrounded by living flesh.

She kept digging, tearing the entrails of the animal, wreaking havoc on the internal systems.

A Doanx can take a lot, but there are limits.

The beast's contortions were becoming more sluggish, its roars of pain less and less powerful. With a last effort, it reared up on to its hind legs, collapsed onto its side, burying D'Ktuan in its dying flesh, crushing her with its weight.

A long ovation saluted the victor.

The very first one in Hhruahran history who killed a Doanx bare handed.

It was a good fight.

**

The old woman showed no signs of tiredness.

Kiara could not help but admire the old warrior as she watched the council meeting through the transparent plex-metal window.

The meeting was an exceptionally violent one and the plex-metal barrier was more for the protection of the people observing from the outside. No known energy could cross that barrier. The sounds came through speakers on the outside wall and even the apparent transparency was due to the electronic transposition of the photo images from the inside surface to the outside surface - creating the illusion of a window to look in.

The First Person appeared to be in full control of her energies, without the slightest colour shift to denounce exhaustion, which Kiara knew she must feel.

The meeting was going, nonstop now, over three full axial rotation and Kiara received the order to go to sleep twice. Both times the First Person mentioned "I want you to be rested when I need you".

What does she need me for?

This time Kiara was directly requested to attend the meeting through the witness box, which was highly unusual as her presence in the political circles and activities was barely tolerated by her superior. She was told several times that she should concern herself with what she is trained for - matters of health, especially that of the First Person.

Politics in Hhruahran were considered a more dangerous affair than war -combat. You have more chance of surviving an interplanetary war affair as a first liner, than to survive as an active participant in the meeting of the First Council.

But this time Kiara was told that the planet's health policies would be discussed, especially the recent dispute around the de-legislation of the healing pods, which would directly affect her.

What does she need me for?

Kiara could not imagine any way in which she could be of help. Especially not like this, standing outside, with no means of direct communication, with the plex-metal wall separating them.

The issue of the healing pods was of no importance on the national scale, but as an issue which involved deep emotional arguments, the opposition intended to use it as a spearhead to break the First Person's long-standing power control. They intended to put all energy available to bring the new legislation in, the same way as the First Person's intention was to block it at all cost. The matter of health was utilized as an excuse to bring this power struggle out into the open.

Something had to break, to give.

For Kiara the issue was important, although not very clear. The main argument against the use of the healing pods was the apparent invasion of privacy. The healer was sharing the subject's emotions and thoughts during a pod session and there was no way to block it. Still, Kiara could not see a problem. If you do not trust your chosen healer, do not choose pod healing. Pick an alternative to solve your problem.

Because the alternative healers seemed to be more and more abundant recently.

Especially the physical contact healers. The persons who, when they find a problem/hurt, try to correct it by actually touching it with dirty hands. Kiara shuddered, they were talking about how some of them even tried to use chemicals to influence body functions…

And anyone could become a physical healer

When they were old enough to decide that they want to heal, they congregated in large numbers around a few teachers who showed them their ways.

Not like the crystal healers, whose special talent was the result of carefully-planned breeding programs and developed by a one to one teaching contact, practically from birth.

And they claimed that they can do everything - Kiara sneered in disdain at the thought. How could they? They have no talent and no proper training. All that they have is greed, to be able to put their hands into the pockets that, until now, were only open to the Healing Houses.

But why is this so important that they need to discuss it in the presence of a full Planetary Council meeting?

Kiara shrugged her shoulders. One could never understand the way politicians get around things. But this thing about the pods...

A sudden movement caught her eyes through the plex-metal window. Council KornD'Ku, of the polar territory, jumped to her feet, sending her chair back crashing to the floor. The young warrior, who always intensely attacked the First Person's health policies, stood there with her legs shaking, holding herself erect by grabbing the edges of the table with both hands - the pale whiteness of her face-plates expressed her suffering vividly.

For a second Kiara perceived the intense whiteness of her pain, until it faded into the dark blackness of death.

The swift efficiency by which the body was removed and the total indifference with which the rest of the Council continued their discussion was a clear demonstration that this kind of thing was not unusual in this room.

The violent power of that pain was far too excessive to be natural, Kiara concluded to herself. It had to be drug induced, and it had to be very powerful to override to such an extent the warrior's natural defences. It was probably a nerve enhancer, carried to her by the aroma of the food recently served to her. There was food and drink in front of everyone - but no one touched it for obvious reasons. The poisoning of the foodstuff was practically a rule in here. She probably did not protect herself against the smells carrying the poison.

Kiara felt uncomfortable with the knowledge that she would not survive long in that room.

She would have probably protected herself against the poisonous smell, but before her last rest period she did not notice the slight colour shift in the light filling the Council room.

Only when the blue council collapsed in violent convulsions did she notice that all the others had extended their surgically implanted colour filters for protection. (I would be dead by now) The thought was sickeningly uncomfortable. (Still - convulsion is a better death than that violent white pain I felt…)

(I FELT!)

Kiara sat up straight in her chair (I should not have felt it. There was a plex-metal wall separating us, and no energy could…)

Her eyes were drawn to the window. The First Person was looking directly at her -(She is not supposed to know where I am) with warning sparks in her eyes.

(She knows! She knows that mental energies can cross the plex-metal. That is why she wanted me to be there.)

(But what does she want me to do?)

Before the meeting she asked the First Person about this several times, but the only answer she got was that she will know when the time arrived. And that she was expected to do the right thing.

(But what is the right thing? How will I know?)

A sudden silence called her attention back to the Council room. All eyes were directed to the central seat, and as the First Person was preparing herself to address the assembly, Kiara felt a tightness creeping around her throat.

There was something wrong. Although there was no visible colour shift - knowing her control, Kiara would not have expected to see one - there was a clumsiness, a hesitation in the old woman's movements, so out of character for her.

As she got to her feet, with noticeable effort, the long chain hanging from around her neck got caught on the side of her chair, broke, and, slipping from her neck, fell to the floor with a loud thump. She picked it up from the floor - chain and medallion - and put both of them on the table in front of her.

There was suddenly a nearly touching thickness in the air, as everyone looked at the sparkling jewel with tense expectation. Then came the relaxation of the muscles as the multiple sensors reported the innocence of the shining object. There were even a few degrading comments about how she was getting old and weak, taking a dress ornament into the council meeting.

Kiara's eyes met with the First Person's (She is doing it again), as she was standing erect now, gathering her thoughts for her speech, with her right hand resting on the large, green stone of the medallion...

(GREEN! So this is my signal. And I can get in contact with her now - as long as she has her hand on my impression stone.) Kiara closed her fingers around her own stone and, closing her eyes, allowed herself to flow towards the other...

WHITE! Searing white pain!

The intensity of the unexpected pain nearly pushed Kiara out of phase with the green energy. She needed all the power of her bloodline to stay in control, to stay with the green, to survive the waves of intense pain.

'No one can stand a pain like this!' She said to herself, while suddenly remembering that the First Person showed not even the slightest colour shift.

She has far more power than I, she thought, while using these feelings of awe and respect to stay in the green, away from the white.

And the green was gathering around her, thicker and stronger, and she flowed ahead - soothing, pushing away the burning white.

(Thanks Kiara - the thought came to her mind - I can breathe again. Quick I need your help...)

(What can I do?) Her mind was screaming to her amidst the pain.

(It is a directional audio disruption focused directly on me. I cannot localize its origin. Help me...)

Kiara could perceive pulsations in the white now. It was not still - it was flowing in waves - it had a directional flow - it was coming from...

(The Council of the Green Region to your left! The flow is coming from her!)

(Where does she keep the sonic disruptor...)

(In her mouth!)

(Thanks Kiara - now get away girl. I do not want you to distract me in the fight.)

The white was difficult to leave behind; it was sucking on her energy. It took quite a lot of effort, but the moment Kiara felt she was back in her space, she forced her eyes to open to look through the window.

The old warrior showed again that she deserved her post. She must have been very fast - as the first visual image Kiara received from the room was that of the Green Council's inert form laying back in her chair, with her neck broken and the First Person forcing open her mouth with her bare fingers, fishing out the metallic box of the audio disruption.

Putting it on the table, she took a deep breath and recited, 'Observe! Remember the Law! The Law was done!'

Her victory was complete. The opposition had plenty of opportunity to eliminate her, as the Law required that the aggressor be killed. When she attacked the council member sitting next to her, she was open prey to all the others.

But she was too quick and she had the element of surprise. The moment she produced the sonic disruptor, she was the victim and not the aggressor any more.

The Law protected her.

Her triumphant eyes, which looked into Kiara's, were quite eloquent. She was not needed any more. The victory was complete.

All what was left now was for the First Person's party to establish their policies and put forward their terms.

The fighting was over.

The power was theirs for another turn.

**

'Mother, what are you doing here?'

'Kiara dear - remember - you called me.'

'I mean - what are you doing here at this time, in the middle of the dark period. You are supposed to be asleep, like I was.'

'Sorry to disturb your sleeping, but your call was quite impressive. Actually, I did not know you could send a crystal call over such a distance. Besides, there was an unmistakable urgency in your call - so here I am.'

'There is a certain urgency, but…'

'While you decide how urgent is your problem, can I come in?'

'Oh, sorry mother. Please come in. Can I help you with your case?'

'Yes, thank you. You see Kiara - we are all creatures of habit. You insist on keeping me at the door, forgetting to let me in…'

'Sorry mother, but you keep surprising me with your

unexpectedly-timed visits…'

'…and I keep getting hungry as soon as I arrive. What do you have to eat?'

Kiara burst out laughing. 'Nothing much - as you see - I am a creature of habit too.'

'But don't worry - I will find something for you.'

'Anything but those sandwiches you gave me last time. I don't think I am that hungry.'

'What about some salad and cold meat?'

'Fine. That looks quite acceptable. And while my mouth takes care of this, how about you tell me why you called? By the way, what are you staring at?'

'At you, mother. No one should be so bubbly and fresh at this late time.'

'I am not really that bubbly. Matter of fact I am quite tired. Remember that our house is not just around the corner. But I will be damned if after all this rush I have to wait until the next light for you to tell me about your problem.'

'Okay mother. You feed your mouth while I feed your ears.'

'It is about my pod. The crystal one. I finished it.'
'So?'

'So…well. Come and have a look at it…'

The room was filled with the pulsating power-humming sound originating from the crystal pod. The large, box-shaped object was brightly illuminated by the green light which came from the inside. It was closed on all sides, but the light was so intense that it shone through the walls, giving the impression that they were completely transparent.

Deep in the centre of the pod there was a pulsating focus of light - bright and of immense power.

Daira put her plate down. 'Suddenly I am not so hungry. What is this thing?'

'My pod…'

'I gathered that much. But again, what is it?'

Kiara did not answer. She had no answer to give.

'When you described the pod you intended to build, I pictured a pod-shaped box with walls of green crystal, with all the mechanisms and properties of a healing pod. I thought it was meant to be a healing pod - built of a new material. But this...this thing...it is astonishing. How did you do it?'

'I do not know exactly. Really mother - I don't. What I intended to do was exactly what you described. This...just happened.'

'There must be more to it.'

'Well...yes. I think I understand what happened, but only now, looking back. I was really not planning to do this.'

'I am listening.'

'Well. You know I put a lot of effort into choosing the right crystals. I went personally to the quarry itself, selected the rocks containing the crystals by going through the whole place, bit by bit, checking every little part of the crystal for flaws, for metallic impurities which would interfere with the flow of mental energy. Only accepted the perfect ones. Perfect on the surface and in the depth of its structure. Believe me, mother it was not an easy job to find the right ones.'

'Keep going.'

'I was also very careful in selecting the adjacent stones. They had to fit perfectly - not only on the surface but also in the directional crystal pattern, so the emisional energy flow could cross the interface uninfluenced. When I put two of them together you could barely distinguish the line of separation between them and the energy flow was like through one stone.

'Right through, the construction was like putting together an ordinary healing pod made of the usual materials. Until I put the last piece in its place.'

'What happened then?'

'I felt a jolt, like something clicking into place, switching on a powerful function. The feeling was more physical than mental. I am sure I felt a fine trembling, which went right through me.

'Then this light – power started to build up, I did not know what to do.'

'Why did you allow it to build up to this level?'

'There was nothing I could do. I could not turn it off unless I dismantled it piece by piece.'

'So why didn't you do that?'

'To dismantle it? Mother - I could not do that. Can you feel its power, that pulsating force emission? It has a life force. It is alive.'

'I can feel its power and it is fantastic, but its emission is completely inanimate. The life energy you feel is a rebound resonance of your own.'

'You are probably right, but could you dismantle it?'

'No. And I don't think it should be. This is something too important to miss. What do you intend to do?'

'What do you mean? What should I do with a healing pod?'

'You are not serious about entering yourself into that thing?'

'Mother, it is supposed to be a healing pod. It is the result of a very long and hard work. Am I supposed to just forget about it?'

'I guess you cannot do that. But if you are not afraid to mix your life energy with that green - you are a braver person than I am.'

'I am not afraid. I am terrified. That is why I had to call you. I cannot do it alone.'

'How can I help you? You know that I would help in any way I can, but I do not see a way in which I can help you to get into that energy vortex you created.'

'Mother my problem is not getting in. While I am standing here, I can feel the pull of the crystal energy, trying to draw me inside. I have to make a conscious effort to resist it, to reject the urge to flow. The problem is that I do not know what to expect once inside. How will I react when I mix with the green energy? Will I maintain enough individuality to separate on the way out? I am afraid I will not have the strength to do it. I will probably need you to get me out.'

'How can I help? The power of this thing is overbearing.'

'Mother - you control the black. The most powerful of all the known crystal energies...'

'Hold it Kiara! You just said the key word. The most powerful of all the KNOWN crystal energies. What you created here is something unknown. Something far beyond my experience...'

'Mother! You are not answering me. Are you going to help me or not?'

'Of course I will help you. I think it is recklessly dangerous, but I agree with you. You cannot stop now. We will probably be absorbed by that green, but you have to do it.'

'You are hard to pin down Mother - but thanks. I feel safer when you are around. And this is not your little girl speaking. I have a lot of respect towards that black crystal of yours...well - the next thing we have to clear up is the question of the subject.'

'What subject?'

'Well. You cannot just enter into an empty pod. You have to have an objective, an aim to direct your flow into. You need a person in the pod.'

'It does not have to be a person. It could be any animated object - an animal, even a plant, to practice with. I would recommend a plant to start. I do not have personal recollection of plant energies, but persons I know say that it is a very soothing experience to mix with plant life energy.'

'It sounds a good idea. I have some pot plants in the garden, we could use them.'

'You mean now?'

'Why not? You do not look very tired now, and I certainly am too excited to sleep.'

'Well, why not? Go and get the plant.'

**

It was nothing like she expected.

It was everything she expected.

It was so much more than anything she expected...the green had the familiar soft feeling, but so much more of it. Mixing energies with the green, fusing together like two currents and merging as one was always a soothing, pleasing feeling. But mixing with this energy was a pleasure heightened to unbelievable levels.

The explosion of ecstasy was far beyond the tolerance of the responding mind.

Kiara was caught in the power of the torrential energy flow and unable to resist, unwilling to resist, was carried deeper and deeper into the crystal structure. Like a pebble carried by fast waters, felt like she lost her foothold, felt carried away, could not see, and could not feel her way in the turbulence. She tried to resist, but the ecstasy of the flow washed her willpower away, she did not want to fight it. Just wanted to flow with the river, mix with it - to dissolve into its vastness...

Kiara's dissolving awareness felt the tugging of something solid in the middle of the green flow. There was black around her. It was a soothing blackness. Something solid to put her feet down, to find her own way in the green...

(Thank you mother - that was really close.)

(Closer than you think.)

(I am okay now. I know my way. I just did not expect such a power. It took me by surprise.)

(Want to come out?)

(Not yet mother. I have to find out what is at the end of this flow. Come with me. Let's explore it together.)

The black and the green exploded into ecstasy.

**

Kiara slowly became aware of her body. Stiff and aching everywhere, her hand still on the pod. With great effort, she opened her eyes.

'Mother - are you alright?'

The faint sigh which left Daira's lips was the first sign of life from her rigid body which stood on the other side of the pod. She also had her hand on the green crystal, brightly illuminated by the energies from within.

'I do not think I will ever be all right.'

'How do you feel?'

'Drained. I can understand now the lure of the mind benders. After an experience like this, the plainness of reality feels painful.'

'Mother, we did it. We went into that plant deeper than I ever thought it was possible. I could understand the function of every organ, the structure of every little part. I could feel the energy transference between the structural and functional parts. Mother, do you understand what that means? I could have made it bloom, I could have made it grow twice its size or made it wither and fall apart into dead particles. We have to try it with an animal now to see if…'

'Now just hold it there. Maybe you have to try it. Leave me out of all this in the future.'

127

'How come? I thought you enjoyed the experience.'

'I did. I am sore. I am stiff. I am starving. I was afraid like I was never afraid in my life when you made me melt the black and fuse into the green. I don't know if I can ever use my crystal as before…but yes, it was an experience worth living through.'

'What is wrong with fusing with the crystal flow? It was the only way to get that deep. It was always my way to…'

'I know Kiara. But it was never my way.'

'But mother…'

'Kiara. Listen to me. I have always used my carbon-based crystal as an instrument. A very precious instrument. An instrument which is very much a part of my life - but nevertheless, it was always an instrument. An inanimate object. An object that was valuable only due to the services it rendered. Can't you see the difference? When you made me fuse…I correct myself there. When I fused with the green to be able to follow you, I had to accept your crystal values. The black and the green were no objects any more. They came alive and they seemed to have a life force equal in quality to mine. I was not using the black any more. I was going with the black hand in hand.'

'That is why you were able to go where only crystal energies are able to go.'

'But can't you see where that leaves me? How can I use my crystal again, allowing it to focus my mind like a mechanical object - when I know of the energies that are lurking in the depth of it?'

'Well you can ignore it on one hand, and keep using the black crystal, utilizing the crystalline resonance structure, as up to now. On the other hand, you can learn to go deeper into the structure and accept the energies you find there as equal to your life energies.'

'Nobody does that with her crystal.'

'I do.'

'You do not count. Your whole crystal training was twisted from the very beginning. I am just starting to realize that through your training period, while I was teaching you one thing you were learning something different. Whatever I said, whatever I showed you - it had a different meaning for you. Like talking in two different languages.'

'Yes - it must have been like that and neither of us realised that the concepts we were discussing had a different meaning for each of us. But I cannot see your problem mother. Just because you are aware of other ways of operating with the crystals does not mean you have to leave yours.'

'It is not that simple. I know I can still do what I was doing before. But until now I operated with the knowledge that my black was the most powerful of them all. That I can do things no one else was able to do. And now you showed me that there is more, much more. And the worst of it is that it is within my reach. That I just have to reach out and find the way... I think you just caused me to have a lot of sleepless dark periods in the future, until I learn to operate the deep energies.'

'I am sorry mother.'

'You will be sorrier later, when you realize that I intend to spend those dark periods with you. You will have to teach me. And this time, we will both speak the same language.'

**

'Kiara D'Charkoon!' The doorman announced her name with a quite unnecessary loudness - as the ambassador was sitting at his desk in a rather small room.

He looked up from his papers appearing rather annoyed, until recognizing his visitor.

Then his impression changed completely, which might be normal in human standards, but was quite startling for a Hhruahran to watch.

Kiara had contact with humans before, but she could never quite get used to the sight of constantly changing faces, without the minor expressions of colour shift.

'Come in please - sit down. Would you like something to drink?'

'No thank you. I'd rather not.'

'Of course. I have to get used to the idea that on this planet the people do not take nourishment for the mere pleasure of it as we do. But anyway, I was expecting you, and I am really glad to see you again.'

'Mr Ambassador. You know very well that I am not a politician, so before I say or do something wrong - I would like to clear up a few things on my mind.'

'Go ahead. I am listening.'

'I am here on the orders of the First Person herself...'

'I know that.'

'...and when she gave me her instructions, she mentioned that you have an eye problem for which you will need my help. She also instructed me to assist you in anything you require of me - and although she was quite vague about it I had the impression that besides healing sessions, she expected me to do other things. So - could you tell me more clearly, in what way can I be helpful to you?'

'Your First Person is very kind to me.' There was a smile in the Ambassador's voice. 'Let me explain what I mean. I do not know how much information you have about my people, but we Lanornaians have a very bad reaction to physical violence. Although our body is second only to the Hhruahrans in physical power, and we are very able to carry out warlike activities, we are not used to violence. We find physical violence very distasteful, almost frightening, and are trying to avoid it as something strange to our ways of living.

'Now imagine how we feel when suddenly we find ourselves on a planet in which physical violence is an essential part of life. Amongst a warrior race that are born, live and die in violence. Whose every work, every thought, and every action we perceive as a direct threat to the very basic feelings of our existence. If you can imagine this - you know how we feel on arriving to your world.'

'It must be a pretty awful feeling.'

'It is. There are a lot of us quite unable to adapt.'

'Like your predecessor.'

'Yes, like him. His mind was not able to accept the sudden change in environmental emotions. In a situation like this, you bend or you break. He broke.'

'Somehow I cannot see you breaking.'

'Thank you Kiara. I appreciate that - especially coming from a Hhruahran. But this is exactly what your First Person understood well, and out of kindness she sent you to me to soften the blow.'

'I cannot see how.'

Well - as she must see it, and I agree with her - being a healer, used to the mental pathways that are an important part of your life - you are probably one of the least violent people on this planet. By being my guide, even if for a short period, to learn of, and get used to, your people, the impact I receive would be a much softer one, much easier to accept. Can you see her point?'

'I can see her point, what I fail to see is yours. Actually there are two things I do not understand.'

'Let's see if I can help clear them up.'

'Well, one is the reason why human Ambassadors

are chosen from your planet. What I mean is that there must be a lot of human populated worlds out there with a more violent background. It would be much easier for them to contact us.'

'You are right on that one. The human race cannot be very proud of its peacetime achievements. But, there is no choice really. Our worlds - yours and mine - are the only inhabited planets this far from the spin centre of the Galaxy. The other races could not possibly survive the gravitational pull of your planet.'

'I did not think of it in this light, and I agree that it seems logical to select your race to be humanity's Ambassador. Although this still does not clear your personal position in here.'

'What do you mean?'

'I mean - I knew several of your past ambassador's personally - and one way or another I know a lot about others. I also know that to be an ambassador with us was always a distasteful, avoidable work. As far as I know, every one of the ambassadors coming to us had no choice in the matter. To be an ambassador in our world was always considered as a kind of punishment, like serving a sentence for something wrongly done at home.'

'In a way this is quite true.'

'However, I have information that you volunteered. Not just that, but you really forced the situation by putting the politicians of your world in a binding situation in which they had no alternative but send you to fill the so unexpectedly vacant post.'

'I was not aware that this was common knowledge - it was supposed to be a very closely-guarded personal secret.'

'It is not a common knowledge - but I know it to be true.'

'It is true - but rather complicated to explain.'

'You do not have to explain anything to me, Ambassador, but it would help me to assist you if I can understand you better.'

'Well, in a nutshell, the thing that brought me here came to me when I read my predecessor's report.'

'He left in a state of panic, quite convinced that we are all insane.'

'Quite true again. But he was also a very meticulous man. In his report, besides presenting his arguments and opinions, he reported everything as it happened. He also presented your side of the story.'

'Strongly disapproving it of course.'

'Of course. However, there was a conversation he had with your First Person, described in detail, which grabbed me very deeply.'

'You will learn very soon, that everything she says has a similar effect on you.'

'I quite believe that. She must be a very intelligent woman.'

'What did she say?'

'Well the conversation was about the way your Government establishes its power. The fights and deaths in the council room.'

'And that made you come here?'

'Yes. In that conversation your First Person pointed out that yes, there are a few deaths during every policy change - but then the new law brought out is completely obeyed by a unified planet.'

'I fail to see your point.'

'The point is that while reading the transcript of this conversation, I could not help but compare it to the function of our so called civilized way of governing. Like - our Government presents a new law to the public, a fraction of the public does not accept it, political parties form, fights start, war - and then thousands die.'

'Very civilized.'

'Exactly the feeling I had. I felt that I had to come to your world personally to understand your ways of living, to try to learn your "barbaric" ways and apply it to produce more peace in the human world.'

'This is the first time anyone came to Hhruahran's for a peaceful solution. It seems unreal, unnatural.'

'It would seem more real to you if you knew the capacity for violence of the human mind. I feel…'

'I apologize for disturbing your Excellency - but there is an emergency call to Kiara D'Charkoon from the First Person herself.'

'Put it through.'

The first Person's face appeared on the screen.

'Sorry to interrupt you Kiara, but I would appreciate it if you would come immediately. I need you urgently.'

'I am on my way First Person.' Kiara was bewildered about the unusual request, but really there was no other possible answer to it.

'Ambassador - you will understand that I have to leave you.'

' Of course. Good-bye Kiara D'Charkoon - and I expect to meet you again quite soon.'

'Good-bye Sir and thank you.'

**

'I came as fast as I could First Person.'

'Thank you Kiara. I am sorry to disturb your meeting with the Ambassador, but I need you here.'

'What can I do for you My Lady?'

'There was an accident in the Green Sector. The Council member from this section was trapped under the collapsing wall of her home. Her chest was squashed under the weight.'

'I am sorry to hear this – but cannot see how…'

'There are two blue healers with her now, keeping her body functioning until you arrive.'

'I cannot see the point. If her chest was squashed...'

'Before you make a decision, I want you to know all the facts. Is that fair?'

'Go ahead, I am listening.'

'As you know, the Council member from their Green Sector was always a strong supporter of my ideas. Recently, she resigned from politics.'

'She did what?'

'Yes. I know it sounds incredible, but this is just what happened. She did not change sides. She did not want to belong to the other sector - I would understand that. But she simply resigned from politics and retired from public life.'

'Retired to do what?'

'Mushroom farming, I believe.'

'First Person, if it would not be you telling me this, I would not have believed it.'

'I do not blame you for it Kiara. It would probably shock you more knowing that she is the fifth Council member doing just that – all during the last turn.'

'This to be a coincidental happening would be a statistical impossibility.

'Exactly my point.'

'Would it be anything to do with the opposition?'

'Two of the council members belong to them.'

'Then this must be a...'

'That is what we have to find out. The directing powers of the Council are being neutralised one by one. By whom and for what purpose? The Green Council member, while alive, refused to give us any information. So did the others. But now - when she is dead - her living flesh might give you the reason behind the strange behaviour.'

'But spying on the dead, it is like...'

'Kiara, use your head. We are not talking about personal gain or power. Something or someone from the outside is systematically eliminating the power structure of our planet. Do you understand what this means? Someone is preparing an invasion of our planet - and we don't even know who is doing it or how. I am, as the acting First Person, the head of our world. Do you really think that what I am asking you to do is dishonest? Is it not my duty to gather the information, which is probably vital for all our people?

'I understand your desire for information - and it honours you. But please - see my side. The very basic structure rule of our functioning is to not to violate a person's privacy. The Green Council cannot give me her consent, and without it...'

'Kiara, listen to reason. You knew the Green Council for many turns. You have seen her on the battlefields when you were a child, and you knew her in politics recently. You knew her well. You knew her dedication to her people, her concern for their welfare. Do you really think she would refuse your consent to probe her tissue memories when the very survival of our people is at stake? Do you really believe it?'

'No, I do not. Someone else maybe, but not the Green Council. I think you have the right to your request, and I will try my best to give you the answer you seek. Where is the Green Council?'

'At your quarters.'

'My quarters? I do not understand...'

'Kiara dear, I know you are a first grade healer, but even you could not do what is needed without your crystal pod.'

'How do you know about that? You have been spying on me! First Person - I think you owe me an explanation.'

'To start with, I call your attention to the fact that I

136

do not owe anyone any explanation. Not to you or anyone else. Is that clear?'

'I stand corrected, however...'

'And the second thing is that you have to learn to look at things in the proper perspective. Due to the office I bear, I have to know about a lot of things other people do not count on. Amongst other things - I have to know about the persons around me, the persons I have to trust, the persons I turn my back to. I have to know how far I can count on them, how far they are willing to support me. So I have to observe, to watch everyone. No one in particular, but everyone. One of the reasons I am in the office for so long is that no one, even those most remotely connected to me cannot even sneeze without me knowing about it. So - yes, I did watch you - but you were not selected out in any way. I watched you because you are part of my household, you are quite close to my person, and if you cannot accept this idea, then you better go home. If you stay with me, you have to accept the idea that being watched is a part of your office.'

**

The slow, green pulsation started the moment the lid was locked in. The lifeless body of the council member could be seen only vaguely through the crystallised walls of the pod. The moment this was closed the blue healers retired to the far end of the room. Their function had finished. They had kept the physical death away from the body long enough; they could not reach it now in the embrace of the green energy.

Kiara wished her mother were there. There were too many unknowns to be faced, every one of them representing danger. She was quite confident about the handling of the crystal pod. The merging and flowing with the enhanced green energy was a familiar feeling by now. But she had to send her life energy into a destroyed body – which, lacking its own sustaining life form, was perfused with the artificial blue. (And blue was never her favourite energy.) So she had to submerge deep, to the particle level of cell functioning, and retrieve a small fragment of the chemical memory.

She felt unprotected without the support of the black, but there was no time to waste.

The body was dying.

The First Person was watching the scene from the far corner of the room. Her solid emotional control did not allow a visible colour shift, but inside her the emotions were raging. Every death/danger sense, so acutely developed during her long, fighting life was alive, warning her not to proceed. Danger, directed to her, but directed especially to Kiara, the green healer, and in spite of her showing harshness towards Kiara, she got close to the old woman's heart.

But in the odds they were facing, Kiara was expendable.

The stakes were too high - emotions had no part in here. The decisions were made.

She watched Kiara's tense body standing next to the pod with her hands lightly on the lid. The pulsating green reflected a sick paleness on her face. Her eyes, fixed on the depth of the pod, on the pulsating energy centre, slowly closed.

Time was passing, no one moved. All eyes were fixed on Kiara and the luminous green pod. Their slow breathing sounded disturbingly loud in the profound quietness.

The First Person was painfully aware of the falsity of this apparent calmness. Although not a healer herself, her long and violent life, the experience of so many fights and the anticipation for it, gave her an extra feeling, to perceive the tension building up in the room. She was aware that Kiara's figure had the stillness of the spring before jumping and the calmness in the room was the calm before the explosion.

Then Kiara's body tensed up with a violence that made her skin plates crunch. Her fingers hard like talons dug into the stone lid. With her eyes open, and her face to the sky, the animal scream, which left her mouth, was the expression of ultimate terror.

Her body emptied into the pod. Drained of all colours, the soft emptiness that was left collapsed in a heap next to the pod.

The crystal pod exploded into violent, burning light. The fantastic intensity of luminous energy was far beyond the Hhruahran's body tolerance, and they fled the room, falling over each other in blind panic.

As the last act of sanity, the First Person grabbed Kiara by the shoulder and dragged the limp body behind her out of the room.

**

Behind the closed door, the room was filled with a solid block of light. The pod, the presumable source of the massive energy output, was invisible in the centre of it.

**

'Daira dear - you look awful. You need a rest. Let me call my blue healers to look after your daughter for a while.'

'Thank you My Lady, but I will be all right. I have to stay.'

'You don't look all right to me. I am worried about you…'

'I appreciate your offer, but it is really not up to me.

139

I could not leave Kiara even if I wanted to. You need a black source to supply her energy needs.'

'You lost me there dear. I always thought that the green was a low energy stone. Even the blue has more penetration.'

'Ordinarily you would be right. The green is a low-grade energy. But the green and Kiara together - it is quite a different thing. Believe me, the only reason the black can penetrate the barrier is because she is comatose due to her energy output. Even at this stage, I can only infuse small amounts of energy at one time.'

'Amazing. I was always wondering how a traditionally black healing House could be so proud of a green bearer daughter. Now I've got my answer.'

'My Lady, there is reason to be proud of her. Until recently, not even I, her tutor, could understand the extent of her power. We made a lot of plans to explore this power, to harvest it and we will do it if she recovers.'

'If she recovers?'

'The condition is serious. I am not sure that I can help.'

'Which brings me back to the reason of my coming to you...'

'I do apologize for not responding to your summons. Please understand the situation - I cannot leave her, she would die.'

'I do understand your situation, what I do not understand is hers. What happened to her? I had two blue healers with me at the time, witnessing the whole thing - and neither of them can come up with an explanation.'

'It's natural. They were only visual observers; they could not have followed the green into the pod. Only Kiara knows why she did it.'

'Why she did what?'

'Why she attacked.'

'Kiara attacking? My impression of the situation was that it was she who was being attacked.'

'That may be so on a deeper level. I can only perceive the superficial levels of what was happening.'

'Daira you are confusing me again.'

'Sorry, My Lady. What happened was that Kiara found something very frightening in the Councillor. Something which took her by surprise, but something which must have been hostile as it precipitated a panic reaction.'

'Panic in a Hhruahran?'

'I know that it seems to be contradictory, but it must have happened that way.'

'Even a warrior can panic if the situation exceeds her capacity to cope.'

'The warrior in her responded to the threatening situation in the only way available to us - which is by force, by attack.'

'Then what happened?'

'I do not know the details; the situation must have been very special if Kiara responded to it by hurling, in one searing bolt, her whole life energy to her attacker. That is why she is comatose. Her body doesn't have enough energy to survive. If I break contact with her - she dies.'

'I did not think it was possible that somebody, even a healer, could send all her life energy out. All logic dictates that exhaustion would stop the fight much before this could happen.'

'Ordinarily you would be right, but in a panic situation everything happens differently.

'In a panic situation - there are no logical thoughts, there are no feelings, and there is no tiredness or pain. The body responds to the fear in an excessive way, without involving the brain in the process. Normally this means to escape from the danger situation - in an Hhruahran, due to our special upbringing, this means an all-out attack. Which was the way she responded. She found something so extremely threatening, so absolutely powerful and frightening - that it was beyond her capacity to endure. She panicked, and attacked her enemy with a mental bolt, which carried all her energy inside. Literally. Due to her training in crystal control and due to her panic - she managed to empty herself completely.'

'That frightening enemy, was it real or was it just in her mind?'

'I cannot answer that. It was real for her. That is the only thing which is important at the moment. On the other hand, remember that Kiara is a highly trained crystal healer. As such, she is not likely to have hallucinations.'

'Could someone have influenced her mind at that moment? To make her perceive something which really was not there?'

'Theoretically that could have happened. In practice, it could not. Remember, I control the black energy which delivers the most powerful mental penetration known to us. Now - when Kiara fuses with the green, I feel like a weak little girl at her side. I cannot think of any mental power which could influence Kiara in the pod.'

'What about a non-mental power?'

'Did you open the pod yet?'

'We cannot get close enough to that damned thing. There is no possible shield against that solid light, and believe me – we tried.'

'Then stop trying. That is Kiara's life energy, augmented, multiplied by the green. No physical force can survive that combination. Only she can open the pod without being destroyed by it, by absorbing the excess of green energy into herself.'

'Did she succeed in destroying her enemy?'

'I do not know. We have to wait for Kiara to be able to tell us – but now – excuse me My Lady, I do not mean disrespect towards you, but I have to eat. Kiara's energy demands are huge, and I have to keep absorbing high-energy concentrates to be able to handle this demand.'

'Please, disregard me and do what you are supposed to do – and by the way - this answered my next question. My supply officer was questioning your energy supplies for more than twenty to a habitation of only two beds.'

'He? You mean to say your supply officer is a male?'

Yes. He is male. I have several males employed in my household. You would be surprised how some of them are able to turn out quite reasonable work if you give them some responsibility. Think about it, try it at your House.'

'What a novel idea. A male having a job with responsibilities. I certainly will think about it, but to do it at home? Well, let me get used to the idea first.'

'I think you would be pleasantly surprised. Anyway - I better go now and leave you to your work. Please let me know the moment any change happens.'

'I will. And thank you for caring for my daughter.'

'I care for her very much, and also feel very responsible for what happened, as it was me who sent her there. Besides, the reason I asked her to do this was that I suspected there was something inside the Green Councillor and wanted Kiara to find it for me. She obviously found what I wanted to know, but she has to tell me about it somehow. Look after her please.'

'Goodbye, Daira.'

'Goodbye First Person. The Goddess be with you.'

'Thank you for coming so soon.' Daira opened the door for the First Person and her group, inviting them inside. Several axle shifts had passed since their last meeting, and in that lapse of time she had lost a lot of weight. In spite of her firm colour control, it was obvious to anyone that she was unwell. She was extremely thin, with the edges of her skin plates grossly overlapping. Her movements were sluggish, insecure, and there was a hint of shaking in her hands. But her eyes shone with a bright inner light, very alert, expressing a readiness to any situation.

'I came as soon as I received your message. I also brought with me five blue healers – as you requested.'

'Thank you my lady – Kiara is waking up, and her energy requirements are increasing. My energy level is very low and I do not think I will be able to cope with her awakening.'

'I thought you said that the blue cannot penetrate Kiara's green.'

'It is true. Even black is just enough to infuse her with energy. So far I managed well, but I am not sure what will happen when she wakes up. She may remember the pod and panic again, which would mean a very large increase in her energy demand. I do not have enough of my own anymore and will probably need all of your five healers to back me up so I can draw on their energy while Kiara draws on mine. It could happen at any minute now.'

As to confirm her mother's statement, Kiara changed position in the bed.

It was her first movement for a very long time. Also, due to her lack of conscious control, her colour was shifting freely up and down through the whole visual spectrum, expressing the different emotions her mind had to cross while fighting her way towards consciousness. The dominant colour was that of anger.

The blue healers, like one person, stepped closer to Daira, fusing their minds, establishing control - ready to supply the energy, as she needed it.

Kiara opened her eyes. They were very tired, but bright and alert,
'Thanks for the black, Mother. It fills me with peace.' With her hand she was searching for her Mother's, when she noticed the others in the room.

'First Person!' She was too weak for control, and her voice demonstrated her surprise.

Then she remembered.

'You were right. There was another mind inside. It was...'And the memory hit her fully.

Kiara sat up in her bed, rigid, staring blankly ahead with a silent scream frozen to her lips.

The colour shift showed extreme fear.

No one moved. For a long time the only sound in the room was the increasingly harsh breathing of the six healers.

Then, with extreme concentration on her face, Daira slowly sunk to her knees...'I cannot keep up with her. I don't have enough energy.' Her breathing was fast and gasping like that of someone producing an extreme physical effort.

'Disengage!' The First Person's voice was tense and urgent.

'I cannot. She has a hold on me. She has a hold on all of us - too strong...to break free.'

One of the blue healers collapsed, in a soft, empty heap on the floor, followed very closely by another one.

The rest did not move. Daira's head was slowly approaching the floor, as if the weight on her shoulders was beyond her capacity to resist.

The old warrior moved with the fluidity of her battle-sharpened reflexes, lifted the heavy chair next to her high above her head - and with all her strength brought it down on Kiara's head.

The noise of the splintering of the chair was underlined by the sickening crunch of Kiara's broken head plates.

**

For a short time - nothing happened. In the complete silence no one moved. Time itself seemed to be frozen. The solid feeling of tension, due to the enormous amounts of mental energy on display - suddenly disappeared from the air.

Just behind the frozen figure of the First Person, still clutching the fragments of the chair, Daira slowly sunk to the floor. Her colours were of an extreme exhaustion.

'Daira - How do you feel? - Daira?'

The answer was nearly inaudible.

'If...I am not dead now...I...don't think...I will ever die. What happened to Kiara? How come she suddenly let us go?'

'I am sorry, but she is...'

'No!!' The sound was like a harsh, barking denial, with the deep red of anger displacing the pale weakness.

With energy she did not know she had, Daira hurried to her daughter's side. Putting the black crystal on top of the green stone resting on Kiara's chest, her red slowly shifted to a quieter blue-brown. With her anger gone, the exhaustion was again clearly felt in her voice.

'Thank the Goddess - she is still alive!' Then continued much calmer, as the healer voice/instinct was taking over, 'I need help. Have not enough energy on my own.'

There was silence again, but not for long. One of the blue healers separated from the group, which was still trying to revive the two fallen ones.

'Kiara is my friend, I will help you. What do you want me to do?'

Daira's voice was very low - as if she had no energy to spare to speak.

'Back me up while I heal the damage on Kiara's body. I need to go into her and have not enough energy to do it. Establish contact and allow me to borrow your strength. Come with me and let the blue flow through the black.'

'You want me to establish the same contact that nearly killed us all just now? I learned to respect the green too much to do that. The six of us, with you being a black - were no match for her.'

'This time it will be different. There is no danger for us. The brain is damaged and there is no more seat for the mental energy. The green is no more.'

'And after the brain is repaired?'

'We have plenty of time before that to put a compulsion into her mind, to wake her up only when ordered. Then we can plan her awakening with safety.'

'She will resist.'

'She cannot. Ironically, the damage to her brain probably saved her life.'

'And ours.'

'True. Without the damage we could have never been able to overpower the green. Now, with physical damage, the non-functioning brain is unable to keep the green energy flowing. There is no resistance to our healing.'

'Also the brain is unprotected, open to us to manipulate, and we can programme it for a safe awakening.'

'Correct - except that she is open for me to manipulate. No one else may enter into her mind.'

'I accept that. You are her mother, and you are the black. I am happy that at least she has a chance to survive.'

'And a good one too. At the same time, we have a good chance to find out what really happened in the pod - without exposing her to further danger.'

'Are you with me?'

'I am.' The healer joined her blue crystal to the black and the green on Kiara's chest.

**

And time seemed to stop again...

The First Person left the room unnoticed.

Her further presence would have only disturbed their work.

**

'Mother – I am back!'

'And about time too.'

'Thanks for the calmness of the black.'

'You are welcome. How do you feel?'

'Like coming back from a long holiday and not being sure what happened in my absence. Did I miss much?'

'Well, that depends. A lot of things happened that you are not aware of, but actually I do not think you missed much.'

'How come the First Person is not here? I would have thought she would be anxious to get some answers.'

'Anxious is not a word you can relate to the First Person. Anyhow - how do you feel talking about what you have found?'

'Fine. Although it is a strange feeling. It is like I feel I should be terrified, going berserk, but at the same time I feel calm about it. As if it was someone else's problem. It is as...MOTHER! You have put a compulsion in my mind. You know how I feel about that kind of tampering.'

'Do not touch it! Kiara, I know you can remove the blocks I put there - but do not do it for now. First let's see if you can handle the emotional impact of your memories. Then you can remove it if you still want to.'

'Mother – I trust your judgement.'

'Thank you. Now – what did you find?'

'The First Person was right, as usual.'

'She was right about what?'

'The councillor was not acting on her own decision. She was made to behave like that.'

'There was another mind inside...by the way – you were right. Even through your blocking compulsion, I can feel a tremendous pressure building up inside as I am talking about this.'

'Can you handle it?'

'Yes. Thanks to your barrier.'

'Good – then keep talking – but what about starting from the beginning?'

'Right. To enter the councillor's body was no problem. The mind was not there – but the physical energies were well preserved and the basic print of the mental functions were easy to read on the flesh. I opened to maximum receptivity, as the recent memory prints were quite faint, as if they were consciously erased. It was then that it hit me.'

'What do you mean by, "hit you"?'

'It is hard to explain. I was suddenly aware of the presence of this other - other...thing.'

'Thing?'

149

'I do not know. It was obviously a very organized, involved, rational mind - but it was so different, so alien in texture and motives that I fail to classify it as a mind of a living being. It was a profoundly malignant presence. The meaning of causing harm was so deeply embedded into its texture that the first thing I was aware of was that something very, very bad was attacking me.'

'Why don't you use the word hostile?'

'Because it is not enough. I can understand wanting to produce harm to someone. We Hhruahrans live by doing that. But when we hurt - we do it for a reason. We do not hurt for the sake of hurting.'

'This mind had plenty of reasons to hurt you. You found it.'

'Yes I know. But that is not all. It was a dark mind - its main power source was this wish to harm, just to feel the suffering caused. And it wanted me, badly. Its host failed by dying and it wanted me for its host. By the time I realized what was happening it had passed my barriers and I had no possible way of defending myself.'

'And you panicked!'

'Mother! I was told before, that by being a successful healer - I am one of the least warrior –like people on this planet, but still I am a Hhruahran. And proud of it. We do not panic. We die…but do not panic.'

'I apologize. What happened next?'

'I knew I had very little time left to be in control. The idea of spending the rest of my life acting like a puppet on a string was intolerable. To have that…thing inside me was-well-I had no real choice. Had to burn it out of my mind - and knew that I had only one try. And if I died - I still won.'

'You are more of a warrior than you think you are!'

'I am a Hhruahran.'

'And you are my daughter - and I love you - and you are killing me with the suspense.'

'The rest, I think you know better than I do. Gathering all my energy, my intention was to burn out both of us, in one blow.'

'And?'

'And I don't know. Have no way of judging the amount of harm I inflicted on that alien mind. I certainly succeeded with myself - or at least would have, without your help, for which I am grateful. I think.'

'You do not have to worry any more. It is not in you. I was there, in your mind, for a long time now. Healing you, feeding you with energy, controlling your mind functions. If I tell you I did not find anything like that in there - it is because it is not there.'

'Remember mother, there were two blue healers in the councillor's body, and had no awareness of the alien.'

'I am black.'

'I know and I do not doubt you. But at the same time do not think I did not notice you changing the subject on mentioning the First Person. What is happening with the old warrior?'

'She is probably getting older! What do you mean what is happening with her?'

'She should be here. By everything I know about her, she should be here right now – squeezing me with questions. Mother, there is something wrong in here.'

'I do not have an answer for you, although I agree with you. Until recently she was always around here. Some place. I could not get rid of her. But since your last, very short-lasting and disastrous recovery, she appears to be changed. She will not come here anymore and says that you told her everything she wanted to know. The rest is up to her now, and she does not need you anymore. She even refused to help me by sending a few healers when I asked her to help me with your awakening.'

'She was probably afraid of losing them. I would be also weary of repeating an undertaking that recently cost me two healers.'

'Kiara! You were deeply unconscious when those two healers died. You have no possible way of knowing about it. What is happening in here?'

'Mother! Do not try to re-enter my mind. She is not in there.'

'She. Who is she?'

'Junkorian.'

'Now, let me see. If I remember correctly - Junkorian was the first puppet you had. At an age when you didn't even reach the height of your father's knee. Am I right?'

'You are, but there is more to it than that.'

'I am listening.'

'It is a bit long.'

'I am not going anywhere.'

'Well all right. It sounds a bit silly to tell it to you now, but when I was small, I always had this fear that something would happen to my body while I am in a crystal trance. That someone will do something to my unaware body, and when I came back, I would find it damaged. So I made up this game, that Junkorian was looking after me, that she was protecting my body. And after a while, she was.'

'I think you had better explain this bit.'

'I was very much attached to this puppet, although I was trying not to show it. It had an important emotionally-charged representation in my mind. And this Junkorian - the one in my mind, started to watch over my body. As I was growing, the Junkorian in my mind was also growing. She was not involved with crystal energies. Her only role was to observe my body while I was not around. She became, in a way, to be like a separate person, with a function of her own.'

'So?'

'So, this means that I had a small part of my awareness staying always with my body, relating to me everything that was happening.'

'You mean this Junkorian is still functional?'

'Yes. She is. She did not have enough energy for action, but she recorded everything.

'When I "woke up" I opened my eyes with a complete memory of everything that happened close to me.'

'She is a very handy person to have around.'

'Yes, she is. But this is not the answer to my question.'

'It is to mine. Well, what was yours?'

'The First Person. Why isn't she here?'

'Hello Kiara. How are you, dear? You look much better than the last time I have seen you.'

'Thank you My Lady. I am feeling better.'

'How is your mother?'

'She is fine too. Thank you.'

'What can I do for you dear?'

'I got this notice from the bank today, it is for a very large amount of money.'

'So?'

'So I would like to have some sort of explanation.'

'Didn't the bank send you a letter with the money?'

'Yes, they did. The letter says it is for the sale of my pod, but…'

'Isn't enough? I mean the money.'

'It is a very generous sum. But my pod is not for sale.'

'Kiara – the word sale was put in the letter to soften the blow. The word should have been compensation. The amount was calculated based on the value of the crystal used, the time and work involved in the assembly and there was also an allowance for the personal loss involved. It was not generous. It was a calculated compensation.'

'Compensation for what? What happened to the pod? I could not even get to see it. My own place is closed to me, under guard.'

'The compensation is for the loss of your pod. The Council decided that for reasons of planetary security the pod and its present contents should not remain under private ownership. You yourself implied something like this in your report.'

'What is being done to the pod?'

'I really don't know. You know that scientific matters are not under my direct supervision. All I know is that a committee was formed to investigate the pod and your report of its contents.'

'My Lady. Do you realize that I am the only person who can approach the crystal pod with reasonable safety?'

'Now, that was the least conclusive statement in your report, as I remember. Kiar. Do not underestimate the capacity of your peers. Besides, if the Committee agrees that you are the person who should be working there, I am sure they will contact you. Is there anything else you wanted to say?'

'Yes My Lady. There is another matter, which I hope will be of some help to you.'

'I am listening.'

'I was working on some questions with the Central Computer. I fed into it all the facts related to this affair with the Green Councillor. Added to it my feelings and opinion about the facts.'

'What was the question?'

'Trying to predict the alien's next step. I got a very high percentage probability prediction about their/its next target.'

'And who is the lucky person?'

'You are, My Lady.'

'It is the only logical conclusion.'

'You do not seem to be surprised.'

'It is because I am not. And before you feel bad about it, I tell you that I put the same questions to the War Computer quite a few axle shifts ago, getting the same answer.'

'But how could you? You have just received my report, and…'

'Kiara dear – you are very good at healing, and I am very good at politics. Let us each stick to what we are good at.'

'I do not follow.'

'I asked you to do a check on the Green Councillor, because I had some suspicion about him and about other things happening around me. Remember? Now, you confirmed my suspicions, but there was nothing in your report that was news to me. You only converted my theories into facts. And when you are responsible for the welfare of a whole planet, and beyond, you cannot wait until all your opinions are confirmed. I have been working on this alien problem a long time before you confirmed their existence for me. Does that clarify your doubts?'

'Yes, My Lady. And I will stick to healing from now on.'

'Good. Now, can I have your computed figures? I want to see your personal approach index. In your report you have only put the bare facts.'

'I thought that would be better. Anyhow - here they are.'

'Thanks. Sit down Kiara, while I go through these.'

'Thank you, My Lady.'

Kiara was fuming inside. (When will I learn not to underestimate her? Every time I talk to her I end up feeling like a schoolgirl.)

At the same time - she could not help but admire the old warrior. (She deserves her position. She is really good. No wonder she had survived so long in that deadly job of hers.)

She tried to sit more comfortably on the hard seat. The empty simplicity of the room and its furniture spoke of the habitat of a full warrior.

The First Person was sitting at her desk - across the room - and while she was concentrating on the computer printouts, her right hand was resting against her temple in a familiar gesture. (She is in pain - but would not call for help) Kiara understood the gesture as she had seen it many times before.

She wanted to help. With a familiarity, which came out of an established habit, she flowed with the green, to meet the white.

The pain was surprisingly intense. The white was everywhere.

(How can she appear so calm with so much pain?)

The green started to push the white back - to soothe the pain.

The reaction was instantaneous, and unexpected in its violence. The white was replaced by the deep red of anger, breaking contact with the green with a startling suddenness.

'Never, ever do that again Kiara!' The sound of anger was hissing in between the words. 'Next time you approach my mind, I destroy you!'

**

'Mother, it just cannot be. There is something wrong. There is definitely something very wrong in here.' Kiara was pacing up and down in her mother's room. In her excitement, she did not even care to control her colour shift. The purple-red of anger was dominating her colour scale, and Daira was astonished to see streaks of fear in the red.

'Mother – I need some answers or I'll burst.'

'I am sure you are exaggerating the situation Kiara. There must be a logical explanation to all this.'

'Logical? You should have felt that burst of hatred. There was no logic in there, but pure emotional energy.'

'And how would you react if you found somebody in your mind, pushing levels and energies? I think the reaction was quite normal for someone who is under a lot of pressure, and suddenly finds someone interfering with the low threshold function of her mind. You would have reacted the same.'

'I would have reacted much worse. But mother, you are missing the point. I was in her mind many times before. Remember? That was my job. To stop her pain when I noticed that she needed me. She always welcomed my presence.'

'Well, you must have startled her.'

'Mother! Let me finish. The point I am trying to make is that she very rarely called for my help, because she knew that I perceived when she had problems. It was an established practice after a while that I entered her mind, soothed her headache and got out, without her even interrupting what she was doing at the time. Most of the times she was not even aware that I was there. Only when the pain had gone did she realise that I was.'

'I cannot see your point.'

'Look at it this way, mother. She is a full warrior. A primarily physical person, with not even a hint of functioning mental capacities. When I said that she was not aware of my presence - it was not because she ignored me, but because she was not able to detect my presence. She had no capacity for it - none whatsoever.'

'Then how do you explain what just happened?'

'That is just it. It does not fit. She detected my touch instantaneously, and the wave of red I received was pure mental hatred. The physical words came only after. But most of all - remember mother – it was her who broke the green contact, and she is not supposed to be able to do that.'

'Then how…'

'I do not know. I cannot explain it. It just does not fit. It is as if there was…'

'Don't. Do not say it!' Daira's voice carried the pale fear what her colour range did not show. 'Do not even say that!'

'I do not have to say it. You know what I am thinking about. I hope to Goddess I am wrong – but I have to know it.'

'What are you going to do?'

'I am going to my room to check on the crystal pod. Are you coming with me?'

'You are not leaving me much choice – are you?'

**

The two soldiers guarding the door to Kiara's rooms were unaware of their presence, as Daira was holding her daughter behind the corner at the end of the corridor.

'Let me go mother – you know I have to go in.'

'And how do you intend to achieve that? Will you

158

go there and ask them nicely to let you in?'

'I do not know yet, but I will not find the way while I am hiding here.'

'Kiara – why don't you use your head? Remember that stone hanging from your neck is not just an ornament.'

'And what do you want me to do? Hit them on the head with it?'

'Not quite. I keep forgetting that you are not trained in the offensive use of the crystal energy. Well, this is as good a time as any for lesson number one. Just watch your old mother perform, and tell me what you see.'

Kiara looked around the corner carefully. The guards were standing on both sides of the door in their usual combat - alert stance, so deceivingly relaxed looking at the first glance.

Kiara knew that from that half-crouching, comfortable-looking position, they could jump instantaneously to any direction.

'I cannot see any change-'

Daira transmitted the mental equivalent of an impatient stamping of her feet

'Enhance your vision!'

Touching her stone with her hand, through the green haze Kiara could now see the whirling black mist around the sentries. It was slowly getting thicker, and more solid until both soldiers were enveloped in a thick, black swirling mass about which they seemed to be completely unaware.

'Mother, you are amazing. It would never have occurred to me to use the crystal's special energy-relocation properties to distort the sensory input of a person.'

'Lesson number one. The next move is yours.' Her voice was somewhat hoarse, as if the deed has cost her

159

more effort than she wanted to show.

'Let's go mother!'

They passed in front of the sentries, who showed no signs of being aware of their presence. On approaching the second door, Kiara slowed down. Behind that door was the crystal pod, and the intensity of its solid light was still fresh in her mind.

She opened the door very slowly.

The room was in darkness.

The pod was open.

It was empty.

**

'Come in Kiara!'

'Thank you Councillor. I appreciate you receiving me.'

'I could hardly refuse to see you, after the way you contacted me.'

'What do you mean?'

'Come on Kiara! Put yourself in my position. The personal healer of my political opponent contacts me, asking me for an urgent meeting, which she wants to be kept secret. What do you expect me to do? I would have died of curiosity if I did not agree to see you straight away.'

'I can see your point Councillor, but let me repeat to you that my visit has a very serious objective.'

'I think you should tell me what it is all about.'

'Councillor, if I tell you straight away what I came to tell you, you would not only disbelieve me, but you would doubt my mental sanity.

'I would prefer, if you agree to it, present it to you point by point.'

'Go ahead.'

'First of all - I present you with these documents -

please study them. They are the exact description of recent happenings. Please read them carefully. Ask me anything if you need explanation on some of its contents. At the end of it there is a list of names. Those are the names of the persons witnessing these events and who you can contact to confirm the accuracy of the documents.'

'The way you say all this Kiara - I don't think I will like what you are showing to me.'

'I am sure you will not like it Councillor, but please read it.'

For a long while, the quietness of the room was only disturbed by the rustling of the document sheets and the restless pacing of Kiara.

How different were these rooms from the First Person's habitation. There were signs all-around of comfort seeking. In the floor coverings, the softer lines of the furniture, the clothing she was wearing…

'Amazing! Absolutely amazing. I do not doubt the authenticity of the facts as it would be very simple to check them. What I do not understand is why you brought this to me? Especially as it says that the First Person herself witnessed most of those events. Unless you have something more to say.'

'Yes. I have. Please study these documents next. They are computer printouts from the Central. The answers to my inquiries about the probable future plans/actions of the alien mind.'

'Fascinating. Absolutely fascinating – although the First Person being the next target is fairly logical. And I wish for the Goddess you have nothing else to show me.'

'I am sorry Councillor, but I do have more to show you, although on a different level. The first two sets of documents presented you with cold facts only, leaving the interpretation to you. This third set will provide you with my personal observations and opinions on the First Person's recent personality changes. Naturally the points made here are very much up to discussion.'

'I am not sure I want to read it.'

'Please do. It was a very hard decision for me to present these opinions of the person I most admire to her principal enemy, but I felt I had no choice in the matter. I feel that you have no choice either but to keep on reading.'

There was a long silence again while the councillor went through the documents, checking and rechecking every piece of all three sets. After which she just sat staring into the air with non-seeing eyes until Kiara was nearly aware of the furious pace in which her mind was working, analysing the information presented to her. At the end - with a deep sigh, she faced Kiara, her eyes seeing again.

'Kiara - I do not think you are aware of what you have just done to me. I wish I had avoided this meeting. The responsibility you just put on my shoulders – well…I do not think any one person should be carrying it.'

Kiara nearly pitied the woman, although an inner voice cautioned her. She was a high rated politician and the emotions shown by a person like her were unlikely to be the real ones.

'I am sorry councillor, but what else could I have done. I lack the political training or power to do anything about it.'

'You did the logical thing Kiara dear, although the smartness of it is up to discussion!' The First Person's voice sounded harsh in the quietness of the room.

Kiara jumped to her feet, her hand automatically on her crystal. She could clearly see the energy blast coming from the old warrior's hand – like in slow motion – and the Councillor surrounded by the bluish, devouring flame.

The flash of the second energy blast reached her quicker.

**

'Kiara D'Charkoon – you are accused to conspire with the opposition against the leading person of the government of the United Hhruahran Worlds. How do you respond to this charge?'

'I accept full responsibility for the charge.'

'Kiara D'Charkoon – do you understand the seriousness of the accusation?'

'I do.'

'Then you do not leave me any other alternative but to apply the sentence required by law. Kiara D'Charkoon – I...' 'Wait!' The interrupting voice was soft – but there was a command in the tone.

'Identify yourself!'

'I am, by office and popular vote, the First Person of the Council of Control.'

'The council recognizes the First Person. Please state present intentions.'

'I wish to talk on behalf of Healer Kiara D'Charkoon - before the council announces its decision.'

'The Council already reached its decision.'

'Then I exercise the power given to me by law as the First Person of the Council of Control, to over-ride the finality of its decision.'

There was a mounting excitement in the room. Although within the law, words like these were not spoken in a court setting for many generations. In the ensuing quietness Kiara could hear her own racing heart. (What does she want now? Didn't she do enough already?)

'The Council recognizes the First Person's right to speak. The Council is listening.'

The old warrior's voice was unusually soft.

'I do not want to interfere with the Council's decision – but I feel I have to bring some facts to light in order that the Council's decision be a just one.'

'The Council is listening to what the First Person has to say.'

'Thank you. The first thing I want to call the Council's attention to is that Kiara D'Charkoon has no political affiliation, indeed, has no inclination at all to take part in any political activities.'

'The Council is aware of this fact.'

'I know. But it was needed to state it again to draw light to the fact that the Green Healer's motive to contact the opposition leader was completely selfless. She thought, or said, that she was convinced her planet was being invaded by alien minds; and the leader of the planet, me, was already on their side. Accepting this as her firm belief, she then did the correct thing to do.'

'Please. Get to the point. '

'The point is that what the Green Healer was doing is what we would all expect from any Hhruahran to do in the same situation. Hardly a punishable thing.'

'Does the First Person suggest a full pardon for the accused?'

'No. What she was doing was wrong and has to meet its punishment, but I feel that her motives to do it have to be considered when applying the Law.'

'The letter of the Law demands death.'

'The letter of the Law applies for treason with intention. This is not the case with Kiara D'Charkoon.'

(Why is she doing this?) Kiara had a careful control over her colour shift - but could not help feeling confused on the inside. (She would benefit greatly from my death. What is she planning? I do not trust her, she is too cunning.)

'First Person, the Council accepts your statements as valid. The Council also recognizes your right to make these statements official, both as leader of the Council of Control and also as the intended victim of the accused. The Council will now retire to consider its verdict.'

**

'Kiara dear - I would like to talk with you before the Council announces its decision.'

'I am hardly in the position to go anywhere My Lady.' Kiara's gesture showing the room around her was self-explanatory. The room where she had to stay to await for the Council's decision was quite small, but they still managed to put in four fully armed guards. There were doors and windows - all open - and through them she could see several dozen of the fully armed guards of the same special task force. The eyes of every guard were constantly on her, their hands on their weapons in a permanent, full alert.

(If they knew how weak and tired I feel - Kiara was thinking to herself - they would not bother with so many guards.)

The old warrior could see the funny side of the situation.

'I can see that you have grown in importance. I do not think they would use so many soldiers to guard me.'

'It looks like somebody is very afraid of me, although I do not know why.'

'Be fair with them Kiara. Anyone who survives a full, close-range blast of an energy weapon is to be treated with respect. One of these days you will have to teach me how you did it.'

'My Lady - I do not think my future will extend long enough to be worth making plans. You have interrupted the Council's speaker in announcing my death sentence, but you have just postponed it.'

'That is entirely up to you.'

'My Lady - I cannot see your point. As far as you are concerned, I am sure it would be better if I die.'

'Kiara dear - if I wanted you to die - you would have been dead for a long time by now.'

'I am aware of that My Lady, and that is why I do not understand your actions. I certainly cannot see any reason why you would want me alive.'

'During the recent events, you and your mother taught me many things. I was always aware of the power of the black healer, although your House was trying to hide it and lower it to the level of the other healers. But the Green Power, the one that you yield - well - I am sure that not even you are able to comprehend the full extent of it. And that is the reason I want you alive, not a sentimental one. I want that power, and I cannot have it without you. But I want that power on my side, not against me.'

'My Lady, I cannot promise you that.'

'I suppose you mean the alien mind you met.'

'Yes, My Lady.'

'Kiara dear, without that happening, without your meeting with what you call the alien mind in your crystal pod - would you put the Green to my service?'

'My Lady - the Green was always at your service. Fully and without reserve.'

'Thank you. I brought you some documents I want you to study. Do not worry about the time it takes, the Council cannot proceed with its decision without me, so you have plenty of time.'

'What kind of documents?'

'It is the report of the committee, which investigated

your crystal pod. I know that you are aware of the fact that they opened it - and this is the result of their study. By the way, that is another thing you have to explain to me one day. The monitors showed that you and your mother just walked in front of the guards, as if you were invisible.'

'Perhaps we were.'

'Not for the monitors, but of course, they have no minds to be affected.'

'My Lady, this is a very long document. I cannot see the point or the need to go through it. I am sure you will understand that under the circumstances I have very little capacity to concentrate on a scientific study on pod energies.'

'You will see the point if you read their final conclusion. Before opening the pod, they studied your reports, and the objective of their investigation was to prove or disprove what you describe in it. Namely - they were looking for your alien mind.'

'And it was not there. Right?'

'Wrong. It was there all right. Just it was not an alien mind.'

'No living person could enter the green pod and survive it. Much less to analyse its contents.'

'No one tried to enter it. The energy was released and stored, its components analysed and traced back to its origins. There was only one life energy in that pod. Yours.'

'And what I have seen, and was nearly killed by, was just a figment of my imagination?'

'Just about. You see, you have done a perfect job in building that crystal pod. The energy flow patterns show a flawless continuity, the self-resonating circles complete. Any energy you feed in that pod goes through those resonating circles, growing each time around, with tremendous feedback capacity. And that is exactly what happened to you. When you entered that pod, by some freak accident the crystals picked up a small, hidden fear from your subconscious mind and fed it back to you increased thousand fold. The alien mind you thought you met was your own subconscious fear increased to enormous proportions. That is why you could not possibly find a way to deal with it.'

**

Kiara felt a sensation of unreality. So this is it. The whole thing was just a technical mistake. All that suffering. The death of the blue healers, the way she herself was brought back from death's door – all this was for nothing! The explanation was very plausible. She knew the members of the committee, they were not the type of people inclined to make mistakes. But neither was she. She could feel again the reaching out of that mind in her memory and only the soothing blackness of her mother which followed it stopped the panic reaction. It cannot be. She just could not be that wrong about this – whatever the committee says.

'My Lady – I really wish I could accept the committee's comment as to the explanation of what happened.'

'Meaning that you do not accept it.'

'Meaning that I cannot accept it. It is not enough.'

'Do you distrust the persons forming the committee?'

'No. I do not. But I also know that you are able to make the committee come up with any explanation you desire.'

'Tell me Kiara, is there any way in which you could be convinced to work with me? I am really trying hard not to finish this affair on a point we will be both sorry for.'

'I appreciate that My Lady. But to be able to accept the committee's report, I need more proof.'

'What kind of proof?'

'The kind of proof, which I can only get by myself. If I could deep check your mind with the green…'

'My dear girl - you are out of your mind. I just showed you a report from the most eminent scientists of our planet, stating that your pod is unstable, that you cannot control it, and that just about anything can happen once inside, and you want me to let you use it on me.'

No way, my girl. If this is the only way that you can be on my side, then forget it. I am sorry to lose you; we could have done fantastic things together.'

My Lady, it is me who is sorry. Remember, it is my life on the line.'

'Believe me Kiara - your life is not in danger.'

'What will be my sentence?'

'The committee did not decide it yet.'

'My Lady - you are the committee. The rest are just your puppets.'

'Very well. Although you declared yourself my enemy, I cannot take your life. You will be exiled from the Hhruahrans' world.'

'My Lady - I do not wish to fight you, but if you leave me with my life, I will have to…'

'You will be in no position to fight me.'

'The Green will be able to reach you from anywhere.'

'You will not have the Green.'

The last words sank very slowly into Kiara's mind. Being without the Green was something for which there was no concept in her mind. She was without her crystal now, as it was destroyed on absorbing the blast from the energy weapon, and although very little time had passed, the tension due to this separation was approaching an unendurable level.

'My Lady - I don't know how you could enforce your sentence and stop me from getting a green stone in whatever world you are sending me. But if you are able to do it, do not think that you are doing me a favour by saving my life. I could not possibly survive the separation. The Green Crystal and I are one.'

'Your mother told me something like that, although she did not appear to be affected by the loss of her stone.'

'What did you do with my mother? She has nothing to do with all this.'

'I did not do anything with your mother. She is my friend from way back and I would trust her with my life. But not now, as she is also your mother and I know the bond between you two. She was just taken into custody and separated from her crystal for the duration of your trial. I wanted to prevent a situation in which I would have to fight with her too.'

'She uses the crystal as an instrument only. The separation from it does not affect her. For me - the Green is part of me, a part that I need to survive.'

'Your mother said you could learn.'

'If she said so, then I got a chance. But even so, I cannot see how you could stop me from getting another crystal.'

'Kiara dear - you have still a lot to learn about the things I can do.'

**

(All this is a dream. It is not really happening. I will wake up soon.)

Kiara concentrated on the idea of waking up. " I am not really walking up on to the shuttle terminal which will take me to the space ship. This narrow, covered passage way is only part of my dream. I can feel this tubular structure swing and bend under my feet - only in a dream could a structure so high be so flimsy. It must be much more solid and firm in reality. It has to be a dream. I am not leaving my home. Why would I leave home? Everything I want is here. I have no reason to go away, especially not forever. Oh Mother - I do not want to leave! But it is just a dream. It must be. Why would they exile me? I was always the best in my class, always working hard. My teachers liked me. I was always a good girl. My family loves me. My mother...

Oh mother - help me now! - It is a dream - it must be. It is not me who is being exiled.

Why would they exile me? I am needed here. I am the First Person's own healer. She needs me. She could have a headache right now. I should be there to help her. To soothe the pain with the green...oh Goddess, how much I miss the green! She is sending me away. The First Person is sending me away. Why would she send me away? She is not, what is inside of her is. She is not herself. It is not the First Person who is sending me away. Then why should I go? The others don't know it. No one knows it. No one understands.

Except perhaps my mother...oh Mother - where are you now? She cannot help me either. The only person who knows. Besides, of course, the First Person. But she is not there anymore. Someone else is inside there now. Where is the First Person now? I cannot leave now. I have to find her. They make me go. They do not understand. They will be sorry. They will be sorry to send me away – but it will be too late by then. They will also have to go where the First Person is now – and there will be someone else inside. Perhaps they are doing me a favour by sending me away. I will be the only person saved. I will not have anyone inside - Oh

Goddess! Why am I so tired? I cannot think clearly. What am I doing here? Oh yes. I am walking towards the terminal...

But I don't want to go! I am so weak. It is hard to walk. It is lucky that no one walks with me - so they cannot witness my weakness. My head is cloudy. I cannot even think clear...the green! It is the green I am missing. I have never been so long without the green. My mother was right in using her stone only as an instrument. I wanted more. I fused with the stone – now I pay for it. Goddess – the crystal pain is tearing me apart. I never thought this would ever happen. The same way I did not believe them when they said the separation would be permanent. I laughed in their faces. I can get a green stone anywhere in the galaxy. Until they said the name Jeshtar. That accursed planet. Dominated by their technology - I heard about them. People there consult their computer to know when to spit.

And I have to go there. Of all the planets of the Galaxy - they are sending me there. The only planet where the Green is not permitted entrance, due to the electrical interferences it would cause to their machines. That is why they are sending me there. They are afraid of the green...oh Goddess - I cannot survive without my green. I'd rather die. I will die. My mother said I can survive - but I know I cannot. Mother - you are wrong – for the first time - but you are very wrong...mother, help me! I cannot think clearly. Where am I? Oh yes, the terminal. That black mouth there is the shuttle's doors. Once inside - good bye. It will be all finished for you Kiara dear. Beyond that door lies a world where green does not exist. Where you cannot exist. A greenless world. I don't want to go there. I cannot stop. I have no strength to fight any more. I lost – and the loser always pays. But it is so unjust. I was doing what I thought was the right thing for the others. Nothing for me. I am being punished for trying to help. For trying to save them…oh Goddess – I am tired. Perhaps it is better this way. It is quicker – it will be over quicker this way. I will not live much longer without the green…what? Someone is calling. I have to wake up. I cannot show weakness. They will not see weakness in me - I am a Hhruahran!)

'Kiara D 'Charkoon!'

'That's me, soldier. What do you want?'

'I am sorry to disturb your thoughts - but I have a parcel to give you before you enter the shuttle.'

'Who is sending it to me?'

'Your mother.'

'My mother? I thought my mother was not allowed to contact me in any possible way.'

'That is true. The orders were quite strict about that. Your mother did not directly send this parcel - she requested officially a departure present to be given to you. She named the present - I was only told by my commanding officer to get it and to deliver it to you.'

'What is it?'

'I think it is a toy.'

'You think?'

'It is a toy. A puppet.'

Kiara's heart was beating in her throat in mounting excitement. (It could not be. Even she couldn't get away with it.)

'Give it to me please.' (I must not show colour shift.)

With controlled, uninterested movements Kiara opened the box. It was Junkorian. An exact replica of the first puppet she had. And, deep inside it, under the fierce warrior outfit - there was the tiniest of the green crystals - an integral part of the complicated mechanism.

There is also a message with the toy - the soldier's voice made it obvious that she did not think much of this demonstration of emotion.

'I am listening.'

'Your mother said that this is the toy with which you started your life on this planet - and she wishes that you would do the same on starting your new life. If you ask me, I would...'

'Thank you soldier - you can leave now.'

Kiara turned, and continued her walk towards the dark entrance at the end of the corridor.

There was a spring in her steps now. Her head clear, and high. Green was flowing in her veins again. She was ready to face the universe...

Thank you mother! You gave me life once again.

When she entered the door - she was very much alive.

CHAPTER NUMBER THREE

The blue sphere approached the white one - then stopped - starting to move to the right, went around it, then again. Then kept going around the white ball, picking up speed, faster, faster - until there was only a blue circular blur around it. Then suddenly like hitting a wall, it stopped. Now the white started to move.

'Okay - have a rest.'

Carlos wiped the perspiration off his face. 'This is hard work Doc!'

'If you could do it easily, there would be no need to practice. It is hard because you have not mastered it yet.' Doc Holdgen tried to give his words a reproaching sound, without much success. He liked his pupil, but that was no reason to go soft on him. If his present enthusiasm to learn will keep, he will go places...

'I know you are right, but I wish we could do something more practical. These balls - day after day, get a bit boring.'

'The moment you control the balls, then you are ready to move to the next stage. Not before.'

'I know you are right, but still it seems so slow. There should be a faster way to have the power - and before you say it, *yes* I know. Having the power is useless without adequate control.'

'What would you like to do?'

'Teach me the use of the medallion.'

'What do you mean? There is not much to learn there.'

'There must be. I have seen Andronicus use it to communicate with a person in another room. I have seen you obtain information from the central computer through your medallion. There must be thousands of other uses for it, which I would like to know.'

'Oh that. As I said, there is nothing there to learn.

You are using the medallion right at this minute, without being aware of it. Otherwise we could not understand each other's language. You can read and write our language. Know how to handle all household equipment although most of them should be quite strange to you. You know lots of things that, if you stopped to think about it, you have never learned. Where is the knowledge coming from? You do not need to know how to use the medallion because the medallion will always give you, automatically, everything you need at that moment. The same thing happens with us.'

'But I cannot do the things you are doing.'

'Of course not. You are black and I am gold.'

'What does that have to do with it?'

'Everything. Remember - the medallion is a computer terminal. A machine. Its functions depend upon its programming. The different colours of the medallion indicate the different functions they are able to perform. That I am able to communicate with someone through my medallion and you are not is not because I am better than you, but because I have a computer terminal, which is programmed to do more than yours.'

'And how does somebody go about getting a better medallion?'

'For us, generally speaking, the only way would be to be born again. In your case, I am not sure.'

'Doc. You are confusing me more and more. Remember, you are supposed to be clearing my mind, not the other way around.'

'Okay. Okay. I just wasn't sure how much Andronicus explained. It looks to me that he dropped the whole bundle into my lap. Okay. Now - in our multicultural society, the personal computer terminal is an essential item for the survival of the individual. I call your attention to the word multicultural. Its meaning is markedly different to the one you are used to. Our planet is in permanent, active contact with over two and a half thousand worlds in this galaxy, and nearly the same number of other galaxies, having over eighteen races as permanent residents and hundreds passing through on a daily basis. Keep in mind this meaning of our multicultural society, and you will understand that absolutely no one could function in a society as such, without a permanent linkage with a central computer.'

'Dr Andronicus did tell me something about this. But why the different colours?'

'Well, imagine the computer terminals like a service your government gives to its people, like the roads, waste disposal, electricity etc. Except we do not pay for it. We do not pay taxes. With the medallion, the government - in our case the central computer - decides who deserves which model of computer terminal. And as it is not a paid service, money has nothing to do with it. The computer decides the value of the person based on the value of his work for the society - and hence the colour of the medallion.'

'So this is why everyone is wearing it outside - to show. The better the medallion, the better the person.'

'Yes, it is true. Knowing the weaknesses of the human character, it was inevitable to develop a cast system, which as you will learn, is a very rigid one.

'However, bad as it is, you have to remember that it is based on real values. The people who show the higher colours, are not the ones who happen to have the richest parents, but the ones who are really the best.'

'Then how come I have seen young, very young children wearing gold? They were too young to be of any practical value to society.'

'It is simple. Our values and capacities are analysed at birth, sometimes even before. The ethical structure of our society makes sure that we always function at our maximum capacity. Those children you have seen have the potential of being valued in the future, and they will be one day. Hence their colour.'

'Do you know of anyone who changed colours during his life?'

'Very, very few. I had a friend, rather an acquaintance, who was an actor, and quite mediocre at that. He was in a car accident in which he smashed his face to pieces, amongst other things. The bones of his face did not heal properly, and the loose fragments allowed him to produce facial expressions that were absolutely bizarre. He became a famous actor - his value jumped and his colour was changed.'

'So his previous valuation was wrong.'

'No, it was not. It is not in your chromosomes that you will have a car accident when you are forty five.'

'Which means, that if I want to get a more functional medallion, I have to smash my face or do something equally radical.'

'Not true. You are under different rules. You are given black - which means that your value is not established yet - until you find your place and function in our society. Only then can you have your real colour - whatever that will be.'

**

'I do not know what the hell I am complaining about.' Carlos was talking to himself again, as was his habit when something was upsetting him. 'A few months ago I would have given an eye to be here. To be on a different planet, to meet and study different people, to learn different ways…but that was a few months ago. Things have a changed appearance when they start happening.'

He was lying on his bed in the darkening room, staring at the ceiling. By now he knew every spot, every mark on the ceiling. He spent enough time during the last few weeks looking at it to memorize every detail.

'There is so much to learn outside - and I am losing my mind locked up in this blasted room! But what else can I do?' He felt like screaming to the building-up shadows on the opposite wall. 'This damned planet has practically no written record system. They don't even have audio or visual recording except for entertainment, and that is useless for me.

'Everything goes through that hell-hole computer - and it works for them - because they are all connected to it. But I am not. If they want to blow their nose, the computer tells them which pocket they put the tissues in, while I cannot even tell the time, as my watch cannot follow the changing values of their day-timing.'

(The door.)

'I understand now what blind people were feeling back home. But they at least could hear, touch; they had some contact with the life around them. In here I am an outcast.

'This medallion locks me out of society as good as any prison wall would. It keeps me alive, but I am completely alone.'

(Open the door.)

'All I can do is to go to that damned school and repeat those stupid exercises day after day - and hope that one of these days they will give me a different colour, that they would open the doors for me. Until then...'

(Open that bloody door! I am not prepared to wait in this corridor all night)

'What? - Who said that?'

(Open the door stupid and find out).

Completely confused by the persistent voice in his mind, Carlos opened the door. He did not really expect to see anyone there, but he was wrong.

Susoan - his flame headed nurse from the hospital was standing outside.

'Hi there! I nearly did not recognize you without your uniform.'

'That's why it took you so long to open the door?'

'What do you mean' "so long"? I never heard you...'

'Cut it out. You heard me perfectly well, you just did not move.'

'No. I really did not...hold on, did you tell me to open the bloody door?'

'Only after you didn't respond to the previous calls.'

'Did you use your medallion to pass me the message?'

'Of course I did. How else would you know that I was outside the door?'

'Look Susoan, I am sorry. I did get your message, but I did not know what it was. You are the first visitor I have had in this world, and I really did not know that was the way you call. My mind is still set on a good old-fashioned knock on the door.'

Susoan's face softened into a smile 'Sorry to get annoyed with you, I should have understood. I thought you didn't want to let me in. And, by the way, can I come in?'

'Of course. Sorry. Please come in.' Carlos was still fighting inside to regain the control of the situation. It was hard to fully accept the reality of mental images and sounds - and keep the imagination from appearing real.

'Thanks.' - the red brightness of her hair drew his eyes along as she passed him. The fragrance that followed nearly knocked him over.

'I will put the lights on, but please do not look at the mess,' Carlos managed to say. 'I did not expect visitors.'

'I did not come to see your room, I came to see you.'

'What did I do? Did I forget to take my tablets or something?'

'Nothing like that.' Susoan put her large shoulder bag down on the floor, stretching her legs while getting comfortable on the deep armchair. 'Do you mind if I take my shoes off? My feet are killing me.'

'Please do it, but you started to say something.'

'Yes. Well this afternoon we were talking about you at the hospital. Nothing important, you know, just nurses talking about interesting patients, and while we were talking I remembered the time when I was first brought to Jeshtar. Remembered the miserable, lonely days and the even worse, long nights. The nights I passed crying in my room, wishing for someone to extend a helping hand to me. And I told myself - Carlos is probably going through similar things. He is probably stronger than I am, but he is black, which is a direct ticket to loneliness. So - here I am. Please, don't kick me out at least until my feet have stopped throbbing.'

'What is wrong with your feet?'

'Vanity. As usual, the prettiest shoes are the ones that kill your feet. Slowly, toe by toe.'

'Put your feet up and I promise not to kick you out for a while. And by the way - your description of your first times fits very much to my present situation. Except the crying, but I was slowly getting to it. Do you want me to massage your feet?'

'I would love to, but no, thank you. It would take away my feeling of superiority. Remember? I am supposed to help you.'

'Believe me; massaging your feet would help me feel much better.'

'Maybe later - if you are a good boy. In the meanwhile, when was the last time you had a decent meal?'

'I eat every day at the hospital.'

'Yes. Sandwiches. I have seen you. I said a decent meal.'

'What is wrong with sandwiches?'

'You will find out after you have tried these.' Susoan got two large thermo flasks out of her bag. 'And before you say anything - I want you to know that it is you who is doing me a favour. It is not every day that I can prove I am not just a pretty face, but that I can cook too.'

The food was really good, and while eating it Carlos realized how much he missed normal cooking. He was not sure what he was eating, the flavours being a bit on the unusual side but, the combining of the tastes and aromas made the composition hard to resist. Although he was not very hungry at the beginning - he could not stop until he polished off the last scrap of food.

'Oh God! That was beautiful - but I am glad there is no more. One more bite and I would burst.'

'How do you feel now?'

'Fine. Just fine. There must be some truth in the saying that you can reach a man through his stomach. I felt very miserable before you came. I really appreciate your company tonight.'

'It was just tonight that you were feeling bad?'

'No. It started very shortly after I moved here. I am not used to being alone. I mean - I was always alone in my life - but I also had a place in the world, somewhere I belonged, something I formed a part of. In here I really know what being alone means. I am completely excluded with no means even for simple communication. I do not know if you understand how lonely this can feel.'

'Believe me, I do understand it. That is part of the reason why I came here. Look - come here to the window - I want to show you something. Just there - Right. Now, I want you to look down and tell me what you see.'

'The street?'

'What else?'

'Well. It is dark and we are quite high up, I cannot see many things clearly. I can see a lot of people, like ants, and cars, lights…I am not sure what you want me to say.'

The flashing street lights from below painted Susoan's face with changing colours. For a long time she did not say anything. When she spoke, with her eyes still on the street, her voice was very quiet.

'I know what it means to be lonely. I know the feeling very well. I used to live in this same building, at the beginning. A few floors higher up. I was wearing black then. I used to stand in the window with the lights off, like now. No one could see me in the darkness - only I could see them. And I hated them. No. That is wrong. I envied them. The people down there running around, the cars, the lighted windows on the buildings, there were thousands of people around me, and I was alone. They were together, everyone looked busy, everyone seemed to have a place to go…and I was standing there alone. Excluded. Yes, I know the feeling. And it lasted a very long time. A very, very long time - then I got the blue, and doors opened for me. Suddenly people noticed my presence, I was here, I was a part of the world. It was not the world of my choice, but it was a world I accepted and a world that accepted me. I had a place. I was not alone anymore.'

'I know what you mean. I know that the main

reason for me feeling like this is that I am black - and black is excluded from the society, but even if I get the gold, I cannot see myself…I don't know. Tell me. How is it for you now?'

'I am home now. The doors are open for me and I know my place. The most important thing is that I can feel there is a place where I belong. Still…' 'Still what?'

'When I think about this planet, I do not think of it as "us". It is still me and them.'

'You still miss your country.'

'Miss it. You do not know how much. At the hospital, when you were still unconscious, I used to touch your hair and thought to myself, my sun used to touch this hair…'

'Your sun?! - Are you from Earth?'

'London.'

'Thank God I am not alone. How many of us are on this planet?'

'Quite a few…'

'Do you meet?'

'No, we don't. We are spread out very thin on this and other worlds, and when we meet accidentally, most of the time we do not even know that we have the same birthplaces.'

'This is a truly multi-cultural society - it discourages segregation. What are you looking at me like that for?'

Carlos shook his head like he was trying to wake up. 'I still cannot believe that you are from Earth. When I saw the twin moons and realized that I am on a different planet, I felt that the door closed the past behind me.'

'It did.'

'You are from what was my past.'

'Yes, that is true. I am from that past. But we both passed that door, and the past is still locked away from both of us. Look down; see the ant-people down the street. They are the people we should be a part of. There is no way back.'

'I was told that when my training is over I can return to Earth any time I want to.'

'It is safe to say that. They know you will not want to.'

'I would not bet too much on that.'

'I would. Look Carlos, I am a free citizen. I am free to go anywhere I choose to go in this universe. God knows I miss our world; still, I would not go back there.'

'I do not understand.'

'Put yourself in my place. As a blue nurse, my pay is fairly low, but I managed to save enough to have visited four different worlds on holidays, one of them was of a non-human race. I meet everyday people of a dozen races; one of my best friends is non-human. I see our people spread across the universe and I am proud of its position amongst the other sentient races. I feel I belong; I am part of something very big. To go back to Earth now - to forget all this, to be permanently stuck to the surface of one planet only, to not even being able to talk about the stars as I know them, would be a suffocating experience. I could not cope with the feeling.'

'Why don't you go just for a visit?'

'Earth is out of bounds for tourists - at least for the time being. I could go back any time I want- but only to stay. So here I am staying. Them and me.'

'Them and us,' whispered Carlos, putting his arm around her shoulder - and for a while neither of them said anything, looking down to the busy street below, with the flashing lights of the passing vehicles, from the warm, safe, dark quietness of their high window. It all pointed out the differences, the separation.

'Them and us,' whispered Carlos. 'All of them, and only the two of us.'

He felt very small and very vulnerable. But not alone. Susoan was with him, his own kind. He could feel the warmth of her body through the thin fabric, warmth that was reassuring and exciting at the same time. He felt safe with her so close.

He wanted to have her close. His arm tightened around her shoulder, drawing her closer to him, wanting to feel more of the warmth of her body pressing against his.

She understood the feeling. She knew what feeling lonely was. Turning towards him, she buried her face against the hollow of his neck. She wanted to hide her tears, but the wetness of her face gave her away even in the darkness.

Carlos felt her sobbing, and wanted to make things lighter by making a joke about getting all wet, but the words did not come out. He could not tell a joke at a time like this.

It was too solemn, too precious, having her in his arms, feeling her warm body pressing against his, alone...completely alone in a strange world.

The sobs slowly, quietened down. The magic of sweet sorrow passed, to give way to a different kind of magic. It felt good holding each other.

'I made a mess of your shirt.' Susoan did not move her face away. 'I am sorry.'

'My lady - you are welcome to cry on any of my shirts.'

'Thank you, but I hope not to have to use the offer too often. I am really a much more composed person.'

A few minutes back I did not feel very composed myself.'

It looks like good old Earth still has us by the neck.'

'I would have used a different part- not the neck.'

'Don't be rude!'

'Elbow! I was only going to say that it has us grabbed by the elbow.'

'Of course. What else? But let's change the subject. I am supposed to cheer you up and instead of doing just that I try to drown you in my tears.'

'I am still alive.'

'Just lucky. And talking about lucky, you wouldn't happen to have some Earth music?'

'I just happened to borrow some from Dr Andronicus.'

'And…'

'And what?'

'Put some on!'

'I cannot. I have to let go of you to do that and I do not feel like doing that.'

Come on – move.' Susoan pushed him away gently. 'Be a good host and put some music on for your guest.'

The soft melody filled the now nearly dark room. Only the flashing lights from the street broke the shadows. Susoan's face was in darkness as she sat on the windowsill.

'I have missed this very much. You can say everything you want about our Earth, but its music is not equalled in any universe.'

'It is beautiful, but I still prefer the music I had before.'

'What music? There was no music I had before.'

'Yes there was. I had you in my arms…'

'Come on Carlos. Cut it out!'

'No - I am serious. Feeling you so close to me was very nice. I don't know, there seems to be something special about you. Come here and make me feel human again.'

'Yes sir! Agent Susoan is coming up to lighten the suffering of a fellow earth-man.' Like a spoiled kitten she found a comfortable nest in Carlos' arms, sitting on the sofa. 'However, I think we should talk.'

'Talk? About what?'

'Remember the reason behind my visit. I came here to help.'

'And you are helping me.'

Carlos buried his face into her hair, breathing in deep the intoxicating perfume. 'Believe me; you are helping me a lot.'

'Cut it out! I am serious - I remember when I was black, the main reason I felt so isolated was because I was so cut off from any information on this place. This is what I meant by saying that I want to help you. You can use my medallion.

'You can ask me what you want to know and I can just relay it to the computer and tell you the answer. Okay?'

'It sounds easy.'

'It should be. Well?'

'Well what?'

'What do you want to know?'

With his arms around her, Carlos pressed his face against the back of her head. The warmth of her back against his chest was confusing his thinking. 'Do we have to?'

'Do we have to what?'

'Talk.'

Turning slowly in his arms, Susoan pressed her face against his.

'Not really. Not now. Just hold me tight.'

'Anything to oblige my Lady.'

'Shut up, just hold me, and don't move. Let me enjoy this feeling drop by drop.'

'Can I enjoy it too?'

'At this moment, you can do anything you feel like.'

'Hey hey. That sounds like a tall order.'

'And? Is big, strong Earthman afraid that little, hot redhead will seduce him?'

'Yes. And be kind enough to remember where you are. This is my place, so if there is any seducing to be done, I will do it.'

'Yes sir. Anything you say Sir. But I wish you would start it, Sir.'

'Well. Now be quiet and let me concentrate. Where was I?'

'Sir, I think you had your arms around me and were nibbling my left ear.'

'Thank you Corporal. As you were.'

'What now?'

'Sir, just for the records - that is not my left ear.'

'Left or right - what is the difference?'

'Sir - that is not my ear.'

'I always flunked anatomy.'

'Sir - I don't want to be impertinent - but if what you are trying to do is to pull my zip down - that is not the way. You have to twist it around, and then pull it down.'

'What a barbaric planet. They can't even produce a proper zip.'

'Sir?'

'Corporal- one more word out of you and I'll bite your nose off.'

There were no more words.

**

'Good morning!'

'Good morning lazy bum!'

'What's so good about it?'

'The sun is shining, the birds are singing and the breakfast is ready.'

'Let's concentrate on that last one. How do I know

189

that it is true?'

'For one, you could smell it.'

'Oh! That's what it is. I thought I was dreaming.' Carlos decided to open his eyes - and closed them with pretend fright. 'All that red is hurting my eyes. I cannot see you. Be kind enough to come closer so I can find out whom I am talking to.'

Susoan did not need an invitation to go into his arms. 'You are a fake and a liar, but any excuse is good enough to get a kiss. And wipe that grin off your face; I am not doing it for you. I happen to enjoy it.'

'Hmm. The things I have to do in this life to make people happy. I have to sacrifice myself so early in the morning. By the way, lady, you taste familiar -did we meet before?'

'You are lucky you called me a lady. Now, give me a proper cuddle and eat your breakfast.'

'Hello breakfast!'

'The breakfast on the table.'

'Anywhere you like it.'

'Get dressed, you sex maniac.' Susoan pushed him back to the bed and escaped into the kitchen. 'Hurry up before it gets cold!' she shouted from there.

Carlos stretched lazily on the bed. 'My God, why can't I wake up every morning like this?' He put on his dressing gown and went to the kitchen.

'If that thing tastes half as good as it smells, you are hired for life,' he commented. 'What did you make?'

'A bit of this and a bit of that. Just things I found around.'

'Well, I am sure you did not find it around here. A mouse would starve to death in my kitchen.'

'It was actually around the corner. I mean the shops around the corner.'

'When did you go there?'

'While you were out of this world, dreaming about

some floozy.'

'She was no floozy.'

'Anyway - I also called your school telling them that you are not feeling well and you will not be in today. And also called the hospital telling them that I won't be in either. Unless you feel that you do not require nursing attention and would rather be alone.'

'I feel that my temperature is rising; I could not possibly be alone today.'

During all this Carlos practically finished breakfast. It was good. He was not exactly sure what he was eating, but it tasted good. He had nearly finished when he noticed that Susoan was not wearing her medallion.

'How come you're not wearing your necklace?'

'Oh - I forgot to put it back. I must have left it in the bathroom when I had a shower.'

'Do you always take it off for showers? I didn't know you were supposed to do that.'

'You are not. Actually I took it off last night.'

'Why?'

'Well, partly because it kept hitting you on the nose. But mainly because I did not want anything to interfere with last night.'

'You mean someone calling you?'

'That too, but mainly I did not want to receive any emotional feedback.'

'What are you talking about? Emotional feedback from who?'

'Are you putting me on, or do you really not know?'

'Susoan - every moment I keep bumping into things I am supposed to know, but someone neglected to tell me. I really don't know what emotional feedback you are talking about.'

'Well, they probably did not mention it to you because it is so much a part of our life that everybody takes it for granted. Our medallions are not just instruments that switch on when used and switch off when unused. They are constantly functioning, picking up and monitoring all your physical or body signs and also your emotional and mental state, moment by moment. And by its permanent linkage it relates all this information to the Central computer. You sneeze and the Central know about it.'

'So much for privacy. But what was that about the emotional feedback?'

'The same way the medallion can pick up your emotions and transmit it to the Central - the Central can send back impulses via the medallion, which can influence your behaviour.'

'And you people like this? It is bad enough this invasion of privacy - but this is like being puppets - made to dance by the whim of the puppet master.'

'You forgot that the puppet master is an impersonal computer, which does the job it is programmed to do. And to answer you - no, we do not like it, but it is a price we are willing to pay for the multiple benefits it offers.'

'Such as?'

'Such as the feeling of complete safety. Safety for your person and safety for your property. In Jeshtar crime practically does not exist. Remember this when you want to steal something. The Central will know your intentions before they are clear to you - and will influence your emotional make up to change your attitude.'

'I still cannot see what this has to do with last night. As far as I remember, there was no crime committed here. Or was there?'

'No. Seducing your nurse is not a crime. Okay - okay,' she interrupted Carlos, as he was about to protest. 'Being seduced by her, if you prefer it that way, either. But the Central also monitors your bodily functions and interferes when you try to do something harmful to yourself.'

'What happened last night was definitely not harmful to me.'

'I hope not - but look at it from the Computer's point of view. If you describe having an orgasm as extreme muscular activity, marked increase of pulse, respiratory rate, blood pressure, intra-cranial pressure, extreme mental tension with the emotional separation from reality - it does not sound very healthy, does it? It is logical for the computer to interfere.'

'Somebody should explain to the computer that it is very healthy. I can vouch for it. But there is more to it - isn't there?'

Susoan was silent for a long time, looking away, not facing him.

'Carlos did I do it again?'

'Did you do what, again?'

'I am not sure. I was told that I do weird things. Like shaking.'

'You did not shake. You went into a full convulsion. For a minute you frightened the hell out of me.'

'That's what I mean. What is it? There is no one I can talk to about it. You are a doctor. What is wrong? Am I an epileptic or something?'

'Hey, hey - stop that. Come here and give me a cuddle while Doctor explains it to you. 'There is nothing wrong with you. On the contrary, you should be proud of it. All it means is that your brain is unable to cope with the excessive intensity of your orgasm, causing a temporary malfunction. The Frenchmen call it "The Petite Morte" - and they think very highly of a woman able to have feelings of such intensity.'

'Thanks. You took away a big worry from my life. You know, you are the first doctor I met who knows about these things, you must be good.'

'I am the best. And if you don't mind, I will have a shower now. Being the best doctor does not make me smell like a rose.'

'Rose or not I was trying to suggest just that. But hurry up, I got a lot of plans for you today...'

Carlos found it hard to concentrate on his shaving. He felt like he were walking on clouds. After the low feeling of the last few days this was hard to accept as real. He was afraid that he would wake up and find out this was just a dream.

The blueness of her medallion gleamed on the shelf under the mirror. It looks just like my black - the same shape and markings. Perhaps a little bit thicker.

He held both medallions in his hands. There was no difference in the touch or weight. The odd thing was that even their temperature seemed the same although the blue was lying on a cold surface for a long time.

'Almost as if they were alive,' Carlos murmured to himself. 'They look the same although there is a world of difference for the wearer. One of these days I will have a coloured one - I hope - and the world will change.'

On a sudden impulse, he took off his black one - and put on the blue medallion.

There was a flash of blinding light, a pain, as if the very fabrics of his mind were torn to shreds.

Then there was black.

Then there was nothing...

**

(Carlos! Talk to me, I know you are in there).

The deep anguish in her voice disturbed Carlos.

(What's the problem Sus?).

(Carlos! Thank God you are back. I knew you would not leave me like that). The happiness in her

194

voice washed over him like a warm wave. But there was something else in her voice...

(Sus, what are you up to now?}

(Dr Alegria - I am glad you can talk to us. How do you feel?)

(Dr Andronicus - I feel fine. What do you mean by...)

(Dr Alegria - please, bear with me for a minute. Describe to me where you are.)

(Why - I am in the...I don't know where I am. Hey - what is happening here? I cannot see a thing, or...)

(Dr Alegria - listen to me. Try to concentrate on what I am saying. You are within the confinements of your body. Your body is not functional at the moment. Your physical senses are not operative - that is why you cannot see, hear or touch.)

(I can hear you.)

(No, you cannot. We communicate with our medallions - from mind to mind. Do you understand me?)

(I understand your words. The rest is a bit hard to accept. Just before I panic - tell me what happened to my body.)

(Do you remember putting on Sister Latimer's blue medallion?)

(Yes, I remember. I also remember the pain. I will tell you one thing - that is something I will not do again soon.)

(I am sorry, but it is not that simple. The medallions are designed upon contact to penetrate the mind on its own wavelength, which is set. To a different mind the penetration of that same wavelength would be lethal. Matter of fact, what you've done by accident is a very popular way of committing suicide here.)

(I am still alive.)

(Yes, you are. That particular psi barrier quality of

yours managed to protect the integrity of your mind. However, it failed to protect your physical body. Every nerve pathway in your body - at the organ or tissue level - was disrupted.)

(That sounds very much like a non-survival situation.)

(It is, and very much so. However, your body is kept functional. With mechanically-assisted ventilation, artificially-controlled circulation and renal function we are able to maintain a near normal tissue perfusion and low-grade function. You do not have to worry. We will keep your body alive, or functioning at least, until you decide to come back.)

(What do you mean when I decide? I have already decided. I want my body back. What do I have to do?)

(I don't know.)

(What do you mean you do not know?)

(I simply do not know - not just yet anyway. You have to understand, that you are the first person ever to survive this kind of contact. There are no antecedents to go by.)

(So what next?)

(Until we know more about the situation - we improvise. You appear to be all right inside - mentally. Your body, cell by cell is in relatively good condition. However, the parts of your body are not interconnected, and you are not connected to your body.)

(You seem to have a lot of information about my body.)

(I had plenty of time for tests. It was over two months ago that you decided to sample the blue. We were just about giving up the waiting when you decided to surface today!)

(Two months! You mean to say, that you kept my body alive for two months without knowing that I was around. Do you do this often?)

(No. We do not usually wait for so long. However, in your case it was different. Sister Latimer insisted that there was a mental link between you two which she was sure was not broken. This seemed to indicate that you were still around somewhere in some place. That is why we decided to wait.)

(Susoan thanks. I owe you one.)

(I will remind you of that when there will be more of you around.)

(So, Dr Andronicus, what is next? Where do we start?)

(To work from within. I asked your teacher - professor Holden - to join us here. He will explain to you what we want you to do.)

(Hello doc!)

(Hello Carlos!)

(Doc - please- show me the way.)

(I will try - but as Theo said - we will have to make it up as we go along. You feel ready to work?)

(Ready? I am more than ready. You have to give me something to concentrate on. If I am not concentrating on something, I do not exist. I feel like I am dissolving into nothing.

There is no sensory input whatsoever. No light, no sounds, no touch. There is not a trace of body awareness. There is no balance or positional sense. There is no up or down. I only feel this deep panic growing inside. I need something to concentrate on in order to control it.)

(For how long have you been aware of this feeling?)

(I do not remember to be aware of anything until Susoan called me. And I was feeling fine until Dr Andronicus made me check my status.)

(She was calling you, practically non-stop, for nearly two months now. You really owe her one Carlos. Okay - now let's concentrate on the problem now. Do

197

you remember the work we were doing at the school?)

(Doc. If you bring here those blasted balls again I will scream. Had enough of them for a lifetime.)

(I do not know why you learned to hate that exercise. You got quite a lot of development out of those balls.

Still - what I want you to remember is the power-building exercise which you were doing before you sent out the energy to move the balls. Do you remember it?)

(Yes, I do remember it.)

(I want you to do it right now. Build up the mental power level to the height needed to move the balls. Tell me when you are ready.)

(I am ready.)

(Now describe me what you see.)

(I am in a green valley. Blue sky above, large yellow flowers around…)

(Stop that!)

(What is wrong?)

(I do not want you to build an alternate reality. It is difficult enough as it is to contact you with this one. Visualize only the energy level you have created, and tell me what you see?)

(Gold.)

(You mean yellow?)

(Doc. I know the difference. When I say gold - it is gold.)

(Project it to me, so I can see it…my god, you were right. It is gold.)

(Of course it is. What is wrong with gold?)

(Nothing, absolutely nothing. Boy. You are full of surprises.)

(Doc, translate please. You lost me again. What is this about the Gold? You are Gold.)

(Now hold it there - My Gold is an arbitrary colour

198

chosen to represent a piece of machinery. Your gold is the visual representation of your aural energy capacity production. It is an inherent quality of your mind and represents a very high level of possible power functions.)

(How high?)

(I knew about persons who had the gold power. I myself have never had the opportunity to meet one. Theo - are you listening in?)

(I am, and as you said, our boy is full of surprises.)

(No wonder he is a psi barrier. He needs to be a barrier to be able to survive such power inside.)

(Doc - cut the mush. Having this gold inside, is it good or bad?)

(My boy - having the power at your fingertips, sorry, at your disposal, I think you have a fair chance to re-enter our world.)

(Good. Now - what do I do?)

(Okay. Now. What I want you to remember is that there is nothing wrong with your body. The problem is that its parts are not interconnected. So you have to go through every neural connection, one by one, connecting them first mentally, then the body connection should follow automatically.)

(And just how do I do that?)

(Mind pictures. Start with your right hand. You are right handed, aren't you?)

(Yes - I am right handed, or used to be.)

(OK - Now I want you to imagine seeing your right hand in front of you. Picture it very clearly, in every detail. When you get it I want you to imagine moving your hand, finger by finger, seeing in front of you every detail of your hand in motion.)

(Imagining that I am moving my hand.)

(Yes in every detail.)

(And what will that do?)

(If you are able to imitate the action mentally - and I am sure you can do it - there is a fair chance that the mechanical connection will follow it, connecting your brain to your hand again.)

(A fair chance? Is that all?)

(Yes. Remember, no one has ever done this before, as no one ever was in your situation. We are guessing. And hoping.)

(Do you realize what you want me to do? To mind-force the re-opening of the neural channels - one by one. You said it would be extensive, but do you realise how extensive? How long do you think it will take me to re-open one nerve path?)

(I do not know. There are too many unknown factors. The whole situation is completely new. The complete disconnection of the entire neural network was unheard of up until now. I am unfamiliar with the power of your gold. The technique I am suggesting to you was never used in this way. I do not have an answer for you, but I imagine it will take less and less time as you go along.)

(Even if you count on minutes to re-connect every interrupted pathway - do you know how long it would take? Only in my little finger, I have hundreds of nerve connections.

Motor nerves, sensory nerves, and pathways belonging to the autonomic nervous system...it is numerically impossible to cover all of them in one lifetime.)

(I can see your point and I agree with you on the size of the task. Still, there is the hope that the time factor will change as you go along and things will speed up automatically, but even if you are right there is no alternative. Unless we find another way later on - this is it.

So stop the mental moaning and start working. I

don't want to hear from you until that right hand is moving. Got it?)

(Got it. And thanks.)

**

(Doc! Hey doc - where are you?)

(What is it? Who is calling?)

(Who do you think?)

(Carlos! What is all that excitement about? And what is the idea of waking me up at this ungodly hour?)

(Sorry for that. You know I have no sense of time. I had no idea that it was night time.)

(Okay. Okay - what is it?)

(I just had to talk to you. Guess what is happening?)

(I give up. What is happening? Hey, did you get it moving?)

(Don't know. How can you be aware of movements if you don't feel the part? But I feel heaviness. Doc, I definitely feel heaviness in my right hand. It might not be much to you, but...)

(What do you mean it is not much?

It is fantastic. It means that our theory is working. If you really feel something there, anything, it means that a nerve connection was established. We have to check it, and right away. Who is there with you?)

(No one that I am aware of.)

(Carlos - who called me?)

(I did.)

(Carlos, cut it out! You cannot call me. You are black.)

(Oh! In the excitement I forgot about that. But...I DID CALL YOU.)

(You are right - I checked with Central and no one was in contact with you recently. How did you do it?)

(I don't know. It just happened. I just called for you -

without thinking - and you responded.)

(Look. Let's go slowly, and start by checking your hand. Something very weird is happening here and I want to come back to this calling business when I am more awake. Okay?)

(Okay. What do you want me to do?)

(First calm down, and then ask Sister Latimer to touch your hand to see if you can feel it.)

(And where do you want me to get her from? You said it was the middle of the night.)

(Yes, it is. But for the last ten weeks she was always with you, even sleeping in the bed next to you to be close by.)

(She did that? She is quite a girl...now - hold on doc, last time I talked to you, you said it was two months since my...let's say accident. How come it's ten weeks now?)

(Last time I talked to you it was two weeks ago. What did you think, how much time has passed since then?)

(Doc, how many times do I have to tell you? I do not have any sense of time. None at all. For me, time does not move. When I called you - I sort of expected you to still be standing next to me.)

(And you have been working on your hand all the time since then? Without rest? Without stopping?)

(Doc. Remember, I cannot feel anything. No hunger. No thirst. No pain. I cannot be tired or sleepy, because I cannot feel it. That is why there is nothing to indicate the passing of time.)

(Fascinating. You could perform a tremendous amount of mental work in this condition. Absolutely fascinating.)

(Doc, could we come back to my hand?)

(Sorry. You are right. Call Sister Latimer...)

(...Professor Holdgen, what is happening? How can

Carlos call me, he being black and all that?)

(When did he call you Sister? I kept tuned in and was not aware of any communication through Central.)

(He is not talking through Central. I do not know what he is doing, but he is not using his medallion.)

(Ask him to call me.)

(I hear you Doc.)

(Carlos, ask Sister Latimer to touch your hand, and while she is doing it give me a detailed report. Every little thing you feel in your hand, I want to know about.)

(Nothing, I know she is touching my hand, because she told me so, but there is no feeling, I can... hold it, I can feel something. Yes. There is definitely a rhythmical pressure change. It's stopped now. Sus, are you still squeezing my hand?)

(No, I stopped it.)

(So it is real. Squeeze my hand three times; see if I feel it right.

Hold on...I felt four squeezes.)

(Correct. I pressed four times.)

(Then it is true. I can really feel something. How do you feel about it Doc?)

(Looks like it is working. Our working theory seems to be the correct one.)

(Doc. I tell you - it's working. And if the rest depends upon time and dedication to work I've got plenty of both. Doc, next time I am talking to you I will be walking.)

(I don't doubt you. But there is another thing you should be aware of.)

(What is it Doc?)

(I am not wearing my medallion.)

(What? Doc, I don't understand you.)

(At the beginning of our conversation I took my medallion off to see if you could communicate with me directly.)

(Without the medallion? But that would mean…)

(Precisely.)

(How can you understand me? Our languages are not even alike.)

(You seem to have established a deeper level of mental contact. You are not talking to me in words; you are sending me complete mental images. There is no language involved in our communication. When you talked about the pressure on your hand, the communication was so complete that I could actually feel the pressure myself; there was no need to understand your words. I am not sure what is happening, but besides re-establishing the electro-neural pathways in your body, there is something else growing inside you. I just hope you will be able to control it.)

**

Carlos kept his word. The next time, he was walking. Well, sort of.

It took him three months to achieve it. Three months of arduous work - in the inside.

From the outside, there was no sign of activity, although this time at least his body was showing physical signs of life. He was breathing spontaneously, his heart was beating on its own sending blood around to feed his organs, and there was some kind of noticeable body temperature, obvious signs of chemical activity. Although all this was of a very low key affair, the monitors showed a definite difference in the composition of the air breathed out, indicating oxygen consumption, and his kidneys did eliminate some waste products.

The supporting team decided to interfere as little as

possible with his bodily functions and accept the vital statistics that normally would be incompatible with life. They all knew that they were dealing with something outside of the boundaries of the known physical rules.

He was fed intravenously with energy concentrates, at the slow rate it was removed from the blood stream. The oxygen concentration of the air he was breathing was regulated by the minute according to the rate of consumption. His body was frequently cleaned and changed in posture and alternate muscle groups were manually and electrically stimulated throughout the day and night to maintain their working capacity.

The body was working. Very slowly, but reasonably well. However, there were no cerebral functioning. The electroencephalograms and all the neural monitors failed to reveal any signs of activity.

No one really knew what to expect. They just monitored everything they thought about and tried to follow the cues of the body, waiting for something to happen. Anything.

And it did.

The first change was a sharp increase in oxygen consumption, followed very closely by a slow but steady increase in body temperature.

A few days later the respiratory rate increased, and very soon after that the pulse started to rise.

But there was still no cerebral activity.

It took a further two weeks before any neural activity began, and even then it started at the peripheries. Sporadic, low wave impulses generated first at the level of the lower motor neurons, not strong enough to cause a discharge at the neuro muscular junction.

Then the EEG monitors became alive, describing strange rhythmical discharges which progressively grew in potency but did not change in character.

'He is waking up doctor!'

Dr Andronicus leaned over the computer printouts. 'There is something happening - yes sister - but I have no idea what it is. What do you think Prof?'

'I don't know why you would ask me. You know damned well that all that data simply does not make any sense. May as well throw all your monitors out and just sit back and wait.'

'You know we cannot do that.'

'And why not? That is what you are doing anyway with your monitors. Sit and wait. The whole blasted thing is ridiculous.'

'Hey Professor, calm down! There is no reason to be upset.'

'What do you mean there is no reason? I don't know about you, but I have had just about enough. I feel ridiculous and I feel impotent and I don't like it. The whole thing doesn't make any sense. I do not understand what is happening. This increase of energy output could mean that he is asking for help, and we are just sitting here twiddling our thumbs.'

'What do you suggest we do?'

'I don't know. I don't know what to do and that is exactly what is upsetting me.'

(Why don't you practice with your white balls?)

'Oh shut up! This is not the time for...CARLOS - is that you?'

(Well, it's not Santa Clause.)

'Ted - what is on the printout?'

'Nothing, I mean there is no change in the brain activity. Still the same, irregular discharges, although they are getting stronger. It seems to be a mixture of alpha and theta activity but with a constantly changing polarity.'

'You know that is impossible.'

'I know it, you know it, but obviously Carlos does

206

not know it. See for yourself.'

'You are right. It is absurd. Carlos, where are you?'

(Now, that was not quite the right question.)

'Sorry. Let me change that. What are you doing?'

(Trying to get up, which I will do as soon as you remove all these connections. I must look like a Christmas tree.)

'You do. But forget about removing the monitors and just stay where you are. There are a few facts I need to know, and I would like to know them now. All right?'

(Anything you say doc. Sorry for upsetting you like this, it really was not my intention. I will try to answer your questions the best I can.)

'First of all - how do you communicate with us? We are all receiving you clearly, but you are not coming through the computer.'

(I cannot answer that. I don't understand it myself. It just happens. It feels the same as when we are talking through the medallion - but much clearer.)

'Then explain to me how it can be that your obvious mental activity shows up as garbage on the monitors?'

(Doc, you are not being fair. You were teaching me. Please remember how much of a novice I am in relation to mental activities. However, I can offer you a guess.)

'Please do.'

(I was trying to re-establish the neural functions in my body, particularly in my brain. I managed to reconnect some of the pathways, but obviously made a lot of wrong, upside down connections and that is why you are getting a changed patterned reading. Doc, you cannot even imagine the complicated nature of our body functions.)

'Can you control your body?'

(I can imitate some kind of a control.)

'Would it be safe to disconnect you from the

monitors?'

(I think so.)

'Sister, please help me disconnecting these tubes. Thank you. No. Not those, I want to leave those monitors functional.'

(Doc. I cannot move about trailing all these wires behind me.)

'Sorry Carlos. I would not dare disconnect everything. I want to know what is happening inside you while we are talking. Don't get up yet – just… what is going on?' The high pitched alarm of the cardiac monitor interrupted the tension-charged calmness of the room. For a long second all the eyes were fixed to the straight green light on the screen. Then all erupted in a fury of activity.

'Sister - put up the bicarbonate please and pass me the…'

(Hold on Doc! There is no problem.)

'Carlos? What the hell are you doing now?'

The alarm suddenly stopped and the monitor screen presented the curves of a perfectly normal cardiac rhythm. Everyone froze in mid movement, awaiting something.

(Sorry Doc - I did not want to startle you - but I had to demonstrate to you that the situation is under control.)

'Carlos! Did you just…?'

(Yes prof. I stopped my heart, then I restarted it again. Doc I do want those wires off.)

'Sister - please take everything off. Okay Carlos, this is your show. I think there is a lot you ought to tell us, so I am listening. But go easy. No more demonstrations like the one you just did, please.'

(Okay - help me get up.)

Dr Andronicus on one side and Sister Latimer on the other, they helped Carlos sit up, then to swing his legs around and sit on the edge of the bed. Professor Holdgen was watching every move from the end of the bed. Nearly forgetting to breathe, his eyes absorbed every movement, every little shake Carlos made. He did not get close to them.

With deepening lines on his forehead, he watched Carlos stand up, with a lot of help from both sides, and then give his first poorly-balanced steps, until he managed to sit down on to a chair next to the small table.

(God - it feels strange to walk again after all this time. I have nearly forgotten how to do it.)

There was no change in Carlos' facial expression. His face was rigid, like it were cut out of marble. Since opening his eyes, except some flickering eye movements, his face was still. No blinking, no shifting his gaze, no movements around his mouth. The stillness extended to his whole body. He moved his arms and legs only when absolutely unavoidable, as if it required great effort to activate the muscles. Besides his very shallow and slow breathing, visually there were no obvious life signals. Even his posture was forced, unnatural, mannequin-like.

(Dr Andronicus - how do you feel about me eating something? I do not really feel hunger although I know I should. If you do not mind, I would like to find out how my body responds to food.)

'Carlos - as prof. said - this is your show. I do not have enough data to be able to offer any comment on your present situation. From a purely medical point of view, it is a good idea at this point to introduce some light oral nourishment. However, the plain medical aspect is the least relevant to your condition. I think professor Holdgen will agree that we are dealing with a basically new mental phenomenon. So - if it is OK with you - I would appreciate if you could answer a few questions until your food arrives.'

(Please - ask the questions - I will try to answer them as best as I can.)

'Thank you. First, I would like to understand the sensory input you are receiving. What can you see, hear, feel…'

(Appear to have a full sensory connection, but only on demand. I mean, I can see everything clearly, but only while I am concentrating on seeing. When trying to hear, I perceive and understand the sounds clearly - but while doing so I do not see anything.

This goes for all the senses.)

'How long can you maintain a sensory input?'

(As long as I want to, but only one modality at the time. While I am listening to you, I cannot see you.)

'Can you see me now? You are not looking at me.'

(I am not aware of which direction my eyes are turned. But I can see you quite clearly.)

'While watching me, what other things do you see in this room?'

(I can see 360 degrees around me if required, like just now, but I am not aware if to achieve this I am turning around physically.)

'You are not. Your sight does not appear to have the physical limitations of your eyes. We will have to come back to this later, but now, tell me about your motor control. Like - I want you to scratch your nose now - and after you have done it, tell me how did you do it and what did you do.'

For a few seconds nothing happened. Then Carlos's right hand rose, shaking, and then stabilized itself, hovering a few centimetres above the table top.

Then, with short, jerky movements he started to lift it towards his face. First it looked like it would miss his nose, but changed direction slightly and touched it.

Then he rubbed his nose, moving his arm from the

shoulder, keeping his wrist and fingers stiff. Then in the same fashion, the hand descended to the table.

(Was this what you wanted?) -

'Yes, thank you. Now please describe to me what you felt controlling your hand's movements.'

(Controlling is not the word. It is more like a hit and run affair.)

'Please explain.'

(First I focused on perceiving the position of my hand and of my nose. Then controlled the muscles to move my hand, but while I was concentrating on moving, had no awareness of the new position of my hand, or how much did it move already. So had to start to concentrate on perceiving the position, while naturally I could not continue with the moving.

When I knew where my hand was in relation to my nose, I would move my hands again, I expect the result was quite visually weird for you.)

'It was - and quite so. Now I would like you to…but here is your food. Do you need any help with eating?'

(I might, thanks. But let me try it first on my own.)

Carlos's fingers closed clumsily around his fork, which speared a potato on his plate, missing it the first time, and then slowly lifted it towards his face. Then obviously he had a bit of a problem co-ordinating the opening of his mouth and the moving forward of the fork and depositing the food in his mouth. The biggest problem seemed to be withdrawing the fork while keeping his mouth closed, but he managed it quite well.

(How was that for a start?)

There was no answer from the others.

There was no possible answer.

'How do you congratulate a man about the fact that he is able to eat on his own? The achievement only managed to underline his physical disabilities.'

Radiating almost audible good humour, Carlos

continued to put food in his mouth, but within a very short time he got tired and asked them to help him back to his bed.

(I promise to perform more for you tomorrow, but today, I need more rest. Please forgive me.)

**

The three of them were sitting, speechless, at the nurse's desk, looking at each other and trying to come to terms with what they recently experienced. Susoan was the first to break the silence.

'Dr Andronicus - what is happening to him?' She could not hold her tears back anymore. 'He has changed so much. I expected he would be normal when he woke up. I already got used to the idea that...that when it's over he will be left with some physical disability.

'But this? I cannot even understand what it's all about. He seems so...so alien. Yes, that is the word. Alien.'

'Sorry sister, there is not much explanation I can offer you. However, I do not think the word alien fits him. Carlos did not change. I mean, Carlos, the person inside the body, did not change. His body suffered very extensive damage, and Carlos, inside, is trying to adapt to the changed situation. The way I see things is that, although he did not say it, Carlos realized that he is unable to fix his body and he is trying to cope with the situation and trying to find alternate solutions. He obviously found some way out but I cannot even guess the way towards which he is aiming. What do you think prof?'

'I think you are right. He obviously failed to repair the damage done to his body, and he knows it. What he seems to be aiming for is to bypass the chemical neural-transmitters in between the central nervous system and the peripheral organ receptors in order to…'

'Professor Holdgen. Please keep it simple.'

'Sorry sister. Well, his physical disability is such that the neural pathways that connected his brain to his muscles and his sensory organs like eyes, ears etc., were interrupted, so his body cannot function. For example, all his muscles are well and able to function, but he cannot make them contract, as they are not connected to his brain. He simply cannot tell the muscles to work; so all movements are out of question. The same way for example that his eyes are fully functional, but he cannot tell his brain what they see, due to the broken up connections, so he cannot see.'

'But he can see and he can move. We just saw him.'

'Exactly. He can. But not the way we understand it. He failed to re-establish the normal brain-organ neural pathways - he simply bypassed them.'

'What do you mean?'

'Well, I am just guessing here, but he seems to have established a direct communication between his brain and the outside world. Like, instead of picking up visual images with his eyes and from there transmitting the impulses to his brain to see, he appears to see directly with his brain, bypassing his eyes. The same seems to be happening with his motor functions. He did not lift his hand to scratch his nose. I was watching him from very close. There was not the tiniest muscle contraction in his arm. I think he directly levitated his hand. There was no muscle used in the moving.'

'This would certainly explain his 360-degree vision.'

'It would too. Although there are a few things which are harder to explain.'

'Ted - what are you talking about?'

'About the episode when he stopped his heart

and…'

'That is simple to explain. He did not stop his heart. He interfered with the cardiac monitor, giving out a false reading.'

'That is exactly my point. He lied. Why would he lie to us?'

'Get off the kid's back Ted! Give him some credit for human emotion. He had enough of that bed and wanted simply to get up.'

(Thanks Doc for defending me and you are right, as usual. I just had to get out of that bed and the feeling was too urgent to explain. I apologize though for the lying bit.)

'Apology accepted. Where are you now Carlos?'

(Where you left me. In my bed.)

(Can you see us?)

(Clearly.)

(Do you realize there are two doors and about four walls in between us?)

(No - I did not. But now that you mention it, they do not seem to be an obstacle.)

(How do you explain it?)

(I cannot. It has been a long time now since I stopped to look for explanations. Now I just accept the facts, as they come.)

(Did you hear our conversation in here?)

(Yes, I did. I was not spying on you either - really I was not. But your thoughts were so emotionally charged and directed straight towards me that they found their way to me. I could not have avoided them.)

(And what do you think?)

(About what?)

(About professor Holdgen's explanation of your "talents".)

(I do not think talent is the right word. But in answering your question, I do not know. It seems to be logical. It seems to cover the facts, but I am not sure if it is true. Things just happen to me lately. When I want to do something it just happens. I do not know how I do it. I don't even know if it is me who does the work.)

**

The next few months, although characterized by a furious burst of activity involving everyone, failed to produce any significant change in their position. Carlos kept producing situations which defied all established scientific laws, and the group, including Carlos himself, had no idea how he was doing them.

Carlos advanced very little in regaining control over his body. The autonomic body functions, like breathing, circulation, digestion and excretion seemed to have been re-established quite satisfactorily, like all the hormone-controlled functions, which were not really affected from the beginning. The neural pathways connecting the sensory organs to the brain were partially re-established, so Carlos had some sort of vision, reasonable hearing and a useful, although quite impaired, skin-contact feeling of pressure and temperature. However, the brain-motor organ connections, meaning the control of voluntary movements, failed to respond to his efforts.

(It is hopeless Sue. I got as far as I can - and this is it.)

(Carlos! You cannot give up. Not now. Not after all this work…)

(Exactly, after all this work. Just look at the results. All this work - as you say - and what for? We are where we were six months ago.)

(Not quite. You are not fair to yourself - not even truthful. Six months ago your eyes could not see, you had no touch, you were not aware of your body's

215

position. I think these are things which indicate a very important progress.'

(Not for six months. It is just not enough for six months. And even if it was, for the last two months nothing happened. We are all working like animals, and for what? We achieved what was possible to achieve, and that's it. It's time to quit.)

'Dr Andronicus, please help me. This hard-headed fool wants to quit. Please tell him off.'

'Why sister? Carlos is an adult person, quite able to make up his mind.'

'Dr Andronicus!'

'Of course, he has to consider the alternatives.'

(What alternatives?)

(You tell me. I can understand you wanting to quit. Okay, you quit. Then what?)

(I…I did not think it out that far.)

(No problem. I'll tell you your alternative. You will spend the rest of your life relaxing, enjoying life and doing nothing. Of course, you will also spend the rest of your life in a wheelchair, being a cripple, unable to survive without the assistance of other people.)

(Not quite what I had in mind.)

(It is your choice. I cannot see a third alternative.)

(You are not giving me a lot of choices.)

(Now hold on! I am not dealing the cards here. If you care to remember, my position in here is to try to help you out of situations, which is completely of your making.)

(I am sorry; I did not mean it the way it came out. I know I have no choice but to keep on working to get out of this mess whether I like it or not. But I cannot help feeling guilty about dragging you into it.)

(So that is what it is. Carlos, please understand our position here. We are here to help you - but it is not as selfless from our part as it seems. Sister Latimer, besides being the nurse officially assigned to look after you, making this is her job, something she is paid for, also has her personal reasons to be here.)

(You bet I have, you hard-headed brute. I am not the kind of a girl who lets her man walk out of her life with some feeble excuse.)

(Sus - I really...)

(Excuses - whatever you say, they are excuses. You are not getting rid of me so easily.)

(Okay - Okay - stop fighting you two. Now - where was I – yes, as far as Professor Holdgen and I are concerned, we both have our own selfish reasons to be with you.)

(I fail to see how you can get any benefit from the hours of work you spend with me.)

(It is very simple, my boy. For Professor Holdgen you are an extremely valuable source of information. Your whole situation is so new, so unusual, that he would not part with your company for anything on this planet, until he managed to squeeze every little bit of data out of you.)

(I can understand his point and I am glad that he finds me useful. And what about you?)

(I am the one who will benefit more from this whole unfortunate episode. Carlos, I have very important plans for you. After your recovery, and naturally, if you agree, I will need your newly-acquired talents to help me with a project of mine. This is why I asked you and the others to keep your situation and your progress a secret. Besides the four of us - you, Sister Latimer, Professor Holdgen and I - to everyone else you are an ordinary, everyday, private patient receiving special treatment. So, as you can see, there is nothing selfless about my trying to help you.)

(Thank you. I feel much better knowing that I am useful for something. Except you, of course Susoan. I fail to see what you are getting out of your work with me.)

(I am going for the jackpot, stupid. You.)

(At this moment I feel more like a handicap than a jackpot.)

(Dr Andronicus, I don't think Carlos is in the mood for working out today. Could he have the day off?)

'What do you mean Sister?'

'If it is possible, I would like to take him out. Just him and me, we could manage quite well in a wheelchair. He's spent more than a year now on our planet and all he knows is the hospital and the three of us. I would like to show him around. I think I know just the thing that will cheer him up.'

'What do you have in mind?'

'I know a place close to here, a small inn to be precise, where you can have a very reasonable meal and a few drinks - all quite cheap.'

'I fail to see the effect of an outside meal.'

'This Inn, besides its good food, is famous for being frequented by off-planet people. It is the usual meeting place of human and non-human races just passing through…'

(Hey Sus - I would love to go there.)

(I thought you would. But it is up to Dr Andronicus.)

'Okay Sister, take him for a walk. In the state he is in now it would be a waste of time to try to do anything. I do not feel happy about him leaving the hospital - but it just might be the thing that he needs.'

(Thanks Doc. Well Sus, when are we leaving?)

**

Halimer's Inn - just like its owner, Joshonhua Halimer - had seen better days. It was an impressive building in its younger days, and some say it was one of the first built in the area.

Since then its majestic appearance has been dwarfed by the newer buildings around it. Inside, it was reasonably clean, reasonably ventilated and always packed full with people. People of all sorts.

Inside, the four walls were completely covered, without leaving a finger's width of exposed wall, with photographs, holograms, paintings and signatures all witnessing its past glory.

The Inn's and Halimer's.

Most of the photographs were old, but so was Halimer. Sitting behind the bar or mingling with the customers, his tall white-haired figure still bore the dignity of the past.

Susoan managed to get a small table for the two of them just behind the door, where she could manoeuvre Carlos's wheel chair without too much fuss. It was not a small feat, considering the place was so full that some of the younger people were sitting outside on the footpath, finishing their drinks.

Susoan placed the wheelchair in a way that let Carlos observe the whole inside of the tavern, practically without having to move his head. With his face frozen in a placid expression, his eyes drank the scene before him. The place itself was exciting enough, like something that came alive right from the history books.

The action was interesting, but the people, well, the people definitely belonged to Halimer's Inn.

'Look at those two albino characters at the side table, the ones with the white hair and white eyebrows.' Susoan was supplying the explanations to the visual experience. 'They are from Taliz, a world without atmosphere where people live under the surface of the planet. As you watch them move, it is hard to believe that those pink eyes are practically blind.'

(They reach for their drinks, they walk in the crowd without bumping into people - are you sure they are blind?)

'Not completely - but just about.'

(I cannot see how that could be. They act normal.)

'Tell me Carlos, if you would move amongst all those people with your eyes closed, would you bump into them?'

(You know I would not, but that is different. I do not need my eyes to...I see what you mean. They don't need their eyes either. Hey - it moved!)

'What moved?'

(That - I don't know what it is. I thought it was a statue of a woman, now it is drinking, at the other end of the bar. I don't know what it is, but she is beautiful.)

'Who? Oh, I see. Carlos boy, you are lucky today. You can feast your eyes on a real, live Hhruahran. They look like a statue when they don't move because their skin is rigid and hard as steel. They are a warrior race, and the hard skin is part of their natural weapon. People say that a bullet cannot penetrate it.'

(And why am I so lucky to see her?)

'Hhruahrans belong to a galaxy quite far from ours, and although they are a mercenary race, we usually only hear about the fantastic things they are able to do. Very rarely do we see them in person.'

(This one has a medallion. A black one. She is not just passing by.)

'True. I only know what I could find out from the Central Computer, and that is not much. She arrived here about a year before you did and I am not sure what she is doing here. The black would indicate that her status is not settled yet, just like yours.'

(People are afraid of her. Just look at them. They are

on top of each other all along the bar - but there are empty places around her.)

'Just because we do not see many of them - we hear a lot about the Hhruahrans. And believe me, there are plenty of reasons to fear them.'

(Still, she is beautiful. And very lonely. I can feel it.)

At the distant end of the bar, the golden face turned towards them. There was a green fire in those eyes, which Carlos felt penetrating through his. For a second, he was all green inside, then the eyes closed and they left darkness behind.

'Carlos, what's wrong? Oh - oh, here comes trouble!'

The door was pushed in violently and a group of soldiers forced their way into the already crowded place. They wore the dark gray-green uniform of the Human World's Confederation and they were behaving like a group of soldiers on short leave - anywhere else, drunk, noisy and looking for trouble. Their presence apparently was something the people got used to, as suddenly there was plenty of room for the soldiers who were still coming in.

Carlos only realized that the rest of the people left when Susoan got up and wanted to leave. But he wanted to stay and watch. He felt safe in the corner, partly hidden by the door, which was left open. His eyes automatically went to the other end of the bar. She stayed there too - eyes fixed on her drink - ignoring the world around her.

It is wrong, Carlos thought to himself, an exotic, beautiful looking female with the reputation of being a good fighter - the perfect target for a soldier looking for some excitement.

However, some order established itself when the captain of the troop walked in.

A tall, solidly-built man who had his past etched on

his face with multiple scars. Without any hesitation he walked towards the table next to the wall quite near to where Carlos and Susoan were sitting. By the time he got there, the table was empty, with a freshly opened bottle and a glass on it.

Obviously he wanted a place where he could keep an eye on his men.

Carlos observed, fascinated. His eyes absorbed the scene and Susoan - although she really wanted to get out - had no heart to interrupt something he obviously enjoyed.

Time seemed to prove Carlos wrong. Besides the boisterous behaviour, the shouting and the singing, the soldiers appeared to be getting drunk quite peacefully. The presence of their grim leader appeared to be enough to keep them under reasonable control.

However, the inevitable had to happen. Sooner or later the alcohol had to cancel the sense of discipline, and one of the soldiers, encouraged by the cheers of his friends, had to approach the golden figure at the bar.

It had to happen. That living statue was too remarkable to pass unnoticed and the battle fame of the Hhruahrans was too great not to be challenged.

The golden statue did not move. With her eyes on her drink, she ignored the rest of the world.

The soldier was drunk enough to lose his inhibitions, but not drunk enough to misunderstand when he was ignored.

Ignored, as one ignores someone vastly inferior.

That, and the mocking cheers from his friends, was too much for the soldier.

He made a mistake.

He put his hand on the statue's shoulder to turn her around.

He was a big man, a solid man - like all the others. Experienced in long years of combat.

Still it was a mistake.

There was a blur of movement, hard to follow with eyes, and the soldier's body flew across the room, crashing against the wall next to their leader, ending in a heap on the floor at his feet.

The golden statue was still sitting at the bar, with her eyes on the drink in her hand. She didn't even spill it.

There was a deadly silence in the room. Time itself seemed to freeze. A confederate soldier was attacked - and beaten - in plain view of all the others.

This never happened before.

Their ferocity in battle, which was nearly a legend, the liberties they were permitted to take for the same reason, prevented practically all violent action against them. Especially when they were all together.

What happened here had no precedent. It could not be tolerated. The world has to be shown that this just cannot happen.

Keeping a deadly silence, like one man, they left their seats and approached the offender.

And she just ignored them. Ignored the lot of them. With her back to them, she finished her drink, put the mug on the bar, and asked for another one.

A word of command broke the silence. Just one word, which effectively froze the soldiers into immobile attention.

The captain stood up, sending his chair crashing against the wall behind him. As he approached, the thick ring of soldiers opened to let him through to the bar.

'Hhruahran - you attacked a confederate soldier. My men want satisfaction.'

'That is their problem.'

Carlos was shaken by the voice, which was deep and extremely feminine.

The Captain too was visibly taken aback by the unexpected quality of her voice.

'Hhruahran - I do not want mob action here - but that is what we will have if they do not get satisfaction.'

'The control of your men is your affair.'

'Exactly. And I feel like they feel. You are a member of a warrior race we only know of by fame. I am offering you a fight, a fair, one to one fight. You owe it to my men.'

'I do not owe you anything, and Hhruahrans do not fight without a reason.'

'Hhruahrans are mercenary soldiers. I am offering five hundred Imperial bonds to the victor.'

'How many soldiers do you have here?'

'Twenty-seven - but you don't have to fear but one.'

The Hhruahran turned her back to the soldier.

'Halimer! Is your Inn still for sale?'

'Yes, it is Kiara.'

'Would ten thousand bonds be a fair price?'

'It would be all right.'

'Okay Captain, if you want to buy a fair fight from a mercenary, it will cost you ten thousand bonds, and I will fight all of your soldiers, together, at the same time.'

There was a shock of silence first, then an indignant uproar. This was pushing the insult too far.

'Captain, your men want my blood. They have access to it for ten thousand bonds. It is me who is challenging you this time.'

'Hhruahran, don't push your luck!'

'Captain, think about their morale. Twenty-seven confederate soldiers refusing a challenge from one Hhruahran.'

'Fine Hhruahran - you asked for it. Finish your drink and we'll meet you at the park across the street, where there is more room to move.'

**

He was stopped at the door by Halimer himself.

'Captain, please renegotiate the deal. Believe me; this fight will do no good for the morale of your troops.'

'Old man don't worry. I will keep the fight a fair one.'

'A fair one? Captain, you misunderstood me. You obviously don't know the Hhruahrans - but I have seen them in action against the Tralafin worlds.

'Believe me, this fight is not a fair one. There are only twenty-seven of you.'

**

By the time Kiara arrived at the park, a big crowd was gathering there. The news of the impending fight was spreading like fire and people came running along the streets from as far as you could see.

There was no way Susoan could get Carlos's wheelchair down close enough but Halimer let them share his balcony with him and from its height they had an excellent view of the park.

The soldiers stood in a rigid half circle, facing the Inn and Kiara, as she arrived.

Kiara faced the leader.

'Captain, before we start, it is in order to warn you that for us Hhruahrans, a fight is not a sport. When a Hhruahran fights - the end is death.'

'Warning accepted. Are you ready?'

'Ready.'

'Okay Brenor - she is all yours.'

The one called Brenor - a huge brute with arms like

a fat man's thigh - advanced in a light crouch. The rest of the soldiers remained behind with a confident smile on their face. They knew what Brenor was able to do.

There was a blur of speed from where the Hhruahran was standing, the blur, with features nearly unnoticeable to the naked eye, passed by her attacker, seemed to touch five of the soldiers behind him, and was back at her place, facing her attacker before the fifth one fell to the floor, lying there in a heap, all five of them with broken necks.

'Come on Brenor - I am waiting for you!'

The soldiers realized for the first time that they had an adversary worth taking seriously. They were all veterans of many battles, they needed no more warning. They closed ranks with Brenor and advanced as one unit, before the command was received.

Doesn't matter how fast she was, there was only one of her.

The Hhruahran was waiting in an insultingly comfortable stance.

As the gray wave closed around her, she moved.

There was no blur of motion this time. She moved amongst them as an armoured vehicle would across a flock of sheep.

When she stood alone again at the other end of the park, a line of dead and wounded soldiers marked her pass.

There were no cheers. This was not a competition.

This was carnage.

As far as the soldiers were concerned, this became a fight for their life. The rules ceased to exist.

As one man, the remaining soldiers drew their energy weapons. The Hhruahran was clearly a problem to be eliminated.

She knew this was the end. She had no weapons, and no means to defend herself against an energy discharge.

She did not move.

Just stood there with her arms crossed over her chest - a universal sign of defiance.

She was expecting her death - defying it.

Then all hell broke loose.

Together with the crackling noise made by the discharging energy weapons, there was the sound as if the ground itself would tear apart. Huge slabs of the pavement tore out as if by themselves, and lifted into the air. Some of them vaporized instantly as they interrupted the energy pathways, the rest, unstopped, found their marks.

There was a frozen silence in the park as the last of the soldiers was crushed by tonnes of rocks.

The Hhruahran was still standing, unmoved, in the middle of the destruction.

The very foundations of the Inn seemed to be shaking in resonance with the explosion.

Susoan had problems keeping her balance.

'How did she do that?'

Carlos could not answer.

Sweat pouring from his face, with a sight of extreme exhaustion, he fainted into oblivion.

**

'I really don't think you should blame yourself for what happened.'

'I should have known better than to stay there. I should have realized the influence she had on him.'

'What do you mean, Sister?'

'It is hard to explain. It was more like a feeling of apprehension. I did not give it any importance, as there was nothing there to support it. At least I did not notice them. Not then.'

'Why? Was there anything to notice?'

'Of course there was. Looking back now - they were quite obvious. I could kick myself for not noticing anything.'

'Come on sister, don't keep the suspense.'

'Well, when we first got there, Carlos was obviously very excited. Commented on things around us, asked questions, seemed to observe everything and everyone in the place.'

'The moment he noticed her, all this changed suddenly. He put all of his attention on her, talked very little and what questions he asked were all related to her. I did not notice his sudden silence as there were so many things happening at the same time that I was distracted. Just assumed that he was observing the same things I was.'

'I cannot see the relation of this to Carlos's present condition. What was he doing during the fight?'

'I do not know.' Susoan was nearly crying now. 'Dr Andronicus, I just don't know. I was so intent on watching the fight…'

'I can hardly blame you for that.'

'…that I just forgot about Carlos. I do not know what he was doing; it could have been anything with those new talents of his. Only at the end, I turned to him to ask if he knew what was happening…just in time to see him go unconscious.'

'Did he say anything? Did he make any comment?'

'Nothing that I could remember. Probably didn't, as you know I could not have ignored him if he wanted to tell me something. Not the way he communicates directly to your mind.'

'Do you think he had anything to do with the fight?'

'I don't know. I do not understand him anymore. He is like a different person, I never know what he will do next, and when he does it, I never know why he does it,

228

or even how.'

'I know the feeling.'

'How is he now, doctor? What happened to him?'

'I do not know. With Carlos I do not have answers - only questions.'

'I only know what the monitors tell me, that he is back in the same condition as at the beginning, with all the vital signs so low that they are not compatible with life. However - he lived the last time.'

'And now?'

'I cannot see why not. I do not know what is happening, but it seems a repetition of the last time, so I hope…'

(Dr Andronicus - sorry to interrupt you. This is the inquiry desk in the lobby. A person is on her way up to visit Dr Allegria.)

(What do you mean on her way up? I do not want any visitors in here. Stop her.)

(Sorry sir, I cannot. She is probably half way up already; I did not let her in. She just informed me that she was going up, and she was on her way before I could stop her.)

(Who is she, and what does she want?)

(She did not say what she wanted, but I think she is an Hhruahran non human. I do not have any other data to supply, sorry.)

(Thank you for notifying me, I'll take over now.)

'Yes - I am a Hhruahran - the name is Kiara D'Charkoon.' The deep, melodious voice from the door startled them.

'Kiara D'Charkoon, judging by the way you entered I assume that you are fully aware of the fact that this is a private treatment room and that you are not allowed to be here. And you are not allowed in this room under any circumstances. If you want to talk to me, you can do it outside, not here.'

'If I leave - Carlos Allegria dies.'

There was a deep silence in the room. Susoan, with a few quiet steps put herself in between the Hhruahran and Carlos's bed, a move that seemed to confuse more the doctor.

'Please, explain your statement.'

The Hhruahran's voice was soft and persuasive.

'I know what is wrong with Carlos Allegria, and you are wrongly assuming that it is the same thing as before. It is not. Unless measures are taken, he will die, and very shortly.'

'How can you know about his condition?'

He did not say it, but the question was obvious. 'What does a woman soldier know about sick people?'

'In my world I was a healer whose word was taken with respect. I am familiar with your patient's condition, you are not, as this kind of problem does not often happen on human worlds. I can help.'

(Dr Andronicus - I checked with the Central - she appears to tell the truth. She was their leader's personal healer until she was exiled.)

'Kiara D'Charkoon, please come in and sit down. I recognize that out of mere ignorance I am unable to help Carlos and I am very willing to listen to anyone who can produce some information. Tell me - what do you know about him?'

'I know about his unfortunate meeting with the blue and the devastating neural disruption this caused.'

The statement was said calmly, but its content made the doctor leave his chair, almost with a jump, and to start pacing up and down the small room, until he felt able to face the Hhruahran again.

'Kiara D'Charkoon - no one, but absolutely no one from the outside world knows about these facts. I demand to know the source of your information.'

'At the Inn, for a very short time, I established

mental contact with Carlos Allegria. Your patient has a formidable natural barrier protecting his psyche, but a few, recently-acquired memories/thoughts were unprotected on the surface. This was one of them.'

'Who else knows about this?'

'No one I am aware of.'

This last statement seemed to help Dr Andronicus regain his bearings and take his seat again.

'Please excuse me for my outburst. My only excuse is the unexpectedness of your statement and the especially stressful time it arrived.'

'Understood.'

'Thank you. Please continue. You said that the present condition is different.'

Yes, it is. He did not suffer any further physical damage. He is only extremely exhausted - beyond his body's capacity to recover.'

'I do not understand.'

'I am sure you were informed of what happened today at Halimer's Inn, but not that Carlos Allegria was involved, or better put, involved himself in those events.

'This involvement of his demanded such an energy out-put that his physical body was unable to supply it, so he used the only thing that was available to him, what we call the vital energy of his psyche. Although this energy is ordinarily not available for transfers, in some special way he managed to deplete himself beyond the limits of survival.'

'You mean he will die?'

'Yes, and soon, unless help is given.'

'How can we help him?'

'I can give him energy.'

Dr Andronicus looked at Carlos first, then at Susoan. It was a hard decision to make. A complete stranger walks in and offers to treat his patient, whose problems are beyond normal understanding. Could he take the chance? There was nothing he could offer, but could he trust her?

'Sister Latimer, I feel that you have a say in this. What do you think?'

'I feel I can trust her doctor...'

'And who will ask me if I trust her or not?' Professor Holdgen stormed in nearly bringing the door with him. He threw himself down to one of the chairs, wiping the perspiration off his face.

'I came as soon as I could. Please, don't interrupt the conversation with formalities. I know Kiara D'Charkoon, and I am sure she knows me. I am also up to date in your discussion, as Sister Latimer kept me informed while I was arriving, so let's get to the point...Ted, what is your decision?'

'I am not sure Professor...'

'What do you mean you are not sure? Come on Ted, what the hell are you talking about? The boy needs help. He needs it now - and you cannot give it to him. What else do you need to make up your mind?'

'It's just that we understand so little about this whole mess.'

'And what does that have to do with accepting the help offered? Look Ted, if someone would tell me that sticking a carrot up his backside would help I would try it. Besides - I checked her credentials and I believe she knows what she is talking about.'

'Okay Professor - I think you are right. Kiara D'Charkoon - please accept my apologies for my hesitation, but Carlos here is just too important for us. Please tell me, what do you require for your help?'

'I have everything I need thank you, but please, we do not have much time.'

'What do you want us to do?'

'First, remove your medallions and place them

outside this room. The instrument I will use might damage their circuits. You will find that you do not need them to communicate with me.'

(Dr Andronicus - she does the same thing that Carlos does.)

(I know sister. Please do what she says.)

Kiara took a heavy chain from around her neck, which until now was hidden under her clothes. There was a white, transparent, glass-looking cube hanging from it. In the centre of the cube shone a very small piece of green crystal.

She placed the cube on Carlos's forehead, and, keeping her fingers on the cube, she closed her eyes.

For a few, tense moments nothing happened, then the green crystal started to shine stronger and stronger until Carlos's whole face was covered by the green light it emitted.

With a deep sigh, Carlos opened his eyes.

'Thank you Kiara for the green.'

As Kiara stepped away from the bed with the still-shinning cube in her hand, Carlos turned his head towards the others.

(Dr Andronicus - please go along with what Kiara wants to do.)

Practically before he finished the phrase, he was fast asleep.

'Doctor Andronicus - look at the monitors!' Susoan could not keep the joy out of her voice. 'They all changed - he is asleep now.'

'Yes sister, in a completely normal sleep, with all bodily functions back to normal.'

'Kiara D'Charkoon, I do not know what you did to him, but we are grateful to you.'

'How can we repay you?'

'Dr Andronicus - I came here to pay a debt. I owed him a life. We are even now.'

**

The tray finished with a loud clang on the table.

'I am sick and tired of hearing that name. If you say it once more...'

'What is the problem sister?'

'Oh - Dr Andronicus. Did not hear you coming in. I do apologize for being loud.'

'Carlos?'

(I am not sure what is upsetting her. She just suddenly…)

'What do you mean you don't know what is upsetting me! You know very well what is upsetting me. Dr Andronicus, since he woke up this morning, all I hear from him is Kiara D'Charkoon is like this, Kiara D'Charkoon is like that. He did not say one phrase this morning without mentioning that name.'

'I am sorry sister, but I too have to mention her name a few more times. Our Carlos here has a few questions coming to him.'

'You are right about that one Ted. And we better get some answers out of him today.'

(Hi Professor Holdgen. You look unusually cheerful today. Is that a good omen or a bad one?)

'A good one, my boy. Today is answer day. I have this gut feeling that Carlos will start providing some answers to the multiple questions.'

'And what do you think sister? How is our golden boy today?'

'Our golden boy definitely does not shine today.'

'Oh- oh . There was definitely a "I want to pick a fight today" tone to that.'

'I am sorry Professor…'

'No. I am sorry sister. Seriously speaking, I do understand that, of the three of us trying to help Carlos

234

out of this mess he managed to get himself into, it is you who carries the heaviest burden, and I really appreciate you sticking it out with us.'

'Thank you.'

'Okay. Now - getting back to the bright side of things - Carlos my boy, are you ready? Ted here looks like he is dying to squeeze some information out of you.'

'Well, I don't know what I look like, but I do have a few questions, if it is okay with you.'

(Doc, you know I am always trying to help. It is not my fault if I don't have your answers.)

'I know Carlos. I know that. Now - do you remember what you said when Kiara D'Charkoon woke you up for a short time yesterday? You asked us to go along with what she wanted. Remember? But you did not say what it was that she wanted.'

'Heh - right on the nose. I was going to ask the very same question myself.'

'Ron - please let the boy answer. Carlos?'

(Didn't she say anything?)

'All she said was that she owed you a life and that now you are even. What did she say to you?'

(Nothing. Well - not quite saying it, but I got the message that she could help me, even cure me back to normal.)

'Did she actually say that?'

'Did she offer to help?' The questions came simultaneously from the two men.

(She did not actually say it. There was not any message directed towards me. I just picked up some stray thoughts from the inside. She was convinced - just for herself - that she was able to fix me up, and I also felt that she would do it if we asked her first.)

'Why didn't she say anything then? Why didn't she offer to help?'

(I am not sure. They think differently to us. They interpret a person's privacy differently, which would be interfered with, if help were offered without being asked for.)

'So what are we supposed to do?'

(I don't know. There was also a thought that you might not agree with the cost.)

'What do you mean we might not agree? How much money does she want?'

(I don't think she wants any money. She says she needs something, some sort of special instrument to use on me. The concept is very vague for me.)

'I have to talk to her. This is an opportunity too important to miss. Ted - how can I get in contact with this Hhruahran?'

'What's wrong with the Central? Did you...'

'Of course I asked. All I am getting is that she requested a privacy code and her present location is not available.'

'How can she do that? I didn't think blacks could do that.'

(When do you want to talk to her professor?)

'I don't care Carlos. Yesterday, if I could. The sooner the better.'

(Okay.)

'What do you mean okay?'

(That she is on her way and will be here very shortly. Better notify the reception desk to avoid complications.)

'Carlos. How the hell does she know that I want to talk to her?'

(I told her. When you said you wanted to talk to her, I called her. Remember, I don't have to go through the Central Computer.)

**

There was a heavy silence in the room. The crystal healer left a long time ago - but the four still could feel her presence. Dr Andronicus was the first to break the silence.

'I think we have a problem here.'

'Ted, my friend, you have this way of stating the obvious. We always have problems of one kind or of another, but this is the first time I cannot see a way to a solution.'

'There must be one.'

'Name it. A crystal of that size. There is no way we can get one in.'

'Hold on Ron. Before you plan to bring it planet side, you better make plans on how to get one. We cannot afford it.'

(Doc - you said I have practically unlimited funds.)

'True, but your funds are granted by the government. We cannot smuggle in the crystal illegally, and then charge it to the Central.'

(I cannot see why we could not get government approval for the import of the crystal. I understand that it is dangerous to have it around, but we could devise some protective system. After all, we can show a very genuine need for it.)

'Carlos dear. What do you think the chances are for a private company to establish a nuclear reactor in the middle of London?'

(Nil. But there is a bit of a difference there.)

'Not really. In a society like ours, in which you cannot sneeze without using the computer, a crystal of that size would mean the same threat as an atomic reactor in London.'

(We could...)

'No we could not. Carlos, I think Ted is right on this one, and God knows I don't like to admit that he is, but we will never get approval from the Central Computer. We should not even apply for it, which would only bring it to their attention.

(So what is left there to do?)

'Dr Andronicus…'

'Yes sister.'

'Why couldn't we move off the planet, to somewhere where the crystal would not interfere with the computer function?'

'It is a logical thought sister - but it would not work. The Hhruahran has some sort of political restriction placed upon her and she is planet-bound. She cannot leave.'

(Officially.)

'What do you mean?'

(I mean that if we are already thinking of doing something illegal it seems to me simpler to smuggle her out than try and smuggle the crystal in.)

'You have a point there, Carlos. It might be worth considering it, but let's leave it for the last.'

(I still can't see the terrible danger that crystal can cause. I mean, you handle radioactive material here, which is as bad as a natural substance can go.)

'Not quite. The crystal that the Hhruahran wants to use is a very special one, a freak in itself as natural things can go.

'You can only find it on one small planetoid in their galaxy, and no one really understands the way it was formed. However, that does not change the fact that it has a spontaneous electrostatic discharge of a very short and penetrating wavelength – which wreaks havoc among machinery - even if they are not of electrical function. And just try to imagine what would happen in here if a crystal of that size interfered with the computer function. Besides interrupting all communication, no matter the distance, all the power functions would cease. Electricity, light, water, all transport would stop suddenly, air transports would crash to the ground, automatic production lines and life support systems would all stop. Just imagine the chaos created - and all that for the presence of just that one crystal. We rely on our computer for everything.'

(This was what Kiara meant when she said you would not accept the costs.)

'There must be a way.'

'Ron - hold on for a minute! Before you get to crystal smuggling, just remember one thing. We did not decide to accept the Hhruahran's offer. As far as I am concerned, I am not fully convinced that we can trust her that far, or that she is able to do what she claims she can.

'Dr Andronicus - we all saw her save Carlos's life.'

'Not quite, sister. We have all seen something - that is true. But what is it that we have seen? We have seen Carlos unconscious, we have seen that before. We have seen Carlos wake up with the Hhruahran's help, but we have seen the same thing happening before, without her help. Then we have seen Carlos go to sleep, quite a common thing to happen. Other than her own words, we have no evidence at all that the Hhruahran had anything to do with Carlos's awakening.'

'That is not quite correct.'

'Ron - unless you have seen something I have not - everything I have said is quite correct.'

'Yes, apparently I did see something you missed. Ted, remember, just before he asked us to do what the Hhruahran wants to do - Carlos turned his head and looked at us?'

'So what? He was moving by levitation like before.'

'Ted that was not levitation. I was looking at him directly and could see clearly the muscles on the side of his neck contract. He moved his head.'

'I did not see that from where I was standing at the time, but we could not make him do that again.'

'Exactly my point. Ted, the crystal healer accomplished more in five minutes than we were able to do in a year. For me, that was convincing enough.'

'It is convincing. I have to accept that. And that also makes the decision easier. We have to go along with her.'

'I agree, the question is how? Does anyone have any suggestions? Ted?'

'My only suggestion at the moment is to sleep on it. This is not the kind of thing you decide on the spot. Myself, I would prefer to think about it for a few days, especially as we have no real urgency .'

(Thank you.)

'I am sorry Carlos. I did not mean it the way it sounded. I know you are in a hurry, but you have to admit there is no emergency situation and also that a careful plan is essential.'

(I am sorry - just meant to be funny. I am more reluctant than you to try something dramatically unknown, but at the same time, I trust Kiara. She is offering something that appears to be the first and only solution to my problem. I cannot help but feel impatient.)

'Could you tell the Hhruahran to meet us here in one week?'

(She knows.)

'How come? You don't mean that she was listening in to all our conversation?'

(Yes, she was, as we maintain contact. She can hear everything I hear. She will be here in one week.)

'I can't say that I am very happy about her listening to everything we talk about, but maybe it proves to be helpful. She may come up with some solution to obtain the crystal.'

(She cannot.)

'What do you mean Carlos?'

(Dr Andronicus - Kiara needs that crystal herself - not just to help me. She was trying to obtain one, even a little piece, for a long time now - and failed.)

'That does not give us much hope - but anyway - let's see what we can come up with. We have one week to come up with a brilliant idea.'

**

(What's wrong professor? The way you stormed in…well you do not look very happy.)

'I do not have any reason to be happy. Where is the Hhruahran?'

(She is on her way, but it will be a while before she arrives. We are all a little bit early.)

'Carlos. Are you still linked with her?'

(Yes I am.)

'Please, break the connection for a while.'

(What is wrong professor?)

'Please, do it.'

(I cannot.)

'What do you mean you cannot? Is she holding you?'

(No. What I mean is that I do not know how to do it. Remember, my training in energy links was…oops - it is done.)

'What is done?'

(She broke the contact herself.)

'She was obviously listening in.'

(Of course she was. That was the whole idea of establishing the contact. Now, can you tell us what is happening?)

'Are you sure she is not listening?'

(Positive).

241

'Well, I might be paranoid, but I hate to make important decisions with unknown factors around. And the Hhruahran is a very unknown factor in our group.'

'You probably are paranoid...okay – okay, you know I don't mean it, but what does her personal life have to do with what she can do for us? You said it yourself that she is able to do what she claims to do.'

'Ted, that is not it - look - judge it for yourself. I spent a lot of time these past days gathering information. There's a lot of data available about the green crystal, most of it useless to us, but it is there. I had full access to the computer banks. However, the moment I started to inquire about the Hhruahran, all that information, like by magic, became classified.'

'I do not understand it.'

'Neither do I. There is a grade A selective blocking *in* the Central's memory banks. Anyone can inquire about the green crystal or the Hhruahrans, but if the same person happens to mention both, even separately, both subjects become classified and inaccessible to that person. Permanently.'

(How can this happen?)

'The how is simple, it was programmed into our Central Computer. The big question is why? There is something here I feel very uneasy about and I think the Hhruahran owes us an explanation.'

'I do not owe you any explanation, but I can give you one.' The unexpected voice from the door startled them.

'Kiara D'Charkoon! Don't people in your world knock or call before entering a private dwelling?'

'Professor Holdgen - if you care to observe, I did not enter. And the door was open.'.

'I am sorry, please accept my apology for raising my voice. My excuse is the last day's failure to find a solution to our problem. Please enter and sit down.'

'Thank you. I do understand your tension and I am sorry for being unable to help. Good morning Dr Andronicus. Sister.'

(What about me?)

'Hi Carlos. I was not ignoring you.'

'Well…I am sorry, but you have to tell me how to address you. I do not know the customs of your race and calling you each time by your full name feels silly.'

'Call me Kiara, please.'

'Thank you. Well now, let's not beat around the bush. Kiara, when you arrived you heard my doubts about you, and you offered an explanation. Please, proceed.'

'I offered the explanation, so you could understand the difficulties you found upon trying to obtain the green crystal.'

'It is quite complicated - but I will try to make it as simple as possible.'

'In my world I was a crystal healer, who is a person born as a result of very careful genetic planning and who from a very early age is trained in the use of a specific crystal to focus and augment mental capacities. After a long string of rather unusual events, the fusion of the energy of the green crystal and my own resulted in an unexpected capacity, which during another unusual string of events became a threat to a group of powerful people on my planet. Due to my social position they could not kill me, so I was exiled. However, the threat to them, which I and the green together represented, would not be limited by spatial distance. That is why the main condition of my survival was their certainty that I could not get in contact with the green. That is why I was sent to this particular planet, that is why all that precaution was taken so that I could not obtain the green, and that is why I am under constant surveillance to make sure I cannot, ever, leave this planet, legally or illegally, and get in contact with my crystal.'

'But you do have the crystal - I have seen it.'

'Yes, I have a small fragment of it, obtained quite by accident before leaving my planet, and I kept it constantly shielded. The only reason that I still have it is that there is no official knowledge of it. It is not large enough to be functional, but enough to help me survive.'

'Survive?'

'Yes. The kind of symbiotic link which was established between the green energy and myself also established a kind of life energy dependence. I could not survive the loss of my crystal.'

'That means exiling you to a life without your crystal was a death sentence. Just like killing you.'

'True, but I don't think they were really aware of that fact. You see, this extreme dependency is not apparent in other crystal healers. I obtained exceptional capacities due to the exceptional conditions of my energy-fusing pattern with the green. The price I pay for it is this dependence.'

'I understand now the risk you have taken when letting us know about your crystal.'

'I owed Carlos a life.'

(I just hope you did not pay your debt with your own.)

'There is no danger - unless one of you talks. I trust you on that.'

'Professor - are you satisfied with my explanation?'

'Yes, thank you. I understand more about the general problem, and it looks blacker than I thought it would be. Any of you come up with a solution? Nothing? And what about you, golden boy?'

(Nothing, which is not surprising. I am the least equipped to find a solution.)

'Do not underrate yourself my boy. Well? Anybody? Any suggestion?'

'Professor Holdgen.'

'Yes Kiara.'

'Sorry to interrupt you, but could you explain to me what you mean by the expression Golden boy?'

'I did not really mean anything by it. It was just a wordplay.'

'I am sorry to insist professor, but I am aware of that expression to mean someone special, someone outstanding in some aspect of life. However, I perceived that you used this expression in some other content. Excuse my insistence, but it could be important.'

'Well, now that you call my attention to it, I did use the expression in reference to his energy level.'

'But he is black, like I am.'

'I did not refer to his medallion. I referred to the colour of how he perceived his own energy.'

'GOLD?!'

'Yes, that was what he said, I have no way of knowing myself. Why?'

'Carlos. This is very important. Please, could you show me the gold?'

(Kiara, what is wrong - you are all...)

'Never mind that, Carlos, please, show me the gold.'

(I am not sure how to.)

'Carlos. Listen. Please listen carefully, this could be very important. Establish neural contact with me and observe what I am doing, and when I tell you, do the same. Will you do this for me?'

(Of course.)

'Kiara placed Carlos's right hand on his lap, palm up, and placed her hand next to it, in the same position. Then closed her eyes.'

For a few minutes nothing happened. The tension in

the room increased till it was almost tangible.

Everyone felt that something important was about to happen.

There was some shimmering in the air above Kiara's hand. A low grade, vaguely greenish luminosity formed in the air and with a very slow, rhythmical pulsation it grew.

In size and intensity.

There was no sound. No one moved or made any noise as the pulsating green light held their eyes mesmerized. Susoan started to get up to go to Carlos's side, but froze in a position half way up, not daring to move, forgetting to breathe.

Then it was complete.

A fist sized ball of green light with an intensely bright centre and the border paling away diffusely into the air.

(Carlos, the gold. Now.)

For a long time nothing happened. Then there was some movement, then a definite shimmer in the air above Carlos's hand. There was a yellowish tint in the air - then it was gone.

(I cannot, Kiara.)

(Follow the pattern.)

The silence in the room was interrupted now by the noise of Carlos's breathing. It was getting faster and noisier.

Large drops of perspiration were running down his face.

Then the yellow - gold was back, getting stronger, pulsating its way into a stronger and stronger glowing ball of light, until it matched the green in size and intensity.

Then they touched. The gold and the green touched, and there was an area of discoloration at the contact point.

With a slow, hesitating motion, the two spheres merged, and the resultant golden-green sphere illuminated the room.

Its light was so intense that the observers had to turn their backs to it, or get burned by it.

(Carlos…withdraw…the gold.)

(I cannot.)

(You…must.)

No one could look at the sphere; its luminosity was too intense. Even facing away from it they had to keep their eyes closed.

Then suddenly it was dark again.

Not really dark, but after that intense golden-green light, their eyes took time to see again in the comparative darkness of the room illuminated by sunlight.

'I have never experienced such power.' Kiara was sitting stiff in the chair, her voice trembling after the effort performed. 'Not even the black energy could match it.'

'Kiara - please explain.' Professor Holdgen's voice was pitched higher again. It always irritated him when things were happening beyond his understanding.

'The visuals were impressive but the meaning of all this is eluding me.'

'The meaning is very simple professor. We do not have a crystal problem anymore. We do not need the crystal. Carlos here is more than enough to supply the energy required for the healing.'

'Kiara, please, go slowly. Better start at the beginning. Like explaining what is so special about the gold?'

'The gold. Oh yes. I do apologize professor for not being clear. I will try to explain it. We all have measurable mental emissions, which, when sent to a suitable receptor is perceived. Naturally, like in anything else, the intensity with which we are able to send or receive impulses varies from person to person. But besides the intensity, the capacity to emit, there is also the mode of emission, which is comparable to the wavelength of electromagnetic impulses. Each person has the capacity to send out impulses in one modality which is fixed for the same person right through his or her life and which is as personal as a fingerprint. Also, this same thing greatly reduces the number of possible contacts for the person.

'The gold, besides its exceptional intensity, has this unique capacity to be able to mould to any modality. A person whose mental energy status is the gold is able to contact or share energy at any level.'

'How does this apply to our present problem?'

'Dr Andronicus - it applies beautifully. I have the knowledge of how to restore Carlos's interrupted neuron pathways. I know the way, but lack the amount of energy required. Due to my specialized training I am able to absorb and use any amount of energy from the green crystals, but only from the green crystals.'

'And the green crystals are not available.'

'Exactly. This is where Carlos comes in. He just demonstrated that he is able to merge his gold energy with my green. That he is able to give me the energy I need to heal.'

'Kiara - how will you...'

(We are wasting time. Kiara if you can fix this body, please do it. Sorry Dr Andronicus for being impatient, but you cannot even imagine what it feels like being locked in a useless body. It is worse than being in prison. Kiara, when can you do it?)

'Not straight away, if that is what you are suggesting. The healing process is fairly complicated and I need your help right through it. As you are not very familiar with the use of your mental energies, you could burn both of us out. If it is okay with Dr Andronicus, I could help Professor Holdgen to train you to a firmer control.'

(Oh - not those damned balls again…)

CHAPTER NUMBER FOUR

'I still fail to see why you have to leave.'

'Dr Andronicus – I appreciate what you are trying to do, making me feel needed, but I have made up my mind.'

'I am not just trying to make you feel better. You are needed, really you are. Over the last year and a half we have formed a very tightly-knit group, the four of us.'

'There is no one who could take your place.'

'Carlos does not seem to feel that way.'

'I don't believe Carlos knows how he feels about anything.'

'Anyway, you do not need a nurse anymore. Carlos is healthier than ever. I don't even know why you keep his room. He spends most of his time outside the hospital.'

'You cannot really blame him for that, sister. He spent the last year practically tied to that bed. It is natural for him to want to get out now that he can. Besides, Kiara is taking him around to...'

'Exactly. Kiara.'

'What do you mean?'

'That's just it. Why is the Hhruahran taking him around? Why couldn't I do it? I know this planet better than Kiara does. Why couldn't he spend more time with me?'

'Sister Latimer, you know it is not the same. The mental bond established between those two...'

'That is exactly what I am talking about. That mental bond. It ties them together, and at the same time it locks me out. I cannot compete with Kiara there. I cannot even communicate with him the way she does. Not even through Central. They seem always be in contact – even when they are not together.'

'Last week Carlos and I went to the Stadium to

watch the game, and right in the middle of it he started gesticulating like mad with both hands. You know, the way he does when he gets excited. Apparently he was explaining the finer points of the game to Kiara, and she failed to accept his views. And she wasn't even there. Imagine how I felt. Sitting there like a dummy, thinking that we are enjoying an afternoon together, and all that time he was with Kiara, ignoring me.'

'Well, that was a bit inconsiderate - but I am sure it was not intentional.'

'I know that. I know that he would not hurt me, and I am also sure that he does not know he is hurting me. It is not his fault if he does not love me.'

'Sister – I think you are being a bit unfair.'

'Unfair? Me? If there is anything unfair in here, it is me getting the short end of the stick.'

'Maybe unfair was the wrong word to choose, but I still feel that you should give him a bit more time.'

'More time? What for? To watch him be tied down to Kiara more and more? That bond should have been formed between the two of us. We have been together for over a year. It should have been enough.'

'But that is where you are wrong, sister. You were not together for over a year. You were with him for a year, looking after him, thinking about him. Time enough to learn to love him, I agree with you about that. But please, also remember that during most of that time Carlos was unconscious, not even aware of your presence. As far as he is concerned, he's only known you for a few weeks.'

'I didn't really think about it that way. It does make me feel a little bit better, but it doesn't change anything else. I cannot possibly compete with the Hhruahran.'

'Sister, I think you are underestimating yourself.'

'No, Dr Andronicus. I am realistic. My only hope is that she might be just a passing fancy for Carlos, being a non-human and all that, and eventually he will come back to me. But I don't want to stay around and wait. It hurts too much.'

**

(I can't let her go just like that.)

(I don't see you having any choice in the matter.)

(I do have a choice. If I talk to her, she will stay.)

(And then what?)

(What do you mean "and then what"?)

(I mean, what will happen after she stays? You'll get married and live happily ever after?)

(And why not?)

(Carlos – please - do not try to lie in a mind link.)

(Sorry. You are of course right. I just feel so rotten about the whole thing. I do not want to hurt her.)

(Then let her go free. Unless you really want her to stay.)

(Whatever I do, she gets hurt. You just don't understand...)

(Carlos, I do understand. We share our minds. I feel your feelings. I do understand. You have to let her go.)

(It doesn't make me feel better.)

(I know, but she understands the situation. Especially after what Dr Andronicus just said.)

(I feel like I should talk to her before she goes.)

(You would hurt her more. She wants to get out of your life quietly, with dignity. Don't take that away from her.)

(I still feel like I should say something to her now.)

(Sure, like... I was passing by a mere ten kilometres away and I could not help but overhear your conversation.)

(They know I can do that.)

(They don't know you are scanning their minds

252

without them being aware of it.)

(So are you.)

(Sure, but I also keep my mouth shut about it.)

(You are no help. Just make me feel worse. I don't want her to leave like this.)

(You can help her by making her feel better. You know the way.)

(No, I do not want to interfere with her mind. But I will watch over her. I will follow her from the distance. I will make sure she has everything she needs.)

(I will help you with that.)

**

The two golden medallions sparkled maliciously under the transparent plastmetal cover, reflecting the sunlight from the outside.

'I definitely feel guilty when we do this.' Professor Holdgen was facing the medallions - as if he was talking to them. 'Every time I feel like we are doing something illegal, something shameful.'

'The legality of taking off the medallions could be discussed - but shameful - it definitely is not.' Dr Andronicus was walking around the room with a small, slowly pulsating red light in his hands. 'No bugs,' he declared at the end, sitting down comfortably on a chair near the window. 'Besides, if there is anything shameful here, it is the fact that we need to hide. Hide from our own governmental body.'

'Which makes it illegal.'

'Morally perhaps. Unless of course we decide on a line of action that is against the law.'

'Ted, you worry me. Sometimes you sound like you're enjoying this.'

'I am not, believe me. The idea that we are right, that our suspicion has a real base, terrifies me. Think about the consequences. Think what could happen if...'

'I do not want to think about it. I am not prepared to accept the possibility.'

'The facts seem to point that way.'

'We do not have enough facts. Not one piece of solid evidence.'

'We have enough to be suspicious.'

'Maybe, remember, only maybe. Besides, since the Hhruahran's appearance on the scene, factors became too unpredictable. I am not sure we can proceed with our plans.'

'What has Kiara got to do with all this?'

'She has too much of a hold on Carlos. This communication between them. I don't think he can spit without her knowing it.'

'Could we get her on our side?'

'Perhaps, but are you game to ask her?'

'Maybe Carlos could...'

'Maybe. Maybe. There are too many maybes here. I am not even sure about Carlos anymore.'

'How come? Last time we talked about this you were pretty sure about the whole thing.'

'That was a few weeks ago.'

'What's happened since then? How is his training doing?'

'Training. That is exactly where the problem is. I do not know what is happening to him.'

'Now hold on there, Ron! I feel like I missed part of the story here. Weren't you supposed to continue his training?'

'Me, training him? You missed quite a bit of the story there.'

'Please, fill me in.'

'Gladly. At least I will not be the only one confused here. Anyway -after his miraculous recovery, I gave him a few days to rest – or so I thought – then I wanted to restart his mental training, just as we all agreed. As he was always very eager to learn, it surprised me when he continued to postpone the lessons, always finding some excuse. At the end, when I finally started to really insist, he declared that he does not need to train with me, as Kiara is teaching him much faster under direct mind contact.'

'You accepted this?'

'Of course not. I insisted on checking his performance capacity.'

'And what happened?'

'I should not have doubted him. Asked him to show me what he can do with the balls.'

'Why those balls again? You know he hates them.'

'Partly because it is a very simple exercise, partly because I was familiar with his previous performance with them, but mainly because it is an exercise which is very elaborately graduated to directly measure mental performance.'

'The speed and dexterity of handling them can be expressed numerically and...anyway, I expected some very skilful handling and wanted to have the exact measurements.'

'And? Come on, don't keep the suspense!'

'Well, instead of mentally handling the balls, as I asked him to do, he simply changed the physical mass of the balls into luminous energy, and back, several times. Right in front of my eyes.'

'I don't get it. What does this mean?'

'It means that instead of showing me the control in moving the balls around, he showed me that he could control separately the movements of every one of the subatomic particles forming the total mass of the balls. It means –that on a scale of one to ten –his performance was about two hundred.'

'What did you do?'

'What do you think I did? After a half an hour or so, which was all I needed to convince myself that I am not going mad, I spent the rest of the day green with envy. I would need several lifetimes of hard work to even attempt what he has learned to do in a few weeks.'

'How did he do it?'

'Exactly my question, but it should have been how did she do it?'

'Okay, how did she do it?'

'Direct mind transfer of information. She says that in her world that is the normal way to train a healer, as the amount of knowledge needed in crystal healing would be impossible to absorb in any other way.'

'This is fantastic. This could change the whole...'

'No. It could not. I had the same idea you just had. I wanted to learn the same way. I asked them first to teach me, and then I insisted.'

'They could not have refused it.'

'They tried – I insisted more – and then they did not. I wish they would have refused the mind contact. I spent three days in bed semi-conscious, with a splitting headache. She nearly burned me out.'

'Why would she do that?'

'It was not her fault. On my insistence, she gave me a very slight energy transfer. Actually, it was just a fraction of the intensity of what she was giving Carlos at the same time. I was not able to take it. I am just not equipped to do it.'

'She should have warned you.'

'She did, but I did not believe her. I will from now on.'

'I see what you mean about him being a new factor to be considered. However, I don't think we have much to worry about. Doesn't matter what amount of data he was able to absorb, Carlos, the person, should be still the same. I trust him.'

'What about Kiara?'

'We can talk to Carlos and follow his judgement. The problem is figuring out how to talk to him without her knowing.'

**

'His Excellency says that he is very glad you accepted his invitation.'

'Please, tell his Excellency that I feel honoured that I was invited to his dinner party.'

Carlos was actually glad that Dr Andronicus had to interpret. It was much easier to hide his embarrassing confusion this way, and as he had difficulty in adjusting his behaviour to this completely alien environment, was quite glad that he had to take his medallion off.

For several days now he was told how to address and confront this most illustrious man, one of the Ten, who had in his hands the destiny of countless planets.

On arrival, the building looked just the way he expected. A very large, functional, but elegant house. The lavishness of the large empty space around it was a clear indication of the social position of its occupant. Space was expensive on this overcrowded planet.

The huge and complexly-shaped communication tower next to the house indicated its independence from the Central Computer. A clear sign of luxury.

And then the confusing part started.

It was the great man himself who opened the door. Dressed in a simple, white robe – it was the host himself who poured them their drinks and asked them to get comfortable any way they wished.

It was confusing.

Then there was the affair of the medallions. Everybody had to take them off and leave them outside in a metaplast cabinet, which cut them off from any communicating radiation.

He even had to promise that he would not keep the communication open with Kiara while inside.

Then the monitors. Every room was full of...

The call to the dinner table. The language was strange but the meaning was unmistakable.

During the dinner, Carlos felt really out of place, perhaps for the first time.

He felt for the first time that he was amongst strange people, talking a strange language. He accepted the translating function of the medallions so completely that he didn't even think about the communication barriers before.

Also, while he pretended to look indifferent, trying to figure out what he was eating, Carlos was acutely aware of the frequent glances towards him from the noisy group around his host, indicating clearly that he was the main subject of their conversation.

It was hard to resist the temptation to extend his awareness and to listen in the conversation, but that was another thing he was warned not to do at this place.

There was nothing to do but to eat and wait. He was not even sure what he was waiting for.

**

Their host's private room was, like the rest of the house, very functional and elegant in its simplicity. It was clearly decorated with comfort in mind. The ornaments were useful and pleasurable to the senses. The furniture was absolutely comfortable, and even the colour of the indirect light had a soothing quality. There was everything one could possibly need – and nothing in excess.

Soir Harnilor – their host – sat reclined in his chair with half-closed eyes, staring dreamily into the greenish depth of his drink.

Carlos and Dr Andronicus were occupying similar chairs, leaning back, giving into the sensuous pleasure of the soft, faintly vibrating chairs moulding to the contours of their body.

With their body heavy with the recently consumed meal, the three men enjoyed the dream-like moment and allowed their minds to blankly follow the waves of the soft music.

It was the Councillor who spoke first.

Dr Andronicus translated.

'Your Excellency would like to know if you enjoyed your dinner. He wants you to tell him directly. He knows that you can do it.'

'What his Excellency wants to know is if I will trigger the mental detectors or not.'

'Whatever he wants, you answer to him.

(Yes your Excellency. I did enjoy the dinner, although I am not sure what we had to eat. And no, I will not trigger off the monitors.)

'You are very perceptive Dr Allegria. Tell me, how could you be so sure that they would not detect you?'

(I scanned them on entering the room. They are set on Central's frequency.)

'I am afraid I do not follow you.'

(Your monitors are set to register mental emissions of the wavelengths used by the Central Computer's communicating module. Organic people, producing direct mind to mind contact, use different wavelengths. The monitors are not set to register me.)

'I see what you mean. But how can you be sure that you detected all of the monitors. Some of them could have been set to your frequency.'

(It was a possibility, but very unlikely. The person who installed your monitors was obviously not thinking about natural communications. He was hiding the

259

instruments from visual detection and also made sure that they were not detectable by people using Central-linked medallions, but at the same time he neglected to check them for emissions on other frequencies. Your monitors are shouting at me from their hiding places.)

'Very interesting, and thank you for this helpful information. Ted, your protégée proved himself very useful the moment he opened his mouth.'

'He can be even more useful with his mouth shut.'

'Did you follow our conversation?'

'Yes, your Excellency. I received the same communication as you did. Also even if I could not understand the language you speak, I would have received a translation of what you said. There are no language barriers in mind to mind communication.'

'What an interesting concept. I wish I had your talent, Dr Allegria. You were able to receive my thought concepts as you do not speak the language I was using. Can you perceive my thought patterns without me scanning them to you?'

(You mean can I get information out of you without you being aware of it?)

'Yes. That is what I mean.'

(I do not know, never tried, but even if I could, I don't think I could keep it a secret from you the next time we made contact. You would know – later – that I did it.)

'Does this have anything to do with the privacy code under direct mind link?'

(Yes, it does.)

'Would you be able to communicate with the Central Computer, without this privacy code being involved?'

(I am not sure what do you mean.)

'Could you obtain information from the computer without it registering your presence?'

(I think that is possible, although it would be hard to find the frequency to which the memory banks would respond without triggering off the defence monitors.)

'Please, give me a demonstration. Find out and tell me when and where I was born.'

(I don't think I should...)

'Dr Allegria,. I cannot tell you what you should or should not do, you have a conscience for that, but Dr Andronicus probably mentioned to you that we have a very important job for you . To decide that it is you who we need, I have to know the extent and limitations of your ability.'

Carlos closed his eyes, leaning back in his comfortable chair, with his whole body visibly flowing into a deeper and deeper state of relaxation.

(I will try...) The other two men kept very quiet. Other than an occasional glance towards each other, they had their eyes fixed on Carlos, not daring to disturb him by moving or making a noise.

Their fixed attention revealed how important this scene was for both of them, notwithstanding their previous light conversation.

Breaking the signs of heavy concentration, there was a fleeting smile on Carlos's face, then the expression turned to that of a deepening, vacant relaxation.

Time itself seemed to stop, but it did not last long.

After what seemed like an eternity, but was in fact no more than half an hour, Carlos stirred, opening his eyes and sitting up straight in his chair.

With a sign Dr Andronicus put his drink down, noticing for the first time the pain in his cramped fingers.

'Well? What did you find out?'

(Sorry Councillor, but I could not find your time and place of birth. However – I can give you the time and place where you were found as a sole survivor of the Naroman invasion.)

'Correct Dr Allegria. I was found at a very early age, displaced from my time continuum.

'There is no existing data about my earlier origins. It is incredible. I buried this information so deeply in the Central's memory bank that the physical presence of at least three of the Ten Councillors is needed to call upon it. How did you bypass my blocks?'

(I did not bypass them. I followed a road which was not blocked.)

'Please explain in more detail.'

(I followed the signals of a medallion communicating with the Central of one of the men standing outside in the street. The idea was that once inside the Central Computer I scan the memory banks and come back with the answer. I nearly got lost. This planet does not have a computer. This planet is the blasted computer.)

'Not quite true, although the computer and the related installations do form nearly seven percent of the total mass of the planet. What did you do?'

(I came back and got from your personal computer your access password, and following it led me straight to the memory bank containing the information about you. The rest was easy.)

'Except that you have been detected. The Central must have a record of you using the password.'

(The Central has in its records the data that tonight your computer requested statistical details on temperature shifts alongside water-land lines.)

'Very clever. And what was that smile at the beginning?'

(What smile?)

'Dr Allegria, I do not have to read your mind to understand that you know exactly what smile I am referring to.'

(Sorry, your Excellency. I was not trying to avoid answering you. I smiled when I found Kiara outside.)

'I thought you were not supposed to be in contact with her. Ted, didn't you tell me that...' (Your Excellency – sorry to interrupt you - but I did not make contact with her. I only said that she was outside.).

'And what was the Hhruahran doing outside?'

(Surveying the house.)

'Please explain.'

(She is trying to look after me.)

'I don't understand. How could she look after you from the outside? And why?'

(Her awareness is permeating the outside walls, filtering the emotional flows for a hostile one towards me.)

'And if she finds one?'

(Your Excellency - she is a Hhruahran. I do not know the extent of her capacities.)

'It sounds very touching, but you still have not said why.'

(We are friends.)

'That's a very evasive answer Dr Allegria. Besides, why would the Hhruahran think that you need protection?'

(I am not sure, your Excellency. I did not discuss the situation with her.)

The councillor gave a long, searching look at Carlos then walked to the window. Leaning against the window frame, he looked outside as if he were searching the gathering darkness for the Hhruahran. His voice sounded tense.

'Ted, what do you think about all this?'

'I am very unhappy about the whole situation.'

'What do you suggest?'

'Perhaps we should cancel the meeting and look

somewhere else.'

'You know we cannot cancel. We need...' The tall figure in the flowing white robe turned to Carlos.

'Dr Allegria – let me explain to you the present situation, at least partly. We have a very serious problem on our hands, the outcome of which could affect our entire planetary organization. We need the help of a person with special capacities; otherwise we might be in trouble. This person, besides his special capacities, has to earn our trust, and this work has to be done with the utmost secrecy.'

'We thought, you could be this man. The objective of tonight's meeting was to enlist your help. We feel we can trust you, but this sudden appearance of the Hhruahran outside our door throws doubt on your capacity to keep our secret.'

(Your Excellency - if Dr Andronicus wants me to help you, I am at your side, whatever this is about.)

'Thank you Carlos, and believe me, we really need you.'

'Ted, the problem is not with Dr Allegria. The Hhruahran is an unknown factor.'

(Your Excellency, Kiara is not unknown to me.)

'Could you keep a secret from her?'

(I am sure I could. She respects privacy too much to invade my thoughts unless I wanted to share them with her.)

'Please, tell me more about your relationship. I do not want to interfere with your private life, but I need to understand the situation. Like, why do you keep in constant contact?'

(This is not easy to explain. Our mind contact, at least lately, is mostly a reflex action. There isn't a specific reason to get in contact. We are always in contact. We would actually need a reason to not to be in contact. Is this confusing?)

'Yes, it is rather.'

(Sorry, I will try to explain. You see, Kiara and me, although we belong to different races and different cultures, have many things in common. We are both healers, and we were both brought up from a very early age to be dedicated to a special way of life, with practically identical values. We both dedicated ourselves, from very young, to very similar goals. We both had a very lonely childhood, standing on our own feet with all the odds stacked against us, and we have both beaten those odds. Now our lives have been interrupted in the same way, and we find ourselves away from our home, missing it.

(As you can see, we have a lot in common. We think the same way. We enjoy similar things, and we even like the same colours. When we are in mind contact, her mind feels so familiar to me that many times I have to concentrate to determine who is doing what.)

'Sorry Dr Allegria, this last remark was not very clear.'

(I will try to be clearer. Let me use an example. Suppose I'm sitting at home, reading, and Kiara is walking in the park. When we are in contact, while I am concentrating on my book, I am also aware that I am walking in the park. I can see, feel and perceive everything the same way she does. If I do this with someone else, as obviously you could do with your medallion, the alienness of the situation would be obvious. However, as we think and feel so much alike, with Kiara it is not so evident. When she walks in the park, she walks where I would walk. If she sits down, she sits where I would sit. If she bends down to smell a flower, she smells the flower I would have smelt. So it's not like I am watching someone walk in the park, it's as if I am walking there myself.)

'It is a very interesting experience, I am sure, but I

still cannot see the reason for a permanent link.'

(Because it is not just an interesting experience. By following Kiara's behaviour, , I am living and fully enjoying two lives at the same time.)

'Fascinating . And this obviously works for both of you.'

(Yes it does.)

'And what would happen if we introduced a secret into this situation? Something you cannot share.'

(It wouldn't make much difference. We only share our surface thoughts. Kiara has a very strict privacy code, and we both prefer keeping things to ourselves. In each other's minds we are both aware of doors that we should not pass, and we both respect those doors.)

'I think I understand the situation a little bit better.' The figure in white moved away from the window, picking up his green drink from the table.

'Thanks for explaining it to me, Doctor. What do you think about all this Ted? I bet you didn't know about half of this.'

'I did not know anything about it, your Excellency, but I have to admit that it is my fault. I never asked.'

'Any comments?'

'I am not sure. I must confess I feel happier about the situation, but I need to think about it more before I comment. It's just too complicated.'

'That is typical of you, Ted - always cautious. I myself feel that this would be the right time to get the Hhruahran's point of view. Dr Allegria, do you think you could ask her to join us?'

(I could ask her, but she would not come. She does not want to be seen with me.)

'What do you mean? You are always together.'

(We are always in mental contact, but not physically together. She says she is under constant scrutiny by the people who organized her exile and if our relationship should become known to them we would be both in danger. You two are the only people who know about our link.)

'I do not fully understand it, but I accept your desire to keep your relationship quiet, although it would help if I could talk to her.

(You can talk to her if you wish, your Excellency – she does not have to be physically present. She can talk to you directly, even better than I do. Do you want me to call her?)

'Yes please. Do so.'

(Kiara! Kiara, where are you? His Excellency wishes to talk to you.)

(Soir Harmilor – I salute the One of the Ten.)

'And I salute the green healer of the House of D'Charkoon.'

(Your Excellency, I do apologize for not being corporate in your presence. Carlos probably explained the reasoning behind it. Please, tell me what you desire of me.)

'I desire a formal alliance with the House of D'Charkoon.'

(I am in no position to speak for the House.)

'Then I seek a contractual personal alliance with the healer Kiara D'Charkoon.'

(I can vouch for her, but she does not seek monetary gain.)

'Her services are needed. I would pay with a debt.'

(I am listening.)

(Dr Andronicus – what is happening here, what are they talking about?)

'Carlos – you just listened to a very ancient form of acquiring the services of a mercenary. Kiara, by accepting to listen to the terms, also accepted a pledge to secrecy.'

'Kiara – I will employ Dr Allegria to do a very

special and somewhat dangerous job, and I would like to have you as his bodyguard. You will receive more details if you accept to work for me.'

(Did Carlos accept the job?)

'Not yet, but I did not extend a formal invitation to him. Dr Allegria will you work for us?'

(Your Excellency, I would like to know more details before committing myself, but I already promised Dr Andronicus I would help.)

'Thank you, and due to the time I think we better close our meeting on that note. I would like to see all of you at my office in two days' time. I will also make an official statement saying there was an attempt on your life, Dr Allegria, and for this reason you were allocated a Hhruahran bodyguard.

'This will make it easier for you two to meet in public.'

**

'Dr Allegria – what do you know about our political system?'

(Nothing, your Excellency. Matter of fact, I didn't know that you had one.)

The office, right in the middle of the Central's building, presented the same elegant and simple furnishing as the Councillor's home. Through the large window they could see the beach – tall palm trees waving in the wind with the choppy water extending as far as one could see.

The view was magical, although Carlos knew that if he opened the window he would see a very busy street outside.

He was sitting in the comfortable armchair, next to Kiara and Dr Andronicus, facing their host sitting on the other side of the large desk. As usual, neither of them were wearing their medallions.

'You know, there just has to be one. In any gathering of human beings there has to be a difference of opinion – hence politics.'

(I always understood that your government was the Central Computer – alone.)

'That is partly true. The Central Computer is our government and we all obey its decisions. But you have to remember that the Central is just a machine. A very advanced and complicated one, I grant you that, but still, just a machine. Like any computer it has to be programmed and it has to be supervised.'

(Which is done by the Ten.)

'Correct.'

(And who are human beings, who so, differ in opinions – so there is politics back in the game.)

'Correct. There is a bit more to it, but basically correct.'

(I am sorry your Excellency, but I fail to understand the necessity of this dual decision-making. If you have your computer calculating the next move, what do you need humans for? And if you have the human group of decision makers, what does the computer do?)

'There is no duality here. All decisions are made by the Central Computer.

'The Ten do not get involved in any decision making. All that is done by the computer. We just supervise the computer – keep it in line, so to speak.'

(I am afraid I do not understand.)

'I'll give you a simplified explanation, Dr. On several occasions, our Central Computer has expressed the opinion that many of the projects we are working on are going to fail, or be made difficult, all because of human involvement. Do you know what does this mean?'

(Please, help me.)

'It means that, for a lot of problems, the most logical solution for the computer would be to get rid of the human element. Wipe out the human race and most of the problems are solved'

(Ouch. I never thought about this. So, the role of the Ten is...)

'Yes, to supervise the computer, and make sure its decisions are to serve the human race.'

(It seems to be a tall order for only ten people. To achieve this you have to check every one of its solutions, decisions, actions – even the minor ones.)

'True, but we are not alone. Every one of us has an individual computer at his disposal, completely isolated from the Central and from each other.

'They do most of the work.'

(Obviously someone must be doing a good job. Your world is running smoothly, like clockwork.)

'Well, not quite. At least, not lately. And this is where you come in. There are things that the Ten are unable to do. Yes, Kiara D'Charkoon – you were going to say something?'

(Yes, your Excellency, but please call me Kiara., it is much simpler. I was going to ask you about taking off our medallions. I do not know what kind of job you are planning for us, but it is something you are trying to keep secret from the Central Computer.

'What I do not understand is, wouldn't this secrecy, the taking off the medallions, call attention on us? Everyone wears them constantly - the way I see it, taking them off is so unusual that it has to attract attention.)

'Kiara, normally you would be right, but not when you are with me. And this is the so-called political part I was going to talk to you about. The Ten is divided in opinions about how much authority Central should have. Some of us feel that it should have complete independence of human influence. Some of us feel that humanity needs to always be in control over the machine. I am of this last fraction.

'My political standing is that the Central is a mere machine, and I want to control it. In following this standing I officially avoid any contact with the Central Computer, as much as it is possible.

'It is expected of me not to wear the medallion and not to allow people to wear it in my presence.'

(Which allows you to keep your secret but does not help you gather the information you need.)

'Very perceptive Kiara. That is why we need you. You both have capacities to avoid control from the Central Computer. You can communicate freely without detection and you can retrieve information from the Central's memory banks without leaving traces of your passage behind.'

(Your Excellency I feel that what you need is much more than information.)

'You are right again Kiara, and I think it is time for you to learn what this is all about.

'Ted – you are very quiet in there. Would you like to tell them the whole story?'

'Yes, your Excellency. Basically, there is very little to say. It all started a bit over two years ago when Professor Holdgen and I, working on a routine research project, stumbled onto some unregistered extensions of the Central Computer's memory banks by accident. I didn't give it a second thought, until Ron, who has a very suspicious distrust of all things mechanical, called my attention to the fact that unregistered means that no one probably knows about it. The idea that part of the Central may not be under the Ten's scrutiny was a very distasteful one, and we decided to investigate.

'Needless to say we did not get very far. We were able to establish that the unauthorized extensions to the memory banks were quite widely distributed and that they in activity everyday – however, we failed to break code and find out what it was all about. At this stage we decided to approach the Ten with this information. Your Excellency, do you wish me to keep going?'

'Please do so.'

'Thank you. Well, naturally we approached the fraction of the Ten that was for stricter control over the computer – and the One of the Ten here present.

'I really expected to get a very simple explanation and to be sent home with a pat on my shoulder. Instead, we were taken very seriously. Apparently his Excellency was already investigating a recent increase of authority gain moves by the computer.

'Your Excellency – I think you should take over from here.'

'Very well. Thank you Ted. As you remember, the role of the Ten is to control the amount of authority the Central Computer obtains, and as of course there was never a conscious bid for power, we only had to watch for moves that could have diminished human authority by accident. I can tell you that for the last few hundred years we had more trouble in making the human fractions accept and exercise their authority than having to limit the computer's power.

'Humans are basically lazy and happy if a machine does their work.

'However, a few months before Dr Andronicus's discovery, the sporadic decisions of the Central, the ones that would lead to increasing the computer's autonomy, increased so much and so suddenly that it demanded further attention.

'Every one of them appeared to be innocent but the sheer number of them could not have been accidental.

'Then, to top it all, Ted appeared with his discovery of illegal computer activity. It complemented my own observations, and we decided to work together. Our investigations advanced very slowly, as we had to avoid any direct contact with Central. We were not sure what we were dealing with, or if we were dealing with anything at all.'

(Your Excellency – sorry to interrupt you – but it just does not seem possible...)

'Please, hold on for a few more minutes Kiara before you ask questions. There is more to come. Ted – would you like to finish the story?'

'Yes, your Excellency. About six months ago, there was an important meeting scheduled for all members of the Ten to vote for or against the new educational program, which the Central came up with.'

In this program practically all the decisions were Computer made; and by accepting it, a very important aspect of human life would come under complete computer control. As usual, the opinions were divided, but the program appeared to be getting closer and closer to rejection.

'Then one of the Ten, the person who was most against the program, suddenly died in an accident, and in his absence the program was voted in. Less than three months later, another important increase of the Central's authority was voted in because of the accidental death of a more fervent opponent. It happened twice in a row – still – the most rigorous analysis into their deaths failed to reveal anything suspicious.

'And this is the whole story. The facts at least. The rest is made up by personal extrapolation, imagination and suppositions.

'Now you know why we need a complete secrecy code, and you can also understand why we need your special capacities. Yes Carlos?'

(Dr Andronicus – I must confess I find the whole

story very hard to believe. Not the mentioned facts, but the interpretation you seem to give them. You are investing the Central Computer with very human characteristics. Why would a machine kill for political power? Sorry – but I cannot accept this.)

'Carlos, please remember your own demonstration at His Excellency's house. Although it was only your very first try, you succeeded in removing, from the computer files, an extremely highly classified information, and implanted into the same file false information. You have also mentioned that Kiara could do it even better. Based on this evidence alone, we have to accept the possibility that somebody else has similar capacities and that they can manipulate the computer even more. You yourself are living proof that this can be done.

'Now I want you to extrapolate a bit more. What would happen if someone got to control the Central Computer? Not too difficult a task for someone able to remove and change basic directives.

'What do we have when the Central does not accept human authority – and instead, starts to give orders, someone else's orders?'

There was a long, frozen silence in the room. The black pictures were flashing; from mind to mind.

Carlos was the first to talk.

(Trouble! That is what we have. Big trouble...)

**

'You are very quiet there, my friend. What is on your mind?'

Dr Andronicus lifted his eyes from the blue-green drink in his hands like someone just waking up and trying to connect with reality.

'I feel very uneasy your Excellency. There are too

many unknowns, too many unpredictable factors involved.'

There was a very perceptive change in the room. Nothing visible, but since the very recent departure of Carlos and Kiara, both men were aware of the building tension in the air.

'What unknowns are you talking about?'

'Your Excellency...'

'And cut out that Excellency crap. We are alone now.'

'It is hard to forget who you are.'

'That is exactly what I want you to remember. Like when we were kids and you used to belt the hell out of me – just because I would not do what you wanted me to.'

'That kid was my friend, an equal to me and...' 'Equal my foot. You always beat me up.'

'...and now I am talking to One of the Ten.'

'You are talking to the dress I am wearing. Talk to the man inside. This house is full of crap-talkers. What I need is a friend.'

'I am your friend.'

'Then talk like one.'

'Okay. Okay. I am sorry. You are right.'

'Now, what are the unknown factors you were talking about?'

'Everything is unknown – and so – unpredictable. Starting with Carlos, I do not know the extent of his capacities. As a person, I had him well worked out.

'I knew exactly how his mind would respond in different situations, until the Hhruahran turned up. She changed all his values suddenly and I cannot make him out anymore.

'Then take Kiara herself. I know nothing about her, what makes her tick, and I feel very apprehensive about her involvement. It is impossible to predict how she will react to situations. And then, it is you, today.'

'What about me?'

'Well, we discussed the situation several times and I had a very clear idea about what I consider our problem with Central.'

'So?'

'Your goody-goody, fatherly behaviour today made me think that you have plans I do not know about. Remember, I know you well. When you seem to come straight to the point, you are hiding something.'

'You are very perceptive, but really there is not much to hide.'

'Come on! Are you going to tell me that you made the Hhruahran Carlos's bodyguard just so the two of them could spend time together?'

'And why not? What is wrong with...'

'Councillor, remember please that I know you well.'

'Okay. Okay. You are right. I wanted the Hhruahran with us because she is tied to this whole affair.'

'What do you mean?'

'Remember the difficulties you and Ron had with obtaining information from Central? That you found the computer was programmed to withhold information about Kiara and the green crystal?'

'Yes, I remember.'

'Well, none of the Ten programmed the Central to do so. I checked with every one of them.'

'But that is impossible. Only the Ten has access to...'

'Exactly. So who placed the blocks in?'

'Perhaps the Two of the Ten who died.'

'They did not. Their successors have a complete record of their activity. They did not programme this in. However – the limiting blocks are there.'

'They are in alright, I could not by-pass them. Still, I see no connection...'

276

'The connection is that whoever we are up against is a declared enemy of the Hhruahran, and also afraid of her. Hence the supervision and the limited access to her file.'

'Then why didn't you mention this to them? It could be a very useful clue to start their search from.'

'I do not like to put all my cards on the table. Remember, we are up against someone who knows everything about us, who can monitor every step we take through the Central. At the same time, we know absolutely nothing about him. No identity, no motives, no means. We are not even absolutely sure that our adversary exists.'

'We have pretty good evidence for that.'

'True, but all conjectural. No concrete evidence. The only little ace up our sleeve could be that he does not realize we know he is involved with Kiara. I am not ready to let go of my only trump card.'

'I see your point. Still, something is still missing.'

'What?'

'I do not know, but you would not have gone to all this trouble just because our adversary seems to be hostile to Kiara. I mean, quite to the contrary, this would be a reason to keep her away from us, not to call attention to our activities.'

'You are nearly all right, but you fail to see the broader issue. We know nothing about our adversary, we have no way to approach him. We need to identify him first. The Hhruahran is obviously under close observation and when she starts to investigate, it will be noted. Our adversary has to respond, and when he makes his move, we will be watching.'

'I thought this might be the case. You never wanted Kiara's help. All you needed was for her to be bait.'

'There is a sound of reproach in your tone.'

'And what do you expect? They are friends, they

trust us. The least you can do is level with them.'

'Of course they are friends. And I like them. But they are expendable, the same way you are, or I am. Man, remember what stakes we are talking about. Can you number the worlds in danger if someone takes over the Central Computer? At a level like this, the personal interest of an individual must not, and does not, exist.'

**

People say that Halirmer's Inn is like an island in the river of time – it is not touched by it, it does not change. This might have been so in the past, but Carlos noticed several changes since his last visit here.

For one, there was the large hologram of Kiara opposite the main entrance, standing defiantly, crossing her arms across her chest, while large chunks of rocks flew around her, a picture taken during her now famous fight with the soldiers.

However, the most important change was in the people's attitude towards Kiara.

Carlos still remembered, how, in his previous visit, she was sitting at the bar, isolated, a large ring of space filled with fear around her. This fear changed somehow into respect and everyone saluted her and seemed to have a nice word for her as they moved towards their table.

There was a happy, friendly atmosphere all around them. Still, it did not seem to help melt the ice he felt inside.

'Come on Carlos, stop sulking now. It is not that bad.'

'He had no right to do this to me.'

'You are wrong there. You only see your side. He did not just have the right – he also had the duty to do it.'

'It just does not feel fair. For the first time in a long time I was enjoying life, I felt free and happy. He shouldn't just dump this thing on my lap.'

'On our lap. But yes – it sort of spoiled things.'

'Spoiled is not the word.' Carlos slammed his fist on the table. 'Why do I feel so guilty about wanting to enjoy life?'

'Hey, hold your horses.' Kiara grabbed his hand and pressed it onto the table. 'It is not so bad. You feel guilty because inside you know exactly what you have to do.'

Carlos froze in mid thought, before he could answer. She was holding his hand.

They never touched before. The palm of her hand was unexpectedly soft and warm, sending strange feelings along his spine. It was like a short circuit in his mind, the warmth of that touch filled his awareness. There was a green glow in Kiara's eyes...

'How romantic. Holding hands and all that.' The dry voice whisked the magic away. As Kiara turned to face the tall man with a long beak for a nose, the contact was broken.

'Bartolmer! What are you doing in these parts? The last thing I heard was that you followed your nose to the Thalix Galaxy.'

'Ah yes. That was a nice mission, but I am back now for quite a while.'

'Carlos – this is Bartolmer – an old friend of mine – who – in his own opinion, is the best news researcher and freelance reporter in all the sentient worlds.'

'Thanks Kiara, I did not know you liked me.'

'I do not; I said this was your opinion, not mine. And by the way, this is Dr Allegria, Carlos in short, this wretched planet's latest import from your own Earth.'

'From good old Terra eh – well, welcome to our wretched planet, as Kiara says. And don't take any notice of the way she talks to me. She loves me, although she doesn't know it yet.'

'You still did not answer my question.'

'What question?'

'What are you doing here?'

'What is everyone doing at Halimer's? I came to have a few drinks with friends.'

' Bartolmer, remember I know you. You do not even sneeze without planning it first.'

'That is because it is quite important the way you sneeze. It could very easily be...'

'Bartolmer!'

'Okay, okay – as you said – I am following my nose, and my nose is telling me that there is a story here.'

'Your nose is lying to you this time.'

'My nose never lies to me. And by the way, what are you doing here? I heard you are in the baby-sitting business. Is this the baby?'

'Yes, this is the baby, but do not upset him, this baby bites.'

'He cannot have much of a bite if he needs a babysitter.'

'Kiara – we should be going.' Carlos was trying to be polite but his discomfort was obvious.

The small, sharp eyes behind the nose studied him with a friendly interest.

'Dr Allegria, please forgive me if I offended you. Kiara and I, we are old friends and often talk like this. Allow me to improve the atmosphere by getting some drinks.'

With this, the owner of the impressive nose pulled his long legs under him and catapulted himself towards the bar.

'Kiara, I really don't feel like company today. I would rather go than...'

'I think we better stay Carlos. Bartolmer did not

just happen to be here. He never does. I think he is looking for something, and I want to know what it is.'

'Do you think he could be with..

.' (Carlos! Screen your thoughts. Be very careful of what you are saying out loud.)

(Sorry, you are right. It is just that I am not used to this cloak and dagger routine. Anyway, do you think he is connected to whatever we are supposed to find?)

(I don't know. Probably not, but he is looking for a story and I want to know what he sees in us.)

'Hello kiddos – I hoped you were still here when I came back. Here you are. Halimer's famous beer. I think it is nearly as good as Earth's standard. What's up Kiara, you look very thoughtful.'

'I am waiting for the questions.'

'You got me again girl. Am I so transparent to you? I bet the Dr here thought I just happened to be passing by.'

'You lost your bet. It's obvious that you want something from us.'

'You make it sound very nasty Carlos. I swear on my mother's moustache that I do not really want anything of you. Maybe just some information , as I am the curious type.'

'What are you talking about?'

'Like I would love to understand why a Hhruahran like you would accept a babysitting job?'

'Perhaps for the same reason an earth man wants a bodyguard.'

'Oh no. That is not the same. An earth man, and especially an earth man as important as Carlos - judging by the over publicized attempts on his life - needs protection from the outside world. I can understand that. I can also understand why were you picked for the job - after all, you are the only Hhruahran available here. What I cannot understand is why you would accept. And don't tell me it is for money. I know your financial position. You are not exactly starving.'

'And what makes you so sure that Carlos needs my protection?'

'Well, put it this way. If I had to pick a fight with one of you, I would not choose you.'

'You just might make the wrong choice.'

'Not from the way I see things. Unless, of course, the baby has more teeth than it shows.'

'Do you remember the fight I had with that group of soldiers a few months back?'

'Remember it? I taped the whole thing. Made a small fortune there – thanks to you.'

'What do you think of the ending t o the fight?'

'Now that you mentioned it that is another thing I was going to talk about. It was a fantastic display of energy control. How did you do it?'

'I didn't do it. Carlos did it.'

'Hey - the baby does have teeth after all. Judging by what happened I think I better pick that fight with you Kiara.'

'I think it would be safer for you.'

'I will remember it. But you still did not answer my question.'

'What question?'

'Why did you accept the babysitting?'

'Are you still calling Carlos a baby? He might not like it.'

'Sorry Carlos, it was just an expression – okay Kiara, why are you his bodyguard?'

'Look Bartolmer, you are starting to be a bother. I did not choose to be his bodyguard – and I could have had two hundred different reasons to accept it when it was offered. None of them would be your business, so cut the questions. If you want to talk to me, change the subject.'

'Okay, okay, I did not mean to upset you. Besides, we probably won't have much time for talking. Here comes the entertainment committee.'

The place was filling up with soldiers. They already lined the bar three deep – and more were pouring in through the doors.

'Kiara –I think we better leave.'

'Carlos, stay in your place. I would not give them the satisfaction of seeing me leave just because they arrived. Besides, I do not think there will be any trouble. As far as I know, all the soldiers have strict orders to stay clear of me. However, you can leave Bartolmer. Your presence in our company may not be seen so favourably.'

'Don't worry about me. Besides, Carlos here will defend me if anything happens.' The thin man leaned back comfortably in his chair with a wide grin under his nose.

'Bartolmer – I think you don't believe what I said about Carlos, and now you are pushing for a demonstration.'

'Sorry for being so transparent, but you have to admit what you said was a bit hard to swallow.'

'Carlos, how do you feel about giving a demonstration to Bartolmer?'

'I cannot see how.'

'Simple. Bartolmer – if you want to have your story – then relay a challenge to the soldiers. I will pay five hundred Florints for one of them, anyone, if he wins in a standard arm wrestling match.'

'Common Kiara,. No one is stupid enough to wrestle with you.'

'Not with me. With Carlos.'

'I am on my way...' The long legs lifted and carried the man away before he could hear Carlos protest.

It was not long before he was back with a soldier who towered nearly two heads above him. The rest came behind in a compact group, keeping a safe distance.

(I cannot wrestle this monster. Just look at him. His arm is thicker than my waist.)

(Carlos – a friend of mine said a few years ago that physical power is useless against someone who controls the mind. We were talking about war machines, but you can apply it to the present situation.)

(Your friend wasn't made to face this monster of flesh.)

'Hhruahran – this shrimp here says that you will pay me five hundred Florints to fight this other shrimp.'

'Not to fight, to arm wrestle, under strict, standard conditions.'

'What is the catch?'

'No catch. Win, and you get five hundred, lose, and you get nothing.'

'Fat chance of that. Where is the money?'

'My word is the money.'

'I accept your word. Okay – come on shrimp – let's get this thing over with.'

'One more thing soldier. Nothing fast. I want to enjoy what I pay for.'

'Hhruahran, for five hundred Florints I'll take a nap right in the middle of it.'

(I hope you know what you are doing Kiara. The five hundred Florints you are offering is just about all the money you have.)

(Which should show you that I expect you to win. You had the training –use it.)

They had some problems adjusting the table due to the differing sizes of their arms, but when they finished they sat opposite one another, across the corners of the table, grasping right hands above it. Or rather, Carlos grasping the soldier's huge thumb, his fingers failing to circle around its thick base. The other had his hand open because he had nothing to grasp. Carlos's hand nearly disappeared next to the huge palm. The ridiculousness of the situation was obvious to everyone.

On the signal given, the soldier did not move.

'Come on shrimp – do your best!'

And Carlos was pushing, putting all his concentration into the muscles of his arm and shoulder, draining out the maximum power they were able to achieve. His muscles started to ache, and his heart thumped with the effort.

The hand did not move. Like pushing against a brick wall.

(Kiara, what the hell do you want me to do?)

There was no answer.

Obviously she wanted him to get this done on his own. But how?

The soldier closed his eyes with a grin on his face.

'Wake me up shrimp when it is my turn.'

His fake snores were answered with laughs and cheers from his comrades.

Carlos realized that he could not push any longer; the pain in his strained muscles was increasing alarmingly. He realized that even his mental capacities could not make his muscles endure much more of this. That remark Kiara made about the physical strength being useless... A golden haze passed in front of his eyes..

. A fleeting expression of surprise passed on the round-featured face of the soldier.

Opening his eyes he looked questioningly at his opponent.

Carlos had a relaxed smile on his face now.

There was a sudden quietness. in the place. The circle of observers tightened closer around the table.

Their hands did not move, but the soldier was visibly working harder and harder. His muscles bulged, his breathing growing faster.

Then there was a flicker of movement of the hands.

Against the soldier.

His face was red now, with thick, bluish veins bulging in his temple, partly due to the effort, partly perhaps due to the anger growing inside.

Then the hands moved again – and there was no stopping now.

With a slow but continuous movement the hands descended until the back of the soldiers hand touched the table.

He lost.

No one talked. No one moved.

They watched the huge soldier with the bulging muscles gasping for air, rubbing his sore shoulder.

They watched the much smaller, slim man opposite him, sitting quietly, not even breathing hard.

There was still silence when he left with the Hhruahran.

**

Carlos welcomed the cool freshness of the air outside, but they did not get too far. Bartolmer was running after them, calling their names.

'Your nose is troubling you again?'

'Sort of.' He was trying to slow his breathing after his run. 'You have me confused Kiara. I do not understand the reason behind this demonstration, and it bothers me when I do not understand something.'

(Yes Kiara – I am dying to hear your explanation.)

'You were looking for a story.'

'So?'

'So I gave you one.'

'Just like that?'

'Just like that. Let's say that I owed you one. Your holographic recording of my fight with the soldiers got me off the hook when they sued me for attacking them.'

'I did not do that for you. I sold that recording and was paid for it quite well.'

'And how much were you paid for taking the recording first to the Central's legal headquarters and insisting on an analysis of it before my hearing came up?'

'You were not supposed to know about that.'

'But I do and as I said, I owed you one. And I am sure you taped this whole thing.'

'Of course I did. Okay – so you paid your debt. You Hhruahrans have a weird code or honour – anyway – I am not the one to complain.'

**

It was dark by the time Bartolmer left them. They were walking silently on the street, side by side, ignoring the strange glances from the occasional passersby. As usual, it was Carlos who broke the silence.

(You realize, of course, that I know you lied to Bartolmer?)

(About what?)

(About you paying him back a favour.)

(What do you mean?)

(Kiara! It is me now reminding you not to lie in a mind-link. I felt pretty low back in there. I needed this ego boost to get me out of the hole.)

(Did it work?)

(It must have. I feel fantastic. Let's start working on Andronicus's project.)

**

'What do you think Ted?'

'I do not know Excellency. Everything they say supports what we expected to happen, but I must admit it surprised me how advanced things are.'

'The same thing I was thinking. I did not expect such a large amount of unauthorized memory banks and computer extensions. And this spreading to the neighbouring planets – we didn't even think about that. We have less time than I hoped for.'

(Could one of you please explain what are you talking about?)

'Sorry Carlos, I didn't mean to lock you out of the conversation. Just that the information you two brought us stirred up a few emotions.'

'What Ted means, Carlos, is that your data demonstrated that despite what we hoped, our supposition appears to be correct, and on top of that, things are more advanced than we thought they were.'

(I still don't understand, your Excellency.)

'We made a plan, Ted and me. In reality, it was more like a fantasy than a plan. We thought of a way that someone could take over control of our world.'

(How?)

'It is very simple really. If it was me, I would build multiple illegal computer extensions which would not be under the Ten's control, and when the amount of fraudulent extensions had grew large enough to be able to duplicate the Central's capacity, I would transfer all the data to these extensions and at the same time I would destroy the Central.

'In this way I would have a smooth, uninterrupted function of all the sentient worlds influenced by the Central, but this time it would be completely under my control. My position would be impossible to challenge.'

(This is exactly what seems to be happening.)

'Yes, it is, Kiara. And it is in a more advanced stage than I hoped. Judged by the speed those clandestine extensions seem to be growing, it will not be long before they are ready for the takeover.'

(Can't you stop them?)

'How? Who is there to fight against? Where, and most of all, who is the enemy? I cannot even make an open inquiry as it would reveal that we know about them, which would take away the element of surprise - the only leverage we have.'

(I don't think we even have that.)

'What do you mean Kiara?'

(While following the projection lines of transferred information within the Central, it happened several times that I was blocked off just before I reached the target. By the way I was blocked I had the feeling that it was not a mechanical. blocking. It must have been planned, which means they are aware of our activities.)

'Carlos?'

(Now that she mentions it, there were a few times when I had a similar feeling, although I was sure that I could not have been detected.)

'This is just what we need. A powerful, unidentified enemy aware of our hostility.'

'It may not be as bad as that. The fact that we are not being attacked would indicate that they are not ready to move. This gives us a bit of time.'

(Time for what?)

'Now, this is where I expect you and Kiara to make some suggestions.'

(We have to identify them.)

'Agreed, but how?'

(I do not know...God, this is frustrating. Your Excellency, you have more experience in these things, what do you think we can do?)

'There is a lot we can do, although I have no specific suggestions for you.

'I have a few leads to follow through with the Ten's personal computers, Ted has his own line of work with Ron, and you two, please continue to dig in the Central's memory banks, and see if you can come up with something. See if you can get through to one of the unauthorized segments.'

(Not much chance of that if they are aware of us.)

'Do your best.'

**

'Halimer's?'

'No. Not tonight Kiara. I do not feel very sociable after our little talk.'

'I know what you mean. It wasn't the most cheerful of conversations.'

'Still, I do not think you should feel this low. What about a quiet drink at my place? A glass of red bubbly might cheer you up.'

'That would be nice, providing that is all you have in mind.'

'What do you mean?'

'Every time I go to your place we finish up with a mental data transfer.'

'Do not get me wrong, I am grateful that you are teaching me, just not tonight. Tonight, the only thing I have enough energy for is to curl up and die. Well, nearly.'

**

The drinks seemed to help

Carlos appeared to be pretty relaxed on the reclining chair, which moulded to the contour of his body, giving the soft sensation of floating on air.

'You know, I could never understand your taste in furniture.'

'What's wrong with it?'

'Nothing. That is what is wrong with it.'

'You are not being very clear.'

'Sorry. What I meant was that you have everything you might ever need. Obviously you went to great trouble to make staying at home a pleasurable thing. Everything functions perfectly.'

'So?'

'You know, the last few times I came here I was trying to find something ornamental. Something which is here only because you like it.'

'And?'

'I could not find anything that would qualify as an ornament. Every shade of colour – every shape pattern, sound, scent – they are all here because they have a function to perform.'

'Don't you like it like this?'

'I love it. It is just the way I like things. But it is not the way I am used to seeing a woman's place. And do not come out with that warrior race business. You are as far away from a warrior as I am.'

'That is not a very nice thing to say to a Hhruahran.'

'Sorry. I did not mean offense.'

'No worries. Once I was called the least Hhruahran on my planet by the human ambassador. And he meant it as a compliment.'

'That is a bit pushing it.'

'I don't think he realized what he was saying. He was worried about not being able to adjust to the lifestyle of my people and thought I would soften the blow. Like first to get used to me, the mild one, then the rest of the planet.'

'Did he succeed?'

'I am not sure, I did not stay long enough to find it out, but I know that none of the ones before him were able to cope with the cultural shock.'

'Cultural shock. I know nothing about your planet, but I know you. And you do not look so fearful to me.'

There was a short silence while Kiara sat next to Carlos's chair in her particular half-sitting half-crouching position, putting her hand on his arm.

'I am glad for that. I do not want to look fearful to you.'

That touch!

Carlos remembered the first time Kiara touched his hand. Its effect on him. And how since then he went out of his way to avoid touching her.

He was not sure what he was afraid of, but felt that he would lose control if they touched again.

And now she touched him again!

The hand felt hot on his arm. It drew him to that touch.

His whole being was concentrated, focused on that touch. There was a green fire in his blood, and he felt the gold to surge to meet it.

The energy fusion was complete, the body disappeared. His mind soared in the golden-green lights.

And Kiara was with him.

And Kiara was him.

They were enveloped by the light.

They were the light...

**

'I am sorry...Carlos...I could not...break contact in time.'

Her voice was unusually soft and hoarse at the same time.

Carlos opened his eyes with a sigh.

'I am not sure I am glad you did it at all. If this happens every time you touch me – I will never want to let you go.'

'Just don't put all the blame on me.'

'Kiara – I think we ought to talk.'

'That's an understatement.'

'There is no disputing the fact that something weird is happening to us.'

'The question is what do we do about it?'

'The word "weird" I find a fairly bad choice, but I do not think you can do anything about emotions of this kind. Besides, I am not sure I want to.'

'I am glad you said that, but you are trying to avoid a word there.'

'Yes. In a normal situation I would say that I love you, that you are the only woman for me. But, while true, these words feel utterly insufficient to express what I feel inside.'

'You just find the word, I can wait.'

'I don't even know if we are genetically compatible.'

'Take my word for it, we are. In spite of the grossly different physical appearances, we both come from the same original human stock.'

'What about physical compatibility – our anatomy could be...'

'There is only one way to find out...'

**

Dr Andronicus was quite agitated when he burst into Professor Holdgen's office.

'Ron, I need some information. Tell me what the word "kerdung" means to you.'

'Hi Ted. It must be important for you to charge in

like this, almost bringing the door in with you.'

'Sorry for that – and yes – it is important. So what does it mean?'

'Now, hold on, slow down a bit. Kerdung represents something very special. and mind you, a very little used concept. The gross meaning is a kind of joining together, but the finer meaning is changing, depending on the context in which you are using it. Where did you hear it?'

'Carlos told me.'

'Carlos has no sufficient training in mental sciences to grasp the meaning of kerdung – unless he has advanced more than I thought possible with Kiara's direct data transfer. In what context did he use the word?'

'The context of a relationship between two persons.'

'Not theirs, I hope.'

'Why? Is it that bad?'

'No, it is not that. I know very little about it, but as far as I know it could be something absolutely wonderful for the two persons involved. If it is successful.'

'And if it is not?'

'It has a devastating effect, usually ending in death – by murder or by suicide. Who are we talking about?'

'For God's sake Ron. You still did not answer my question. What the hell is kerdung?'

'Sorry, but I needed to know the context in which the word kerdung came up to understand its meaning. It means a complete joining of two persons. So complete that both persons cease to exist and a new one appears. One person, one personality, one thought process – living in two, physically separate bodies.

'It might not get to this extreme, but it comes close. Sometimes enough personality traits persist that you may not notice any visual changes, but when you dig deeper you realize that you are talking to the same person, it does not matter which body you are talking to. Did I answer your question?'

'I think you did. Just give me a couple of minutes to digest all this.'

'And while you are digesting, could you tell me who are we talking about?'

'Carlos and Kiara. He came to me with a warning. He said they are Kerdung – and when I did not understand what he was going on about he explained that they have "kind of got married". He also hinted that it is not quite what we understand by marriage. It seems to fit with what you just said.'

'What was the warning about?'

'He mentioned our "special work" and said that from now on he will not be able to break contact with Kiara, so if there is anything I do not want her to know, to not tell him either. Or the other way around.'

'It is quite considerate on their part to tell this to us. Considering everything, I think they have a good chance to pull it off. Good luck to them.'

'What do you mean they have a good chance of pulling it off? They have already done it.'

'You cannot know the result until a certain time passes and you see them function in the practical, everyday life. You see, each person has a kind of mental functional wavelength. These have to be very close, nearly identical to be able to resonate and produce a functional kerdung. It means that the basic personalities of both partners have to be very, very similar.'

'The way Carlos spoke about their special contact before, it seems they have a very similar background.'

'Yes, I remember you telling me about it. It is just the kind of thing that might make it successful.'

'And if they are not? Can they, kind of divorce?'

'No. They cannot. It is as with anything else, the higher the investment, the higher the risk. They aim to the highest imaginable point in personal relationships. What they've invested in it is their lives.'

'I am not sure I follow you.'

'They established a kind of a mental contact state which is permanent. There is no way back. If it is a non functional state, they cannot survive it.'

'Neither of them?'

'Neither of them. They are not interdependently functional. Remember, we are practically talking about one person living in two bodies. Half a person cannot survive. This goes for the successful kerdung too.'

'You lost me again.'

'The kerdung, when it is functional, is an absolutely wonderful relationship. But it needs both of the components to function.'

'What happens if one accidentally dies?'

'The other cannot survive. Remember, there is no one or the other. It does not matter how wonderful a person is, half a person is not viable.'

'If it is so, Kiara should not have allowed Carlos to take the risk.'

'I think you got that one wrong. Taking into account that the Hhruahran's life span is nearly twice of ours and that their body is more resistant to sickness and physical attack, I would say that it is Kiara who is taking the risk.'

'I see your point. What I cannot see is how this will affect our work.'

'Aha! The cat is out of the sack. So this is what you are really worried about. You could never learn to really trust the Hhruahran, and now she is in, or Carlos is out.'

'Don't get me wrong, Ron. I like Kiara. She is good to Carlos, she is useful to us, and she appears to be a nice person.'

'But...'

'Yes, there is a but. I have this little voice deep inside me that tells me not to trust her. Something I have no control over. Call it a gut feeling, if you like.'

'You know I take gut feelings seriously.'

'I take this one seriously, although I tried to fight it. Look, I pick up feelings from her. The first time she appeared I knew she would stay with us. I knew she loved Carlos, probably before she knew it. Still, this little voice keeps telling me that there is more to her than meets the eye...'

**

'Your Excellency, I think Carlos here would like to ask you a question but feels it is not the right time.'

'The right time to ask a question is when you want to know something. What is it, Carlos?'

The dinner, as usual, was simple and excellent at the same time. They were relaxing now in the arms of the comfortable plasty-chair, enjoying the somnolent feeling caused by the full stomach, soft music and the tall, green drinks served by their host. Next to Professor Holdgen, who was teasing Carlos in front of the Councillor, Dr Andronicus was relaxing with his eyes closed, obviously not wanting to take part in the conversation.

(Sorry, your Excellency, I was not going to ask you this because it is only a matter of curiosity and has nothing to do with what we are meeting here for. I was wondering about the colour of your medallion.)

'What is it you want to know?'

(The colour. The bronze. It is the colour of the most common metal combination in the galaxy. As far as I know, there isn't a special meaning attached to it. Like, for example Dr Andronicus's gold. Its colour   suggests high value. Your position would surely deserve a colour of some higher symbolic value.)

'I see your point, and the answer lies in your question. The colour of our medallions, except the black, of course, which is a transition colour only, represents the value of the person who it belongs to. Not how rich he is, nor how well he is placed in society. Dr Andronicus has gold because the value of his person is such. He could be earning a living cleaning the street or lying drunk under a bridge; his colour would be still gold. Now, the bronze is the most common substance around and the colour bronze has a symbolic meaning of being worthless.

'This is to remind us, the Ten, that our power, our social standing does not come from personal worth, but from the job we were elected to fill. It is being a Councillor that gives us the power, not who we are as a person. The colour bronze is a reminder for us to stay humble, to always remember that we do not have power, we only represent it.

'Did I answer your question?'

(Well – partly. The thing is, that to be elected to be a Councillor, you had to have some special qualities to qualify. Wouldn't that give you a higher colour?)

'This would be the truth on your Earth, for example, where everyone wants to be a politician. On your planet, a politician has a lot of power with a relatively small amount of responsibility and workload. In our society, it is the other way around.

'Believe me, the two most important things that qualified me to be a Councillor was that no one else wanted to be one, and that I was no good for anything else.

'Hence the colour bronze.'

(You are talking about yourself as someone of a very low personal value.)

'Because it is true. Remember, we measure personal value by the person's usefulness to the rest of society. My original psych evaluation qualified me for manual work only. These disqualified me.'

Pulling back the long, loose sleeves of his robe, the Councillor presented his hands to Carlos. Long, slim fingers, deformed by angry-red swellings at every joint.

(It looks very painful.)

'It is. Sometimes it is not this bad, but certainly it stops me from working with them.'

(Your Excellency, allow me to relieve your pain.)

'Carlos thanks for the offer, but there is not much you can do about this.

'The medical science of...'

Carlos covered the Councillor's hands with his own. There was a growing golden-green haze around their hands which lit up the whole room with a brightening light.

When it stopped, it took several minutes for their eyes to re-adjust to the relative darkness of the room.

The Councillor was still standing in the same position, with extended hands in front of him, flexing and extending, testing his fingers with an incredulous expression on his face.

The redness was gone, and so was some of the swelling. 'Carlos – I do not know how you did it – but the pain is gone and I can move my fingers. They are not stiff anymore. How long will this last?'

(I expect it to be permanent, your Excellency. I cannot change the shape of your hands, but if you wish, I could make them more functional with a few more energy applications.)

'Carlos! What did you actually do? Those hands were grossly inflamed a few minutes ago!'

Carlos faced Dr Andronicus's half-sitting, half-standing form. The set of his jaws and the bulging vein in his neck expressed the frustration the scientist was feeling. It took a while until he was able to control himself.

'I apologize for shouting. I had no right to do it.'

(I understand.)

'No. I don't think you do. You see, I tried, for many years, to alleviate His Excellency's suffering. So when I saw you performing that, well, whatever you did...'

(You reacted with anger.)

'Yes. But it was not directed at you. It was anger towards myself, for failing, for not even knowing that it was possible to fix those hands.'

(You couldn't possibly have known it.)

'Well – I did not know it. But where did you learn it? You never suggested you could do something like this.'

(To tell you the truth, until a few minutes ago I did not know I could do it.)

'Carlos!'

(It is true. You know about our fusion and what it means. Suddenly I acquired such a vast amount of alien knowledge that my own mind was unable to absorb it. I, Carlos Allegria could not repeat the energy transfer I just did, but I could allow the part of me, which used to be Kiara D'Charkoon, do it.)

'Fascinating – but this is not a Kerdung situation you are describing.'

(You are right Professor, as always. In spite of our many basic similarities to form a successful Kerdung, Kiara and I have to fuse two completely alien civilizations into one.

Believe me, it's not easy. I am confident that we will be able to do it, but it will take time. I have all her knowledge, plans, aspirations, and she has mine. There

300

are two people living inside my mind, two completely alien people. I have to find the common factor, to fuse them into one being. And Kiara has to do the same.)

'And until you do it?'

(Well, until then, Kiara, or the part of Kiara which has not fused with me yet, will share my mind and I will be doing things I do not know how to do. Kerdung will be established when Kiara and Carlos cease to exist separately and there will be a new person walking around in two bodies.)

'Are you getting there?'

(Yes, I do not think it is far away.)

'What if you are not able to do it?'

(Then we have a real problem!)

'Carlos – I will not pretend to fully understand what you are talking about, but I am grateful for what you have done to my hands. Please, communicate to Kiara my thanks.'

(Your Excellency – I am happy to be of use to you – but you are asking me to send a message to myself.)

'Please explain.'

(As I said to Professor Holdgen, there are certain aspects of Kiara's personality that still exist independently in my mind, but this is only a small fraction of the whole. For the most part, our lives are already fused together. I am Carlos. And I am Kiara.)

CHAPTER NUMBER FIVE

The rest of the world around Carlos did not seem to react to the changes within.

The sun kept shining.

The beer at Halimer's tasted the same.

And no one showed an awareness of the changes happening to him.

Everything and everyone was a constant reminder that their fusion was not complete. The mere fact that he was able to think about himself as Carlos was proof of this. incompleteness.

He wished for this fusion.

He was working on this fusion.

At the same time, he was always aware of the fact that deep, very deep inside, he was also afraid of it.

He wished to share his mind with her.

However, he was not able to accept the idea of not being Carlos.

He wanted the change.

He wanted the superiority that being Kerdung offered, but he was not able to give up being Carlos.

His friends kept treating him as Carlos, pretending that nothing had happened, even those who knew about the kerdung situation. Mainly because they did not know how else to treat him. Everyone, including himself, was just waiting to see what was going to happen.

As Dr Andronicus said during one of his meetings with Councillor Soir Harmilor, 'I am not sure what is happening. I don't know if we gained Kiara, or we have lost Carlos. We just have to wait and see.'

Professor Holdgen was the only one who found himself in a kind of a paradise. He was actually witnessing the birth of a kerdung. And a kerdung between a Human and a Hhruahran at that.

Before, he never even hoped to meet a kerdung in his lifetime, and now the idea of witnessing the fusion of two so completely alien minds, forming the strangest of kerdungs, kept him permanently on cloud nine, and at Carlos's back with his constant questions and tests.

However, Carlos was spending most of his time in the hospital, where he was trying to find a common factor to join his medical knowledge with the Hhruahran's healing.

'It is absolutely impossible,' he complained one day to Dr Andronicus. 'The very basic ideas, the fundamental concepts, are simply not compatible. The concepts of biochemical medicine, on which all our techniques are based, are completely rejected by the bioenergical healing of the Hhruahrans.'

Dr Andronicus had little to offer to him in the form of help. He just listened, nodded his head as if in complete agreement, then just dragged him along to see the next patient.

For quite a while now, he had given up trying to understand what Carlos was talking about.

He knew the problem Carlos had to face on the inside.

Since that first, miraculous cure he witnessed at the Councillor's place, Dr Andronicus spent many long nights with Carlos as he tried to explain to him concepts which he himself was unable to fully accept, until Dr Andronicus simply gave up asking why and how. Just simply pointed him towards a patient, telling him: "do your stuff".

And he was doing his stuff.

Patients were healed out of illnesses for which there was no standard medical help or understanding.

Healed in a ridiculously short time.

At the same time, the human part of Carlos was applying his medical knowledge to the same patients, to try to find a balance between the two techniques.

He was also using drugs as part of the standard medical treatment, in spite of the rejection of the use of chemicals expressed by his Hhruahran part.

There was no real opposition between the two healing techniques. There was not enough common ground to form an opposition.

How do you discuss with a fish the feeling of the breeze on your skin?

Still, he did not give up, and after a long period of time there appeared to be a hint of light in the darkness.

Not real understanding.

It was too early for that.

But at least there was a hint of acceptance.

His Hhruahran part, which mainly worked on function manipulation at sub-particular levels, producing directional changes of energy flows, was starting to accept the usefulness of the shape-changing reality of some of the human surgical techniques.

The human part, on its turn, was beginning to accept the possibility that a body function might not be related to physical mass. That there could be more to energy level changes than mere chemical reactions.

It was not much, but it was a beginning.

**

(It is working querido.)

(Yes it is Kiara. Much slower than I had expected it to happen, but it is happening. I really didn't know what to expect.)

(Are you disappointed?)

(How could I be? You have presented me with a world far beyond my wildest dreams. Still...)

(Still what? Are you regretting the fusion?)

(I will never do that. But I am not able to accept the

304

idea that I am not me. It just doesn't sink in. It might happen - I do not know...but for the moment I don't know what to expect.)

(I know exactly what you mean. I also find it quite a disturbing concept. It is difficult to comprehend how "ME" can't be "I".)

(There is also the other side of the story. I quite enjoy your company; I like to be with you. I like to touch you. Will I be losing you too, the same way I will be losing myself? What will happen to this feeling between us?)

(I cannot answer that Carlos. I don't know what will happen. Even in my world, the kerdung situation is quite rare. I have never met one personally. As far as I know, and this is only second-hand information, a kerdung relationship is the most pleasurable, heightened physical and emotional state two people can share together. But what happens to the physical and emotional pleasures of communication between the two people who like each other when they join to become one, I just don't know.)

(Aren't you afraid of the possible outcome of all this?)

(Afraid – I do not think that is the right word to use in here, but I do feel a kind of apprehension. It should be expected, considering the risk, and not knowing what I can gain.)

(It sounds a bit unfair – doesn't it?)

(Unfair or not, here we are.)

(There is not much chance of us backing out, is there?)

(No. Not really. Not at this stage. We are too far into the fusion. Whatever is left of our individual personality is not enough to survive.)

(You mean that we will make it or we die?)

(No. I mean we will make it.)

**

'Hi Ron. How are our dear kerdungs doing lately? I lost track of them these last few days.'

'Do not talk to me about that blasted couple! They've caused me nothing but trouble since I've known them.'

'Hey! And good morning to you too! You are getting very moody in your old age. What are you fuming about this time?'

'I was just thinking about my life when you arrived.'

'And what got you this upset?'

'What? What? Everything seems to be wrong lately. I was just remembering how I was feeling on top of the world not so long ago. A respected know-it-all, the scientific world at my feet. I seemed to have all the answers to all the questions. It was a larger than life feeling.'

'So? What has this got to do with the kerdung?'

'Not much, except that since Carlos appeared on the scene – I've felt miserable. I feel low, ignorant, like I know nothing. It is not a nice feeling for someone who used to be at the top.'

'As far as I know you still are.'

'Maybe in everyone else's eyes. Maybe. But not in my own, and that is what counts.'

'I still don't understand.'.

'Sorry Ted, I should not have taken it out on you, but every time I meet Carlos I cannot help feeling low and ignorant. Lately, his mere presence reminds me how little I know.'

'Aha! I get you now! It is the Hhruahran's knowledge that she is sharing with Carlos that's upsetting you.'

'It is not her knowledge that is upsetting me; it is my lack of the same knowledge which is hard to accept.'

'Ron, you are a fake. I have seen the shine of your eyes every time you met them and were able to pump them with your questions. You would give your life for this opportunity, to be able to study the Hhruahran's mind science.'

'Well...in that aspect I guess you are right, I do enjoy the learning bit.'

'As I said, you are a fake. As you yourself told me once, the most stupid thing in life is the feeling that you know everything.'

'Okay, okay. Don't throw my own words in my face.'

'You asked for it, but anyway, what's happened? You must have had a meeting with one of them to start off all this nonsense.'

'He has just left.'

'And?'

'And...nothing. We had a long conversation. He was explaining to me his new feelings as a kerdung.

'I think he was explaining things to me for both of our sakes, trying to sort out his ideas while he was talking to me.'

'So? I still don't get it. What is wrong with that?'

'What was wrong was that he was explaining to me everything in detail, slowly, so I could understand it, but I didn't. I had no idea what the hell he was talking about.'

'I cannot see how it is possible for you not to understand his mind-speech. He is putting the concepts right into the...'

'I know that. That was not the problem. I understood every word, every concept, in a superficial way, but it didn't mean anything to me on a deeper level. Let me put it a different way. Try to explain colour to a blind man. You can explain the different shades of red to him, and he will understand what you are talking about, that the colours are the visual aspects of different objects, but it will have no meaning for him. If he had never seen the colour red, even if he knew the word, it would not have any real meaning for him, he would not have the feeling of what you are really talking about.'

'I see your point.'

'Carlos was talking to me about concepts and emotions, which, although I could understand on a superficial, brain level, as I have never experienced them myself, not even anything close to them, I could not have the feeling, the deep understanding of what he was really talking about.'

'I understood the words he was using, the concepts, but I did not understand at all what he was feeling.'

'Why didn't you ask him for a deeper level of concept transference?'

'No thank you. One near burnout was quite enough for me; I will not try that again soon.'

'You still did not answer my original question.'

'Which one was that?'

'My inquiring about how they are doing?'

'Oh that. I think they are doing fine!'

'What do you mean you think they are doing fine?'

'It is a very difficult question to answer because I do not have any previous knowledge of kerdungs. Nothing to compare them with. Still, I have the impression they are not doing as well as they would like.'

'I don't think Carlos knows enough about the kerdung situation to know what to expect.'

'That is probably true, but even so, I think he started the whole thing with the wrong idea.'

'You are talking about the romantic aspect of the thing, aren't you?'

'Yes. Exactly. that is what I am talking about. His original idea to join with Kiara was based on a male–female attraction. His idea of kerdung was about the ultimate marriage situation.'

'Well, isn't it?'

'In a sense yes, but not in the way he was figuring it out. The very base of the male-female relationship is to enjoy each other's company. What will happen to this relationship if the other does not exist anymore? If there is only one of them. Two bodies but only one person.'

**

'Ted! You are staring again.'

'I am sorry, your Excellency, but your hands are fascinating me.'

'You have seen them many times before.'

'Yes. For many years I tried to fix them up and failed. What I find fascinating is that they look the same as before. The same distorted shape, the swelling of the joints. They look like any other badly arthritic hands. Stiff and painful.'

'They might look it, but they are not. Not anymore.'

'That is exactly what fascinates me. They move, they are agile, they bend even though they shouldn't.'

'Yes. I am very grateful to Carlos for my hands. Since I've had them I've realized how much suffering the old ones caused me. When pain is so much a part of your everyday life, you sort of accept it. as a natural thing. I really enjoy these hands. Imagine, a few days ago my little niece was here and I helped her make a necklace by stringing up coloured beads. Several times, - when she was not looking, of course - I untied the necklace, just for the pleasure of being able to do it again. It sounds silly, but it gives me physical pleasure using my fingers in ways I could never use them before.'

'It is fascinating – I am using Ron's favourite word again – but I would have never believed it if I had not seen it with my own eyes. A hand of this shape to have such a good function.'

'Yes. I don't know what Carlos actually did to them, but it worked. And talking about Carlos, how is our kerdung doing?'

'Confused and confusing. I am not sure what comes first. I do not think he himself understands what's happening to him. He's trying to clear his mind by talking to everyone and explaining his situation, making everybody else confused. The last time I saw him was at the hospital, trying to find someone to listen to his story, and everyone else quietly clearing out of his way.'

'Poor Carlos. Sounds as if he is having a rough time.'

'Poor Carlos, my foot. I think he is enjoying every minute of it. Confused or not. I talked to Ron today. He seems to be a little worried about the outcome of this kerdung situation, although he is confident that they will make it. And talking about results, did you have any success?'

'Well, I am not sure, but I can tell you this much, something is happening out there. Good or bad, things are different.'

'What do you mean?'

'My technicians are reporting that for the last three or four weeks they did not meet any conscious blocking in their way.'

'Did they get through?'

'No, they did not actually get through. The automatic barrier defences programmed into the

Central are absolutely impenetrable. Whoever put them there knew what they were doing.'

'I did not notice any change in the Central's behavioural pattern.'

'The changes are very subtle, but I saw that they are definitely there. Until recently, there did not appear to be a very strong, pre-programmed defence. The barriers found appeared spontaneously, not as a result of previous programming, but like a last minute, illogical change of code.'

'That would mean previous knowledge of our plans.'

'Yes. Just that. Or someone was able to monitor our every move – or someone had inside information.'

'And now?'

'Now, the technicians report that they still can't gain access to the memory parts of the illegal sections. They still find very strong barriers, but there are blockages programmed in previously, and they appear when a warning code is triggered.'

'I am not sure I see the implication of all this.'

'The implication is that we are not watched anymore, or that our enemy has lost his line of information and he cannot monitor us any more, or because he does not want to watch us anymore because we are no longer a threat to him.'

'I do not like the first one, but the second one sounds sinister.'

'Exactly . And to make it worse, it correlates exactly with our findings, that judging by the extent of the clandestine computer network, they should be very near to the completion of their plan.'

'But then something should be happening. There is no reason why they should wait and give us more time.'

'You are right again, Ted. For this exact reason, that there is nothing happening, I'm rather inclined towards the first thought.'

'Meaning that we have a spy, and this spy stopped talking to the enemy, stopping their source of information.'

'It is a tough way to put it, but yes, that is what I have in mind.'

'Who could that be? Our group is so small, so carefully chosen and controlled.'

'Remember one thing, the giving out of information might not be a conscious decision., or a willing one.'

'You are talking about a mind tap.'

'That would just able to do it.'

'No. I cannot believe that.'

'Well, you might not believe it, but you better start thinking about it. Just who do we know who's changed a lot during the last three or four weeks? Who suddenly lost interest and is not attending our meetings and is not aware of our recent plans because of it?'

'It could not be Carlos! He wasn't even on this planet when the whole situation started.'

'Kiara was.'

'Yes. She was. She arrived just before, but I still cannot believe it. It does not seem logical. If she's the spy, why should she disconnect and stop gathering information just when it would be most important to do so. Shortly before the action starts, when the information would be most needed by our enemy.'

'I have never said she was passing on information about us willingly. She might not even be aware of it. This kerdung situation could have happened unexpectedly, throwing off course our enemy's plans.'

'We have to be sure.'

'I agree, but until we do so, we have to keep them out of the picture.'

'That will not be very hard. They are so preoccupied with their own kerdung-related problems they don't seem to care that much about anything else.'

'Good. Let's keep it that way.'

**

'It has to be one of these three combinations.'

'Hold on. Don't try it yet.'

'We have to. Sooner or later we will have to try one of them, you know that.'

'I know. I know, but there is just too much at stake.'

In contrast with the spacious arrangements which characterized Soir Harmilor's home, this basement room was a very small one. Crowded with electronic equipment and shelves, which were bending under the weight of the paper material piled upon them.

The three men were bending over the shoulders of the operator, watching, with unmasked intensity, the small, yellow-green screen.

'Which one would you like to try first, Ted?'

'Your Excellency, I wish you would leave me out of the decision making at this stage. You know only too well that my knowledge of computer technology is down to the very basics only. I think you should ask this question to Phyll – after all, he is the mastermind behind all this set up.'

'Sorry Phyll – Ted is right. This is your show. What do you suggest?'

'Any of the three combinations selected have the same chance to be the right one and get through.'

'Do we have a second chance?'

'We might, but then again, we might trigger off one of the barrier codes if we choose the wrong sequence.'

'Meaning?'

'Meaning the door will be slammed in our face and the whole pathway that took me nearly nine weeks to establish would be erased.'

'Any danger of precipitating a different kind of response?'

'You mean retaliation against the Central's authority circuits?'

'Yes.'

'No. I don't think so. I was extremely careful when building the pathways, not leaving behind any clues for identification. Of course, there is always the chance that I made an error somewhere along the line.'

'Okay. So which one would you suggest?'

'I would try the second one.'

'Why?'

'It is different from the other two and, if there's only one correct sequence, the different one would be the logical choice.'

'Why is this one different from the others?'

'The other two are individual, self-supporting code sequences. The second is just a copy of the Central's own security code system.'

'I know all the Central's code systems, especially the security ones. This one does not look like any of them.'

'The whole system is displaced by two elective time units. Otherwise it has the same components that the Central's that it sounds too simple to be the right one.'

'Well Councillor, this is your baby. However, we better try one of them quickly – before someone notices the pathway and blocks it.'

'Go ahead Phyll. The second one.'

**

'Sorry Ted, but this is all I have for you.'

'It isn't much.'

'No, it isn't.'

'The Councillor, in his white robe and with his ever-

314

present green drink in his hand, was pacing up and down in front of the large windows. Most of the time he faced away from them, as if trying to hide the deep lines of concentration on his face.

Phyll Landrous was following the pacing with his eyes. Although he was talking to Dr Andronicus, he was watching for Soir Harmilor's reaction to his comments.

The fourth person in the room, Professor Holdgen, was not watching anyone. He was leaning back with his eyes closed, enjoying the comforts of his plasty-chair. In spite of his blissful, faraway expression, the others knew that he did not miss any of the conversation.

After a long, tension-filled silence, the councillor faced them.

'Phyll – you are our computer expert. I need your opinion. No. Let's change that. I need your reaction. I need to know your gut feeling about this whole affair'

'About anything in particular – your Excellency?'

'No. The lot. Start from the beginning. When we called you to help us and explained to you what this was about, what was your first reaction?'

'I thought that you were joking. I really did. I mean, the whole thing did not make much sense.'

'And when we showed you the data collected?'

'It frightened the hell out of me.'

'What do you mean?'

'Well, what I mean is that although you did not show any positive proof for anyone statistically minded, the sheer amount of data you presented had to mean business.'

'What kind of business?'

'Well - your data appeared to show that our Central Computer had acquired some autonomous function, which although in itself is an absurdity, as we are talking about a machine, deep inside it is the ultimate

315

dream, and nightmare, of every computer programmer.'

'What was your next reaction?'

'Well – then I became sort of more rational and began to follow up and check your data in more detail. Very soon I realized that there was no autonomous function in our Central but there was a big deal of clandestine programming.'

'Did that frighten you?'

'Quite the opposite. It sort of brought the whole thing into my lap. It was a challenge, and it was within my sphere of expertise. I was quite confident that I would be able to catch him.'

'And when did you change this impression?'

'Yesterday – when we broke the barrier code to the clandestine memory banks.'

'You lost me there. I cannot see why would you lose your confidence after winning a move?'

'This is just it. It wasn't winning at all.'

'You got the access you were looking for?'

'-Yes and no. Sorry, your Excellency let me explain it. When Ted first told me about the idea that somebody was building a new computer to transfer information from the Central to take over the Central's functions – well – the idea appeared a bit childish to me.'

'You did not mention this then.'

'Sorry Ted, but I did not want to hurt your feelings. It seems a logical idea on the surface, but if you are talking on a higher level of expertise, the idea is not practical.'

'Why not?'

'To be able to extract information from the Central you would need to know the passwords, the code signals. But when you have access, you do not need to build a new computer. You could use the Central itself for anything you want. You could input your own barrier code to keep everyone out. You could make the

Central do anything you want it to, and keep everyone else from even being aware of your presence. Why would you need to build a new computer?'

'But there is one being made.'

'Yes. There is definitely a new computer there, functionally linked to the Central.'

'What does that do to the "childish" idea?'

'Nothing. When I saw the irrefutable evidence of the other computer, the only possible explanation I could think of was that our friendly invader could be an expert in many things, but knew little about computer programming. This way, the possibility of the "childish" idea being real was accepted.'

'Until yesterday.'

'Yes. Until yesterday, with our very useless victory.'

'Now hold your horses for a minute there Phyll! As far as I understand, if you break a code and gain access to the memory banks of a computer, all the information there is available to you. Isn't that so?'

'It is true.'

'And you got access to the clandestine memory banks. Right?'

'Right.'

'So you know what is there – right?'

'Wrong.'

'You lost me again Phyll. Please explain.'

'Your Excellency – it is not easy to explain.'

'Try.'

'Okay. We did break the code and got access to the new part of the computer. We did ask questions, and we did get answers. But all the answers are gibberish.', does not make any sense.

'Is there another code? A new language?'

'I do not know.'

'Phyll. I have seen you translate the Regurlian hand-prints with the Central in less than two days. There is

317

nothing more alien to the human culture than that...if you could do that, you can certainly do...'

'Your Excellency, sorry for interrupting you, but you are simply talking about a different language. Common concepts only expressed with different symbols. This is something different.'

'It does not matter how different it is. If you apply computer logic to the...'

'Computer logic. Ted! There is no such thing.

'Now hold on there, I might not have your expertise, but since I was a child I had this hammered into my head, that the computer, and especially the Central, is a absolutely logical thing, it cannot go wrong. If it gives the wrong answers, it has to be a human error.'

'That is true, but only in a superficial way. If you understand the basics, computers are the most illogical things around.'

'Please explain it.'

'Ted, it is not easy to explain it and besides we are getting off the original topic.'

Never mind the original topic. I think it's important to clarify this first.'

'Phyll – I think Ted is right. We need to understand what is going on.'

'Okay your Excellency, I will try to be short. Ted, if you want to record your name in the computer, what do you do?'

'Simple. I start with the code for recording, then just type in the information that my name is Ted.'

'Not so simple if you break it down to the basics – step by step. First of all, tell me where the logic is that the sound, which is your name, should be represented by those three symbols on paper. It was a completely arbitrary process, by which the position of the vertical and horizontal lines of the letter T and E were chosen, also that the roundness of the letter D should represent the sound we know it represents. So, before you are starting to type your name – you have already started from an illogical base. Do you follow me so far?'

'Yes, But...'

'Let me finish before you interrupt me. Now, what you do next is press the buttons on the keyboard representing the letters T, E and D. Am I correct?'

'Yes, you are.'

'OK. Now, what happens when you press those buttons? There is a signal starting off from the contact plate of each button directed towards the memory circuits. But what signals? Tell me. Where is the logic by which you select the intensity, the frequency, and the quality of the starting signal? I tell you now that there is no logic in it.

'The builder of the keyboard scratched his nose and arbitrarily decided on the signal which would leave the keyboard when pressing each letter. Meaning the second stage of your feeding information into the computer is also completely illogical. You still following me?'

'Yes, and before you say it, I will not interrupt you.'

'Good. Now the next stage. The signal from the keyboard reaches the memory circuits, producing a change, an imprint, which is the standard for each letter. Right. But who decides on the kind of imprint it leaves? Yes, you are right. The selection of the quality of the imprint on the memory plates is also arbitrary, and so, completely illogical. Can you see what I mean? The only way I can find out your name from the computer is by knowing the letters T E and D and what they mean. Logic has nothing to do with it. If we do not have this previously-arranged understanding between each other, the meaning of the alphabet, I have no way of finding out your name from the computer.'

'You could compare the frequency by which

different elements appear in the sound and in the written part and conclude from there the interrelations.'

'Ted! You were not listening. Let me put it to you in a different way.

'Just imagine a race which has no written symbols. To whom the alphabet has no possible meaning. And imagine that they got hold of one of our pictorial catalogues. Just tell me what possible way they have to work out the relationship by which we group together Shade, Sheep and Ship.'

'Phyll – are you implying that the programming that went into the computer is so alien to us that the Central cannot find any common ground to even start an analysis?'

'Yes, your Excellency. That is exactly what I mean. And that is why we cannot even guess the reason behind the building of the new components.'

'And what is the connection between the Central and the new parts?'

'There at least I can give you a positive answer. There is a constant flow of information from the Central, which is recorded in the new banks in a way we do not understand.'

'Can we stop this flow of information?'

'Not really – your Excellency.'

'What do you mean?'

'Well – we could put in new codes, new passwords, barriers, but they are easy to break,'

'And the alternative? There must be something we can do.'

'Well – there is this switch...'

'What kind of switch?'

'A manual one.'

'And what does it do?'

'Your Excellency, I would like you to promise me that I will not get into any trouble for telling you.'

'Phyll – I cannot promise you that, but I can promise you that if you help me I will help you with anything I can.'

'That is enough, thank you, your Excellency. Well now. When I installed the finishing circuits on the original Central computer, out of which the present one evolved, I was not very sure about what we actually did achieve there. The whole concept on which the communication and the memory units were based for their functions was completely new at the time. I managed to install a dormant program amongst the basic drive principles - which would only become active if someone physically activated this switch.'

'What was the program about?'

'That the computer identifies me as the only person authorized to access it. Only me, personally, identified by fingerprint, retinal pattern and voice print would be able to give orders or ask questions of the computer.'

'What was the reason behind this programming?'

'Your Excellency, at that time I found that this was the simplest way to neutralize the computer if something would go wrong.'

'Something or someone?'

'Either.'

'And why you?'

'Can you name anyone better indicated?'

'No, you are right. You were – are - the expert in the Central's functional balance. Where is this switch located?'

'In the main building, in one of the lateral maintenance passageways.'

'Who else knows about this?'

'Not a soul besides me. Up to now.'

'And you think we should use this switch?'

'Your Excellency, that is not for me to decide. I cannot see any other alternative, but before you do it, I think there are a few points you should consider.'

'Such as?'

'Number one is a question of trust. By using that switch, you are giving me the same power that you are trying to keep from our friendly invader.'

'I already thought about that one, and there is no question of trust there. Just simple logic. The logic says that you could have used that switch any time in the past had you ever wanted to do it. The next point?'

'The next point is that I would be physically unable to supervise all the Central's functions – meaning chaos in multiple systems.'

'I am aware of that, but I believe that you could delegate the supervision of some of the functions. Isn't that so?'

'It is true, and a very good idea at that. I will need about 250 people selected for briefing on program supervising.'

'You will have them by this afternoon. Anymore?'

'Yes, there is one more, your Excellency. You have to also consider the possibility that if something happens to me, you simply lose the Central. It will not accept access from anyone else.'

'This could be prevented with the same delegating of your authority. Besides, I intend to watch out for you.'

'Thank you your Excellency.'

'Then it is settled. As soon as the selected personnel are in position to operate we will activate Phyll's switch. I want all in this room to come with me and I want five members of the Elite Guard in full battle equipment to accompany us. I also want Carlos with us when we go.'

**

'This is as far as you are getting!' The deep voice was immediately followed by white, flashing lights which were blinding in the confined place.

The bodies of the five soldiers crumpled into charred masses on the floor.

The air filled with the acrid smell of burned flesh.

At the door, the tall figure of the Hhruahran with the gun in her hand blocked their way.

They were trapped. There was no other way out of the room.

Phyll was standing next to the control panel, behind which the switch was hidden. The switch they all came here to find. It was well within his reach.

He just had to extend his hand and...

'Don't!' The warning came. 'I am grateful for you showing me the switch, but do not push your luck.'

Only the Councillor appeared to keep his calm. 'Kiara D'Charkoon! What is the meaning of this?' he demanded.

The tightness in his chest made it difficult for Carlos to speak.

'She is not Kiara – your Excellency. The body, maybe...'

The sudden fear closed his throat, his mind refusing to accept what his brain already knew to be fact.

'Very observant, Dr Allegria, but then I expected you to notice.' The gun holding figure seemed to be enjoying the situation. 'Tell me – what else do you know?'

The other two members of the group, Dr Andronicus and Professor Holdgen, appeared too perplexed to say anything.

Everyone was looking at Carlos, expecting him to come up with an explanation.

'Who are you?' He could barely manage to push those words out.

'I think you know who I am. You have all Kiara's memories. We met at her home planet.'

'Why did you follow her to Jeshtar?'

'I did not follow her here. She brought me here. Matter of fact – my only objective in visiting her planet was that she could bring me here.'

'That could not be true. You were not in her mind. I would have noticed you. She left you behind when she was exiled.'

'Remember her Junkorian, the independent part of her mind. I was there all the time - keeping very quiet. She was not even aware of my presence. She was a useful tool, she brought me here.'

'Where is Kiara?'

'The same place you are all going now. I am sorry. I do not have the taste for physical violence, but the existence of that switch you came here to find forced me to show myself before I was ready. There can be no prisoners in this battle.'

The finger was tightening on the trigger - then stopped.

(Carlos!) The mental scream froze everything. Querido, I am sorry for failing you. Burn my body. Quick. It is the only way to kill him. Quick. I cannot hold him much longer.)

(Kiara – I cannot.)

(Carlos! You cannot save me. He took me by surprise. There is not enough left of me to survive. Please - burn him. He killed me - don't let him get away with it. Hurry. He is too strong...)

As if confirming this last statement, there was a flicker of the eyelids, and there was a tremble on the finger lying on the trigger.

A burning light surrounded the Hhruahran's body. Gold. Angry. Consuming.

There was only an empty place there when it greyed

out.

In the relative darkness that followed, Carlos collapsed in a heap on the floor, helped by Professor Holdgen's narcotic needle on the side of his neck.

He nearly missed the shadow of a mental whisper which lingered in the room...

(Gracias Querido...)

**

'Professor Holdgen – may I come in?'

'Lor! What a nice surprise. I did not know you were back, but I am very glad to see you. Please, come in.'

'I thought that by now you didn't even remember my name.'

'I make a point of remembering the names of the girls who used to sit on my knees, messing up my shirt with their ice cream.'

'I bet you wouldn't let me do that again.'

'I bet I would. And I also bet that I would enjoy it much more this time. But what is Mrs Andronicus doing back on Jeshtar? I thought you were one of Earth's permanents.'

'I am, or at least I was until now. I came to see our friend here. How is he?'

'Carlos? I did not know you were interested in him.'

'Call it a guilty feeling. I am more or less directly responsible for him being here, on Jeshtar, and as so, of everything that has happened to him in here.'

'Well, now that you mention it, I always forgot to clarify that point. What was the original reason for getting him to this planet?'

'It is sort of complicated. It started with him accidentally finding out things he should not have known about. Then moving him here became a question of survival after his latent psi capacities were rather roughly activated by our mentor.'

'How did you get together the first time?'

'Well, we didn't actually get together. He accidentally witnessed my, sort of miraculous recovery after the explosion at the chemical factory.'

'As far as I can remember, there was nothing miraculous about it. I found it even rather slow. It took you over ten months of regenerative surgery to regain the function of your hands.'

'True, but Carlos did not know that. The problem was that shortly after the accident I was to attend an important meeting with the local authorities which I just could not miss. So I disappeared from earth-side, came home to Jeshtar to heal, and after recovering I time warped back to the same day of the accident on Earth.'

'I am starting to get the picture.'

'Yes. And by a simple mistake on our side Carlos was able to see me, completely healed, after what, to him at least, appeared less than one day.'

'The miracles of medicine. It must have been quite confusing for him.'

'Yes, it was. He got into all sorts of trouble, but he just kept digging and trying to find out what was going on, until, well, he finished on that bed next to you. Which brings us back to my original question. How is he?'

'Just look at him, sleeping like a baby.'

'Like a drugged baby.

But he is really fine. At least, as long as he is asleep...'

'When will you wake him up? It's been over two weeks now, hasn't it?'

'Sixteen days precisely since I put him to sleep, and, at least for the moment, I dare not wake him up.'

'That was quick thinking on your part to put him to sleep on the spot.'

'I did not know you were watching. Ted shouldn't have told you where we were going.'

'He didn't. He didn't even know I was watching. I was following Carlos's every move from the beginning, being connected directly to his medallion through the booster station we have earth-side. I was observing everything that happened to him since he was removed from Earth – including this last episode when Kiara died.'

'You did not witness Kiara's death, only her body's destruction. She was dead long before that moment.'

'I know. It is strange how the body can retain part of its life energy, even after mental death.'

'Was Carlos aware of you as an observant shadow in his life?'

'I believe that he was aware of the fact that someone was listening in, but I do not think he knew who or where from.'

'Then you also know why I had to put him to sleep.'

'Yes, I think I do, you probably stopped him before the meaning of the death of his kerdung partner sunk in deep enough to start the self-destructing process. But what are you doing next?'

'I do not know. I really don't know. I know I cannot keep him asleep forever, but I do not dare to wake him up before I am able to work out a survival pattern.'

'His kerdung was not a fully fused one as yet. It is possible that he has enough individuality left to survive.'

'It is possible, yes. But how can I be sure of it? I do not dare take the chance. Wake him up, just to find out that he cannot survive. There are no records anywhere about any surviving member of a disrupted kerdung.'

'This is what I came to see you about.'

'Why? Do you have a solution?'

'I am not sure. I have an idea but I am not sure it is practical.'

'Let's hear it. At this stage I will listen to anything.'

'Could you wake him up – like – not all of him?'

'You mean wake up Carlos and leave the part which is Kiara asleep?'

'No. I do not mean that. I know you cannot do that. But why couldn't you create a time related memory loss?'

'I think I like what you are saying. Keep talking.'

'What would happen if Carlos would wake up earth-side, back in a time when none of these things happened yet? At a time when he doesn't even know about our existence?'

'You mean with a memory block for the rest?'

'Exactly. Why couldn't we take him back in time, and let him live through time again, until today, but this time without us in the picture.'

'Let me think. It is a very interesting idea. The new starting point would be the first time his life crossed yours. It should be the night of your accident.'

'Why not before that? Why couldn't we get out of his life entirely?'

'Because it is much easier to alter memories than to eliminate them completely. I think we can place him in a more permanent blocking if we allow him to meet you, but change the consequent events. We should be able to change the whole sequence of events which lead to him being on Jeshtar just by making very minor adjustments to what happened that night.'

'Well? Do you think it is a workable idea?'

'It has some logic in it. Still - I am not sure it will work.'

'What is the problem?'

'The problem is that I do not know how much of

Carlos's personality was left independent from Kiara. Is there enough left of him to survive? He was working hard on his kerdung fusion, but I also know that he had problems with the idea of Carlos, as a person, not existing any more. This might save his life now. Yes. I have to work out the mathematics first, but I do not think there should be any major problems. Except for you, perhaps.'

'What do you mean?'

'I am not sure yet, without working the details out, but it seems to me that due to the time energy levels needed to be tapped, we would not able to do two time warps so close to each other.'

'Why do you need two time warps?'

'To get you out from there and back to today. Otherwise you will have to go through your years of surgery again.'

'Ouch. I do not fancy that, but if there is no other way I am willing to go through with it. I owe him that much.'

'We all owe him a lot. I will work out the details and present it to the Council for approval.'

'Why do you need the Council's approval?'

'Do you know how much energy you need to warp back one year? You need more energy than this whole planet consumes in three months. We cannot get that amount of energy without the Council's approval.'

'Please, let me know as soon as you know something.'

**

'Carlos! Wake up!'

'Okay. What is it?'

'Ambulance control called. They are sending us a group of casualties from the oil plant. There was some kind of accident. They are on the way.'

'I am going! I am going! Be a good girl and get me some more details, will you?'

With a sigh of resignation, Dr Carlos Allegria threw the blankets to a corner of the bed, and for a second, stared at his shoes. Could they be the same shoes he walked into Casualty only two months ago? They were white and shiny then, not like now. But then, if you want to have nice shoes, you should not sleep in them or, use them in places where people wet, vomit and bleed. on them.

As he walked out to the Casualty reception area, Sister Angelica was just putting down phone.

'There was an explosion in the oil refinery – apparently one of the female technicians is badly injured. There are also a few dozen minor burns and lacerations.'

'That is the ambulance arriving,' she added. 'You check the woman in the ambulance while I line up the rest of them for you.'

'Yes, boss!' And he was on his way. Sister Angelica, no matter how deceptively young and fragile she looked, was always the indisputable authority in this part of the hospital. Even the Medical Superintendent, called Ogre by his residents, and not without reason, smiled when he spoke to her.

For a new resident doctor, if he wanted to survive the insanely hectic six months term of Casualty duties, it was indispensable to be in her good book.

I should not be complaining, he told himself while manoeuvring through the swinging doors. I had nearly one hour of sleep tonight. Damn more than I had last night, he added while opening the ambulance's back door, which arrived just as he got out.

'She is pretty bad Doc.' The paramedic was lifting the blanket covering the charred body of the woman.

'She was right next to the explosion.'

'Let me check her before you move her out...'

As he opened her clothes, her chances appeared to improve. She wore thick, hard wearing overalls which should have protected her body, at least partially. Her hair was charred, exposing large areas of a blackened scalp, with a deep laceration on the left side which started to pump out blood in spurts the moment he removed the dressing. She was unconscious, probably due to a blow to the head, but breathing deeply and regularly, and she had a good, strong pulse.

Although she must have received the explosion right in her face, it was not burned. The skin was blood-stained, but intact.

She probably protected her face with her hands – the very deeply burned, blackened hands, supported this.

As he jumped out of the ambulance to head to the emergency room, Carlos heard the approaching sirens. Please, no more, he mumbled to himself.

'It is a police siren.' Sister Angelica seemed to read his mind once again. I do not think they are bringing more patients, but probably investigating the explosion. As usual, they will get in the way, asking questions of everyone – causing a lot of bother and paperwork.'

The police car, with its flashing lights, switched off now, screeched to a halt next to the ambulance, as the paramedics were removing the burned woman.

The doors opened and the first to jump out of the car was a tall, very distinguished-looking man, who with a gesture of his hand stopped the paramedics.

With two long steps he got to the stretcher, had a glance at the woman, then with a deep sigh of relief, let them pass.

'Thank God she is alive!' With this he turned around and went straight to the Casualty reception area without heeding the protests of the young nurse that he was not allowed to enter. there.

'Carlos! Telephone!' Sister Angelica's voice insisted at the door.

'Take a message will you, please. I have to put up a drip and do something about this head wound.'

'Carlos – you better come now. Dr Manzino is on the phone, and he wants you. Now!'

There was authority in her voice. Carlos knew that she understood exactly what he was trying to do, and if she judged that phone call more important, then it probably was.

On entering the office, he noticed the tall man standing next to the window, talking on the phone. He recognized him immediately, although he had never met him before.

Who could not recognize him? Dr Andronicus's picture appeared in the newspapers and television very frequently. He was like a living legend – if not for the world, at least for this part of it.

He was the Chairman of the National Institute of Modern Technology, which was the humble name of the society formed by the best brains of the continent – all dedicated to research projects related to space travel.

Dr Andronicus's name was outstanding even amongst these people. The media stopped counting the number of his inventions or major scientific breakthroughs in which he was the key figure.

Anywhere anything new happened related to space travel, people expected his name to be mentioned. somewhere along the line.

'What the hell is going on here?' Carlos was confused. He would not be coming here unless something important was happening.

In answering his question, Dr Andronicus, without a word, presented him with the phone, indicating that he take it.

'Hello?'

'Dr Allegria? Dr Manzino speaking – now listen very carefully because it is very important that you understand this..'.It was undoubtedly Dr Manzino's voice, but it sounded strange.

Usually he called him Carlos, had a bit of small talk before starting to talk business. The tone of his voice denoted that he wanted to use all of his authority and that it was very important that he, Carlos, would accept this authority without questioning.

'...the burnt woman you just received is Dr Andronicus's wife. He requested it from me, and I agreed that he take over her care immediately. He wants to take her away. Please – no questions asked now – just stand aside and let him proceed. I'll talk to you tomorrow – is that clear?'

'Clear – but the woman is...'

'No buts. Dr Andronicus assumed full responsibility for her. He brought his own personnel to look after her. Our nursing staff have the same orders as you - stay clear, and do not interfere, whatever they do. Is that clear?'

'Sure, but I hope you will tell me more tomorrow.'

'I will, see you tomorrow.'

More confused than ever, Carlos put the phone down. That woman was dying – needed immediate emergency care to give her at least a chance for survival.

This is the only reasonably-equipped hospital for a long distance around – and he wanted to take her away. It will kill her – and the man has to know it.

'Dr Allegria.' Dr Andronicus's voice brought him back to the office. He noticed all the nurses standing around and the door of the emergency room was closed.

'Who is looking after...' But his exclamation was cut short by Sister Angelica's angry, impotent shrug. He did not remember ever seeing her angry, and he would have never imagined her to be impotent.

'Dr Allegria – I am Dr Andronicus – I am sorry to interrupt your routine like this, but I am sure your Superintendent explained to you what is happening. Am I right?'

'He told me that he agreed you could take her away. But he was not aware of her condition. I assure you that if you move her, she will die. I'm not sure she can survive her injuries even if she stays. Sir, please let's not waste time...'

'Dr Allegria – I assure you that we are not wasting time. My personnel are looking after her and I can also assure you that, now we are here, she will be okay. Now, do not get offended. Nobody is questioning you or your hospital's ability of dealing with the usual type of injuries, but my wife is not the usual type of patient. You see – she had a very major accident years back and in order to preserve her life she has several mechanical devices implanted in her body. To save her now, a medical doctor, no matter how able, is simply not enough. She also needs highly-trained microelectronic and computer technicians, and the people with her at this moment are the same ones who looked after her before. I assure you again -that this – me taking over, is in no way a lack of faith in your abilities. I hope you understand me.'

'I am not sure I do, but my boss says that you are the boss – so you boss.' Carlos was trying to appear cheerful whilst trying to work out how to behave in this unexpected situation –. 'Do you mind if I see what they are doing to her?'

'I do, I am afraid. My wife's life is far too precious to allow any interruption; even I would not go into that room. But it looks like they have finished. Here they come.'

Six men dressed entirely in white were wheeling out the stretcher.

It was a simple ambulance stretcher. No oxygen, no drips, no visible apparatus. The woman's head was completely covered with bandages, as was her neck, shoulders and arms. The rest was covered with a blanket.

Only her face was visible, clean, untouched by the fire.

'You cannot take her like this, I don't care how skilled your men are - look, she is not breathing,' exclaimed Carlos, trying to push one of the men aside to get to the woman, but it was like trying to push a ton of bricks away. He couldn't even move the man.

'Dr Allegria.' The soft voice of the woman stopped him, frozen, looking at her with such an expression on his face that in any other time it would be ridiculous. No one laughed now.

Everyone was staring at the woman.

Her large eyes were open, with a faint smile around her lips. 'Dr Allegria,' she whispered. 'Thank you for your concern, but I am well looked after. Trust them, please.'

No one moved or made a sound while she was taken out. Only the sirens of the departing ambulance made them return to reality and look at each other questioningly, utterly confused.

'Dr Allegria.' Dr Andronicus's voice sounded much more friendly now. 'I very much appreciate you understanding and not interfering with my wife's departure. Speed was essential, and someone with less understanding could have caused delays. Allow me to express my gratitude to you and your staff by giving you a few hours rest. Allow my personnel to look after the patients in your waiting room. This is not a request, this is only an expression of my gratitude – please accept it.'

With a gesture Carlos indicated that as far as he was concerned, he could take over the whole place. He was still shocked about the woman's miraculous recovery. Too many things happened too fast for him to assimilate all of them.

'Sister, I assure you that you will find this place completely ordered and clean after our departure. I know the workload on a Casualty nursing staff. Please let my men help you by cleaning up after themselves.'

'Thank you,' was Sister Angelica's cold answer. She was at least as confused as Carlos, but the idea that someone else was ordering her around in her Casualty infuriated her. However, there was nothing she could do about it but stand aside, fuming, and watch all those men in white moving around.

One thing she had to admit. They were good at what they were doing.

The patients were treated and sent home, the place cleaned until it shone like new. And everything was done in a quick, efficient manner. Not a wasted action, not a useless movement. The efficiency of these people was just amazing. But what really confused Sister Angelica was that all the men were dressed exactly the same - all in white, and all of them seemed to be doing everything.

They were treating patients, writing prescriptions, collecting rubbish and cleaning floors – but there seemed to be no distinction between doctors and cleaners – everybody seemed to be doing everything.

It could not be, decided Sister Angelica, it must be that I find hard to distinguish them, dressed all alike.

Then it was all over. Dr Andronicus and his man filed out, the last people carrying out bags of rubbish.

One of the last ones, a tall, thin man approached Carlos.

'Doctor – you've got some blood on your shoes. I've got a special solvent, would you like me to...'

Carlos watched the man with fascination while he cleaned his shoes. His hands, partially deformed by arthritis, the fingers nodular, swollen... appeared to be stiff and sore, but they moved with quick dexterity.

Carlos could not take his eyes of those fast -moving fingers. They stirred something deep inside him.

(I have seen those fingers before.)

The shadow of a memory.

A feeling.

A pain.

THE END

www.ingramcontent.com/pod-product-compliance
Lightning Source LLC
Chambersburg PA
CBHW030922050726
47498CB00003BA/856